The Southern Campaign

A Novel of Alternate American History

Book 2 of the Finch Folio

Daniel H Lessin

Black Labrador Creations, LLC
Minneapolis, MN

The Southern Campaign: A Novel of Alternate American History
Published by Black Labrador Creations, LLC, Minneapolis, MN

ISBN: 978-1-7347976-4-0 (print) / 978-1-7347976-5-7 (ebook)
Library of Congress Control Number: 2022911082

Cover art by Jason Grossman

To learn more about Daniel H Lessin, visit:
blacklabradorcreations.squarespace.com

Printed in the United States of America

A Note to Readers

As with the first in the series, this book comes with some caveats. *The Southern Campaign* is a work of alternate history. The Revolutionary War did not happen in this fashion. Some of the personalities, locales, and battles are fictional, whilst elements of others are fabricated for lack of information available. The strong language and, at times, morally objectionable viewpoints taken in this book, meant to be historically correct, do not represent the views of the author.

Though the author personally feels that the Crown forces had relative justice on their side in the American War of Independence, he does not mean to suggest that they were the absolute heroes of the conflict. There were many people of courage and honor on both sides. There were many scoundrels, fools, and incompetents on both sides as well.

Alphabetical List of Dramatis Personae

(* denotes a character inspired by history)

Blackhawk: A Shawnee war chief

Joseph Brandt*: An Iroquois polymath—warrior, diplomat, activist, lawyer, and missionary

Harold Brewster: Finch's brigade doctor

Thomas Browne*: A Loyalist colonel in the King's Carolina Rangers

Abraham van Buskirk*: A Dutch American surgeon who formed and commanded the Royal Provincial Fourth Battalion, New Jersey Volunteers

Jack Byron*: A Royal Navy Vice admiral known for his poor fortune regarding weather conditions

Guy Carleton*: The governor of Quebec; a British war hero and strong proponent of Catholic, Native American, and African American rights

Henry Clinton*: A British general with a penchant for activism

Antonio Luisa de Córdoba: A Spanish governor of New Orleans

Titus Cornelius*: A Loyalist partisan, erstwhile officer in John Murray's Ethiopian Regiment, and founder of the Black Brigade

Charles Cornwallis*: A British general known for his hot-headedness

Gerald Cutty: James Simmons's commanding officer, a captain in the Forty-Seventh Foot's light infantry

Patrick Ferguson*: The Scots British inventor of the Ferguson rifle and founder of the Experimental Rifle Corps

Adelaide Finch: Giles Finch's resourceful wife; calm and even-tempered, she is strong-willed and progressive

Archibald Finch: The quiet, thoughtful, artistic son of Giles Finch and twin of Caroline Finch

Caroline Finch: The brash and reckless younger daughter of the Finch household and twin of Archibald Finch

Constance Finch: The sweet and mild-mannered elder daughter of the Finch household

Giles Finch: Our hero—well intentioned and quirky, he nevertheless has made his fair share of blunders; thoughtful and brainy, he serves as an engineer in His Majesty George III's army

George Germain*: The British colonial secretary for the time period

James Grant*: A British colonel of the Fifty-Fifth Foot known for his savage cruelty

Nathanael Greene*: A Continental Army officer known for his excellent strategies, middling tactics, and Quaker background

Sir Charles Grey*: A British brigadier general, very skilled with light infantry tactics and the element of surprise

John Hancock*: The president of the Second Continental Congress and a prominent revolutionary; a smuggler and merchant by trade

George III of House Hanover*: The king of England in this time period

Charles Hector, Comte d'Estaing*: A French general and admiral known for his run of bad luck and middling competence

William Howe*: A British general with some sympathy for the American colonials, having fought alongside them in wars past

Walter Kerr: A friend of the Finch household and apprentice to a blacksmith

John Laurens*: A Continental Army officer known for his passionate interest in the emancipation of enslaved peoples

Charles Lee*: A British officer who fought for the Rebellion; eccentric, indecisive, and incompetent

Benjamin Lincoln*: The second-in-command of the Continental Army, known for his competent staffing abilities but relative inability on the field of battle

Francis Marion*: A vicious backwoods partisan from South Carolina fighting on the side of the Rebellion

Lachlan McIntosh*: A revolutionary general from Georgia known for his cantankerousness

Gilbert Motier, Marquis de Lafayette*: The French aide and brigadier general in George Washington's army; idealistic and aristocratic

Hans Muller: A Brunswicker jaeger

John Murray, Lord Dunmore*: The erstwhile governor of New York, later Virginia, known for his emancipation of Virginia's Rebel-owned slave population

Lysander Peabody: A preacher turned colonel in the Royal Provincial First Georgia Volunteers

Alexander Perkins: Giles Finch's batman

Augustine Prévost*: A Swiss general in the employ of the British as a mercenary

Prince: Commander of the Second Ethiopian Regiment, convened by John Murray

Francis Rawdon*: The founder and colonel of the Volunteers of Ireland regiment; a charismatic and talented but distinctly chauvinistic commander

Frederika Riedesel*: Friedrich Adolf Riedesel's wife; a clever, witty woman who was Adelaide's employer prior to Adelaide's marriage

Friedrich Adolf Riedesel*: A Brunswicker major general who was known for pressing his troops to their limits and fighting fast and hard

Running Deer: A Cherokee war chieftain

Sandsnake: A Creek war chieftain

She Who Laughs: A Cherokee warrior

Benjamin Silverstein: An officer in the Chatham County Militia

John Graves Simcoe*: An activistic and extremely talented lieutenant colonel of the Queen's Rangers

Adam Simmons: Finch's staffer, a major in the British Engineering corps

James Simmons: A private in the Forty-Seventh Foot's light company

Jack Storm Crow: A Cherokee warrior

Banastre Tarleton*: The field commanding officer and lieutenant colonel of the British Legion; a wealthy and violent playboy

Jean-Baptiste Donatien de Vimeur*: A French general working closely with Washington to confound the British

George Washington*: Commander-in-chief of the Continental Army, renowned for his charisma

James Wright*: Royal governor of the colony of Georgia

Ludwig von Wurmb*: A colonel in the Hessian Jaegerkorps

Preface

Saint Cuthbert's Hall, Minneapolis, Minnesota

18 May 2021, 5:21 PM

Greetings, readers! Author Daniel Lessin here, hailing you from my current hometown in Minnesota and wishing you a glorious day. In case you are new to the Finch series or need some reminding, I figured I'd catch you up to speed, a task also done by reading book one of the series, *Defending the Colonies*.

When last we paid a visit to Giles Finch, he was leading a bittersweet but newly empowered life. Having spent the last year and a bit fighting the American War of Independence, he was exhausted by the physical exertion, dispirited by the closed minds and cruelty on both sides of the war, and traumatized by the endless battle. Having been pressed into command by the impulsive decisions of such generals as Thomas Gage and William Howe, he chafed at his position of authority, missing the freedom of choice he enjoyed as an engineer. Though initially able to put into practice some of these liberties as a colonel to great effect, Finch's luck eventually ran out.

Captured in a not-so-clever trap laid by the Rebellion that Finch overthought in his desperation to bring the war to a quick end, our hero found himself imprisoned in Easton, Pennsylvania, where he was treated with a degree of decorum (insofar as prisoners could be treated back then), but his men, emancipated slaves whom Finch himself had assisted in freeing, were tortured and sold back into slavery. Eventually, after his wife and fellow officers petitioned long and hard for his release, Finch was exchanged for infamous Rebel warrior John Stark and released back into British hands.

Now we find Major Finch, demoted and disgraced, in New York City, doing what menial tasks befit him. Fortunately for him, however, his wife, Adelaide, and their children, whom he had sent to live in Britain with his brother, are now back with him in the colonies.

Let the adventures continue!

CHAPTER 1

Construction in New York

Governor William Tryon's Mansion, New York City, New York

12 August 1776, 7:37 AM

The sun shone brightly through the curtained windows, reflecting off the glass-and-mahogany cabinets containing a pair of candlesticks and several sets of silverware. Inside New York governor William Tryon's mansion, two gentlemen, one impeccably postured and lean, with his hands on his hips, the other somewhat stout and quailing under the first one's glare, stood watching each other. The dazzling sheen of the sun enhanced the intensity of the lean man's dangerous gaze as the heavier fellow blinked.

The athletic, aristocratic, decidedly handsome William Howe smirked as he looked down his nose at his ranking engineer. "And so the prodigal son returns," he said coldly. "I hope your time off recovering from imprisonment was satisfactory, Mister Finch?"

The rotund engineer blushed scarlet as his coat, which he nervously stroked with his fat fingers. Giles Finch had failed his empire once, and it was clear the British commander-in-chief was unlikely to let him forget it. "I—I am well, General Howe," he stammered. "I thank you very much for my time off. It was needed to reconnect with my family and—"

1

"Good," Howe interrupted. "I hereby call you into service once more. You are a good engineer, Mister Finch, so long as you know your place as just that. You need not concern yourself with battles so much as the planning before and the outcome thereafter. Hammer this into that thick skull of yours, and we shall get along just fine. Who knows? We may yet even restore the colonies to their sense of duty." He smiled primly.

"Yes, sir." Finch's voice shook as he regarded Howe's expression with abject terror. He remembered well his last interaction with that look, and, indeed, after his dressing-down upon his disgraced return to New York from his last campaign, he did his utmost to avoid General Howe. "So what would you have me do?"

The Corner of William and George Streets, New York City, New York

15 August 1776, 8:00 AM Precisely

"Rally on me, lads. We have pressing business to attend to," Finch announced nervously.

It was a blisteringly hot day, the sun beating down mercilessly upon a collection of pioneers—combat engineers and medics—drawn from soldiers of the Tenth, Fifty-Fifth, and Fifteenth Foot. They had been delegated to Major Giles Finch's command for lack of a present superior officer in the engineering corps. As they fanned themselves, sweating profusely, they scowled at their presiding commander. It seemed as though everyone had heard of his harrowing setback at Post Hill and subsequent demotion by General William Howe. He wished he could have had a chance to justify the acts leading to his fall from grace, but the British Army always seemed more keen on castigation than forgiveness.

Better to put my best foot forward, he thought, *and pretend I am not afraid of high command, lest I cower from them and never redeem myself. I will be more forward and cordial and win their appreciation back—that of both the soldiers* and *high command.*

"G-good morning, gentlemen," he went on. "General Howe has decided that we are in need of a place to safely store our supplies. As winter will soon be here, we must shelter those munitions with which we shall equip our forces. Stashing them beneath dining flies and other tents is no longer sufficient, and I fear stockpiling that which we own in the houses of our loyal constituents would be unwise and lead to a considerable loss of love between our peoples. As such, we shall construct a depot upon this very spot."

"Should we not build it inside Fort Tryon?" one of the pioneers asked, abruptly reddening as Finch turned his gaze on him.

"A thought, Mister Simmons," Finch replied, smiling patiently. "But at this time I believe the placement of a depot here will serve us better. It is closer to the middle of the city, and whilst we may have to post a guard for it, it will be more readily accessible to our forces wherever they are placed in town. Now, as to the work, the day is hot, so I highly recommend you strip down to your shirt-sleeves. This will not be easy labor."

The men sighed with relief as they struggled with their tight jackets, revealing their waistcoats and white shirts beneath. Finch, perspiring as much as his men, laid out his plans for the structure as the building detail gathered around him.

Hexagonal in shape, the depot would have two layers of sloping roof made of red oak wood, used because it would be easy to replace due to the prolific growth of the tree in British-occupied New Jersey. Equipped with six doors, it would allow for easy access from any direction. The structure would be massive and the plans quite ambitious, but both were necessary to cater to a city as large and strategically important as New York.

The soldiers murmured, shuffling their feet and stroking their chins as they looked suspiciously at the sketches prepared for them. Finch sensed unsurety amongst them.

"Come now, fellows!" he said, as heartily as he could. "We are Britons. We've done the impossible. Our few fire ships under Drake have routed armadas. Our brave tribesmen under Boadicea have crushed legions. Did not our thousands under King Henry triumph over the tens of thousands of French on Agincourt's blood-soaked field? Did not Marlborough inspire our allies to defeat them again most soundly at Blenheim? If these men of the army could do the impossible on the field of battle, surely we of the engineers and pioneers can expend time and resources to match their efforts, that our dogs of war be provided with the best support we can give to them. Do they deserve any less? Let us to our labors."

And so work began, with soldiers taking small skiffs out to New Jersey to hew the trees. As the oaks fell with thundering crashes to the great swings of the hatchet, the pioneers, all the while under guard from their redcoat brethren in the off chance some partisan band might raid the operation, dragged the logs back to their boats, the better to float their gains across the mighty Hudson River. The felled wood was then piled high into as stout a structure as could be made. Finch oversaw what he could of this, but knowing he could not be everywhere at once, he called upon Simmons to oversee the work on the building itself. "Stoutly, sir! Build it stoutly, Simmons!" Finch demanded, clasping the officer's shoulder. "We must make it so that it may stand up to the worst the Rebels might throw at it!"

With these guiding words, Finch focused his efforts on the felling of the trees. It pained him to watch these majestic woods, a testament to Nature's own engineering, devastated, but he assured himself that they were giving their lives to a good cause. Just like his many soldiers.

God, he thought, looking out at his charges as they chopped up lumber and began placing it on wagons to be floated back across the Hudson. *How many more need to die before we achieve our objectives?*

The Corner of William and George Streets, New York City, New York

3 OCTOBER 1776, 2:37 PM

Finch tried to contain his excitement as the final plank of wood was nailed into place, completing the depot, which dominated the high ground in town.

He smiled as he addressed the men. "Excellent work, lads. I am sure high command will have very little to say about our achievement here today, and that means we are doing something right. We, sirs, are the unsung heroes of the war, but that makes it doubly important that we do our job, the better to ensure the smooth running of day-to-day labor in our armed forces. I am very proud of you all."

He waited a few moments for his praise to register in his men before straightening his coat. "Right. So. Return to your regiments. You are dismissed for the time. You have proven yourselves all fine men, and should the time come when we need you, I shall call upon you once more. Gentlemen, the king!"

"The king!" the soldiers roared back.

"Finch!" a voice called from the distance. "A word."

Finch, knowing this voice well, brightened upon hearing it and turned to see his friend and superior, General Henry Clinton. The beefy-looking, full-bodied general was squinting at him from about fifteen yards off as he sauntered over from the direction of Frankfort Street with a small entourage in tow. Finch walked toward his friend and took his hand in his own.

"Greetings, General Clinton. What a beautiful autumn's afternoon." He gestured to the towering structure. "Do you see my magnum opus? You have no idea how good it feels to partake in the construction of a great project once more. Why, I haven't done such gratifying hands-on labor since the last war with France."

"Slow down, Finch," Clinton replied, amused at the major's enthusiasm. "Your men were splendid. Unfortunately, seeing to our supplies is but one of many battles we must engage in. It is time we see to another front." He pointed to a carriage with his cane. "Ride with me?"

Governor Tryon's Mansion, New York City, New York
3 OCTOBER 1776, 3:00 PM

After a bumpy carriage ride along the cobblestones of New York City, a footman opened the door for the two officers at the front of Governor Tryon's mansion. Clinton, grinning, tossed a coin to the coachman and led the engineer to General Howe's office. Howe was nowhere to be found; the room was instead solely occupied by a pale, tall, slightly husky fellow with a long-ponytailed powdered wig standing at a table behind a chair, a map unfurled in front of him. He started slightly, then gave Finch an icy glare as the engineer entered the room.

"This is whom you bring me for my expedition, General Clinton?" the man inquired. "A disgraced engineer with a history of questioning orders?" Finch cringed inwardly, taken aback at being recognized, as the officer snorted derisively. "Oh, yes, I've been told of your penchant for disobeying orders, Major Finch. Word gets around fast in the British Army, and my mentor, General Howe, has spoken of you, old boy. Described you in great detail as a man of whom I should be wary."

The brawny elder general smirked at the man and gestured in Finch, who sat himself at the far end of the table from the officer. Clinton himself continued to stand. "I bring you, General Cornwallis, one of our finest commanders in the early New England campaign. True, that does not say much, but Finch here is a man of bravery and craft. He will serve your little outing quite well."

Clinton turned to Finch. "What say you, Colonel? Fancy a jaunt through the Carolinas?"

Colonel? A jaunt through the Carolinas? Finch was taken aback by both the sudden reinstatement and the offer of a new campaign. *Surely Howe has disgraced me sufficiently so as to staunch any career progression?*

"You'd be able to regain your rank and, with luck, garner some further honor and promotions," Clinton continued jovially. "Might be nice to help raise your family's esteem in society's eye, wot wot."

"General Clinton, whilst I deeply appreciate the opportunity to serve, are you sure you do not wish to name a . . . nondisgraced officer to the fore? General Howe would be livid to hear of this development," Finch stated. "What's more, I have just acclimated to being with my family once more. Their company is such a delight, and . . . well . . . I feel my work is best done after a territory is secured. Work that I truly enjoy. I do not think I am so much a combat engineer as a builder." He blushed as Cornwallis glared at him.

"Bravery, General Clinton?" Cornwallis inquired, his tone skeptical.

Clinton smiled impishly. "He uses it judiciously." He turned back to Finch, a twinkle in his eye. "So you don't want to go, eh? Then it is a shame for you that General Howe has given me leave to determine which commanders I intend to use for this expedition."

Finch didn't know whether to be amused by Clinton's antics or terrified by them. Howe had done him a great disservice by demoting him, but he could have done much worse. Now Clinton offered the possibility of redemption.

After a pause, Finch nodded to himself. *This option will likely take me further away from my family, but I am of no use to my wife and children disgraced.*

"Your offer intrigues me, General Clinton," he said at last with a smile.

"Thought it might, lad." Clinton grinned, clapping Finch on the back.

"Do I not get a say in this?" Cornwallis remarked grouchily.

"Not really, no," Clinton replied. "As a marquess, you may outrank me in high society, but this is my command. My project. You assented to being a part of it."

"A part of what, precisely?" Finch inquired.

"Ah! Glad you asked!" Clinton replied, pounding his fist on the table. Resting his foot upon one of Governor Tryon's beautifully upholstered chairs, which creaked under his weight, he announced, "General Prévost and Colonel Haldimand have suffered from a serious lack of support in the South. Their regulars have been beaten back at nearly every turn."

He walked over to Cornwallis's seated position and pointed with a sausage-like finger on the map in front of him to a small city in Georgia. "Though they hold the coastal town of Savannah, recent reports insinuate that their efforts to defend Augusta, the other great city in the region, have failed. Governor Wright has fallen back to the Ninety-Six District in South Carolina, which, apart from Savannah, is our only holding in the deep South. There he trains his Loyalist refugee militias, entirely cut off from Prévost and Haldimand's much-reduced force of redcoats and militia of their own."

Finch did not like where this was going. "Where do we feature, General?"

Clinton scowled briefly at Finch's interruption before continuing. "Prévost, Haldimand, and Wright need our assistance in Georgia," he growled. "Whilst some fancy maneuvering up north will certainly draw the attention of portions of the Rebel forces, we should assume they are intent on attacking their quarry. We must defend what footholds we have and shore up our current defenses before we push onward. This way, we might also have a definitive southern flank against which to push the Rebels from Georgia."

"As General Howe and, indeed, General Gage have remarked in the past, that makes sense," Finch concurred. "Was not Georgia used to house a large quantity of criminals for a time, however? Surely prisoners of the Crown would look upon their mother country with scorn. We need Tory auxiliaries, and quickly."

"A fair point," Clinton admitted, "until one realizes that a prisoner may feel that it is better to live ruled by one king, thousands of miles away, than thousands of 'kings'—that is, citizens held in higher esteem than themselves—who are neighbors. I have been told the Scots and Irish have always felt so. Perhaps former convicts would as well."

"Intriguing, intriguing," replied Finch. "So you would have us reinforce Prévost and Haldimand's regulars as well as what Tories they have amassed, capture Augusta, and move to link up with the Ninety-Six District forces under Wright, before pushing on?"

"It is far from ideal," Clinton pointed out, "but the surprise reinforcement would certainly throw the Rebels off balance."

Cornwallis, at long last, spoke up. "There will be Loyalists, certainly, but how many? We will not be able to hold Georgia very long if we are unsupported by the locals." He grunted, thoughtfully tracing the map, deep in thought. "Tell you what.

Let us sail into Charleston, here. It appears to be a very large port and important town. If we take it, it will mean a devastating loss for the Rebellion and one their men most certainly will not be able to ignore. If Admiral Howe is willing to lend us a few frigates and ships of the line, I'm sure their covering fire could contribute in the capture of this important town, whilst simultaneously the defeat will be near enough to Savannah to certainly catch the attention of the Rebels nearby."

"Begging your pardon, General Cornwallis, but the Rebels will be sure to have entrenched Charleston heavily," Finch cautiously pointed out. "I would think it best to proceed very prudently and with Tory auxiliaries before attacking such a mark. It is the capital of South Carolina, after all, and were they to have constructed a fort, it would like as not be constructed of palmetto wood, which soaks up shot like a sponge. Charleston would be a very tough nut to crack."

"That's my boy!" Clinton roared. He turned to Cornwallis. "You see? He can be of great use to us."

"I see. And what would *you* do, *Major* Finch?" Cornwallis replied sourly, staring Finch down.

"The Rebels expect the Crown forces down south to be rebuilding their armies, not taking the offensive," Finch replied. "As they will be mobilizing their own armies to attack the Ninety-Six District and Savannah, I feel that a surprise attack here, on Wilmington, in the colony of North Carolina, would destabilize them. It would split their forces in the northern and southern regions into a more easily handled size—or, if it didn't, it would at least severely lower the morale of North Carolinian troops, who would want to protect their homes but would be newly bound by the Rebels' most . . . ambitious, yet somewhat . . . ungrateful document."

"What is that?" Cornwallis interrupted.

"Their so-called 'Declaration of Independence.' All men are created equal? Really? Believe that though *I* may, the Rebels' own treatment of the black man and the Indian seems to differ from these sentiments they allegedly claim. We treat those people better, even though we do not cite their liberation in our war goals. And the Rebels dare speak of equality as a matter of whites alone! I'm—" Finch paused, realizing he was rambling. "Regardless. I'm suggesting that if we were to liberate Wilmington whilst the North Carolinian Rebels and their allies fought in Georgia, that could lower their morale. They would have to split their forces to engage us. But if they do not retrace their steps to attack us, it would give us plenty of time to entrench whatever holdings we might take from that point."

"So you wish us to place ourselves, isolated, deep behind enemy lines as an invasion force that will, in turn, also attempt to distract an army of enemies who are newly empowered, enthusiastic, and confident, thanks to their declaration rag?" Cornwallis asked skeptically.

Finch blinked. "You will find that some Loyalists will rise up to greet us as we storm Wilmington's gates. Again, as well, those Rebels who fall back to engage us will take some time to return to Wilmington, allowing us to set up defenses. True, it will divide our forces, but it will allow General Prévost and Colonel Haldimand to break the remaining enemy forces and move about more freely. They should be able to garner reinforcements, possibly from Wright, so they will not necessarily require you to resupply them and bolster their numbers."

Cornwallis grunted.

"Sharp as ever, eh, Finchy?" Clinton remarked. "Threw even our own Cornwallis for a loop, you did. However, I think we shall have to check your intricate battle theories for a time. They are clever, but this time we must be ensured of safe, if uninspired, victory."

Finch's face fell.

"So you have made up your mind?" Cornwallis inquired.

"Indeed. The thoughts you and Mister Finch have put forth are innovative but have all the more convinced me that for this encounter, we shall need direct, blunt force. Your ideas are too risky, you see. So, by God, let us make with all possible haste to Savannah. Cornwallis, you are in charge of the men. Finch, you will survey the battlefields and ensure fortifications and depots are prepared upon request. I want you boarding the ships by sundown. Report to General Prévost, and take with you the infantry of the Thirty-Third, Twenty-Second, Forty-Seventh, Forty-Ninth, and Fifteenth Foot. Bring all their detachments—not just the line, but the lights and grenadiers." Clinton paused to take a breath. "Tell General Howe we are also appropriating the six-pounders from Batteries C and D of the Third Royal Artillery. The last thing one wants in battle is a lack of guns, wot wot. Was it King Frederick II of Prussia who once said—"

The doors suddenly flew open, and the Finch children tumbled into the chamber. First came nine-year-old Caroline, precocious and ambitious, with a chubby stature and a head of curly hair, followed closely by Constance, sixteen years of age, with deep blue eyes and long wavy hair framing a full physique. She was always chastising her younger sister for her misdeeds. Adelaide, Finch's petite, delicate wife, followed, red in the face, with words of caution issuing from her thin lips, as Archibald, Finch's only son and Caroline's twin brother, took up the rear, waddling along with a round physique of his own and looking thoughtful underneath his curly mane akin to his twin's.

General Clinton was the first to respond to this intrusion. He smiled and waved, just as a pair of sentinels appeared, huffing and puffing. "Are—*huff*—these . . . individuals troubling you, General Clinton?" one of the guards asked.

"No, no," Clinton responded, waving the soldiers away. "What have you to say, Missus Finch?"

"My apologies if we have offended, General Clinton." Adelaide blushed. "Please understand, they wished to accompany me today to provide my husband with a meal. Still, I could not help but hear your remark about a lack of cannon and the importance of having them on hand. What of a lack of moral support and family? Will not that, too, cause difficulty?"

"But of course, madam. That, too, would indeed pose a problem," Clinton replied. "It will be, as ever, my firm suggestion for soldiers to bring wives and children on their expedition and for our ranking engineer to ensure he keeps better tabs on his own." He smiled dryly before rounding on Finch. "Now's your chance, Finchy!" he roared. "Show your wife how much you love her, and take her along for the journey. I'm sure it will be very educational."

Finch, a tad embarrassed at Adelaide's bold entry, nonetheless approached his wife and lovingly kissed her hand. "Adelaide, my love. I trust all is well?"

"Passingly so, my husband. I grew weary of gossiping with other wives and doing the washing, and so when the children wished to see where you worked, I indulged them and took them by the depot. Nobody was there, however, so I imagined you were sent for by high command. We wished to surprise you with a loaf Constance baked. Is it not beautiful?"

Constance offered up to Finch a very intricately woven loaf of bread. "Cohen, from the lights, taught me how to make it, Father," Constance interjected proudly. "He says families where he comes from make such a bread every Friday. Can you imagine?"

"Darlings, this is wonderful work," Finch exclaimed. "And it is a delight to see you all again . . . during my work hours . . . in front of my employer . . ." He sighed. "And yet, you could not wait until after hours?"

"Giles Finch!" Adelaide snarled, her sweet face turning ferocious, with the look of a Bengal tigress crossing her features. "You will apologize to your daughter at once! We must be supportive of our children."

"But . . . but Adelaide! This is my profession!" Finch protested. "You cannot just barge in here and—"

"It's fine, Finchy!" Clinton's features lit up playfully, whilst Constance's face fell slightly and Caroline and Archibald looked a bit sheepish. "Shouldn't you let them know of the adventure you will all be going on?"

"We know! To the South!" Caroline replied cheerfully.

Her father stooped down to her. "Educational though it may be, my dear, it will be dangerous," Finch began uneasily, scratching his head. "I do not wish to subject you or the rest of the family to further perils. Why, even being in the colonies alone—"

Adelaide interrupted him. "Remember what happened the last time you *abandoned* us, husband. You were quickly taken by Washington and his men. By *Washington*, dear. I always thought you deemed him extremely incompetent."

"Adelaide, he had thousands of men under him. Lord Dunmore and I had only a few hundred."

Adelaide shook her head. "Nevertheless, we, your family, are here to support you and tend to your camp until the war's end." She drew herself up proudly. "It is what any patriotic woman would do, seeing as I may not fight," she grumbled slightly at the end.

"Adelaide . . ."

"Mummy's right, though, Father," Caroline remarked, nodding and causing her curls to bob energetically. "We're ready for anything!"

Constance smiled nervously. "Father, we are here for you. I'm sure I can make myself useful in the camp."

Archibald nodded mutely and hugged his father.

"Hem hem," coughed Cornwallis into his hand, attempting to bring matters back to the war.

"Silence, Cornwallis!" Clinton bellowed, clapping the general on the back. "This is a sentimental matter. Perhaps we should repair to the tavern and let this family catch up on their lives."

Cornwallis looked at his commander in shock. "But General Clinton . . ."

Clinton glared at him. Cornwallis rolled his eyes to the heavens. "Coming."

The two slipped out, leaving Finch with his wife and children.

CHAPTER 2

Onward to Georgia

New York Harbor, New York City, New York

10 OCTOBER 1776, 5:32 PM

Finch's hands shook as he made his way onto a tender bound for the HMS *Northumberland*, which would convey him and his compatriots southward. Slipping as he stepped onto the boat and nearly falling, he regained his balance and sat down heavily on a bench. He had never been to the southlands before. Whilst he was delighted to have a chance to aid the war effort and win honor for his family once more, he was nervous about the expedition, and it showed.

A wave of nausea hit him as the choppy water tossed the boat about, and he worried greatly after his family. He had heard that the South was even less civilized than the Northern Colonies and possessed of all manner of terrifying creatures in addition to indigenous populations, with whom he had had little contact previously save for a few battles in the Seven Years' War.

Horrible images poured through Finch's mind: Caroline being snapped up by alligators and Archibald being hacked apart by tomahawks. What was more, though Finch had heard the South was more loyal to the Crown than the North tended to be, he wondered how much longer that would be the case as more red-coats poured into the colonies. Finally, in accepting this mission, Finch remained a tad leery of the toes upon which he was stepping. He quaked, unsure of himself, as the flat-bottomed boat was raised onto the seventy-gun ship of the line, men clambering all over the decks like ants to receive the party on board the bateau.

As the *Northumberland* left Manhattan Harbor, rocking on the waves, Finch wasn't sure whether it was seasickness or the recollection of the fire in General Howe's eyes as he saw off the fleet of vessels bound for the South that made his stomach turn. From the conversation at dinner the night before, Finch knew that Cornwallis was also uneasy.

"General Howe does not smile upon this mission," Cornwallis had remarked to Clinton. "I think we should see to our operations with extreme caution and do our utmost to keep him apprised of our actions. I do believe you may have placed Finch here in danger of outright dismissal by stringing him along when he should be serving a disciplinary sentence for his . . . misadventure."

Finch blushed as Clinton laughed until he struggled to breathe. Food had gotten stuck in his trachea, and his face had turned red. Fortunately, one of his aides hit him on the back with a resounding whack, dislodging the food.

"Sod Howe!" Clinton cursed. "This is my personal experiment, and he will hear of our victory, if only you would heed my orders. It is on my head, and not Finch's, if I botch this. In fact"—he pounded the table—"I shall double down on my wager. As you gentlemen set out, I shall prepare and lead a second force of my own to attack Charleston in support of your reinforcement of Savannah. Lord knows I should like to see some action."

Cornwallis grimaced. "I think you should stay in New York, sir. You can conduct the fight from such a distance, and you know it will be safer—"

"Nonsense, nonsense, I couldn't possibly forgive myself if one of you died because I wasn't with you at the front."

Off the Coast of Savannah, Georgia

18 OCTOBER 1776, 2:13 PM

As Savannah's beaches came swimming into view, it was clear to Finch, having left the security of Clinton and his esteem far behind, that he and his compatriots faced a city under siege. Fires burned and masonry crumbled under the artillery brought to bear against the town. Off in the distance, barely visible through his spyglass, Finch noted a brown-coated force of Rebellion linemen and their militia counterparts advancing on the western gate through the swamplands, and a great feeling of contempt overcame him.

He had not forgotten his cruel treatment at the hands of Sergeant McFadden during his internment at Easton, where, in addition to Finch being imprisoned, his men had been tortured. Despite being an officer and a gentleman himself, he was endlessly mocked and jeered for the loss of the soldiers he had led into an ambush. McFadden had caused him great pain, having done far more than was just when Finch was behind bars, and now the engineer vowed it was his turn to do what he could to cause carnage to the opposition.

Finch dashed to the bridge of the *Northumberland* and found Captain Samuel Elway surveying the besieged town with his own spyglass. "Captain?" he inquired, turning to Elway and pointing in the direction of the Rebel forces. "Can we do nothing about those Rebel worms inching ever closer to Savannah's fortifications?"

"No, sir," the captain replied. "We are under strict orders to offload General Cornwallis's men and take our leave as quickly as possible. Admiral Howe wishes for my fleet to be in close support of General Howe's forces further north."

Finch, remembering his vow to himself, leaned into the comparatively young captain and whispered, "Think of it as target practice. You see Cornwallis over there? He will not have much of a city to protect if we do not work to drive off the scum. And then where do you think the brothers Howe will be when the Rebels do not have a distraction in the South to detract from Rebel defenses up north?"

Elway stammered slightly, then frowned. He shook his head, appearing to think heavily on the matter; then he sighed. "You stay here," he said. Stepping smartly across the decks in Cornwallis's direction, he began talking to the general. Several gesticulations and a great deal of hushed conversation later, Cornwallis and Elway nodded at each other. Elway returned to Finch. "Let's inform the gunners." He and Finch dashed down a few flights of spiraling stairs to the decks below, and in the considerable darkness of the lower levels of the ship, Elway addressed the men standing at the thirty-two-pounders. "Gunnery crews, load round shot. We cannot come in too close or we'll run aground, but each crew will fire a ball or two at the oncoming Rebels as we pass them and come into port. Send word to the rest of the fleet asking for their support."

As the men loaded the guns and fired them with deafening roars, smoke enshrouded the vessel. Finch's eardrums were hammered, but he looked on, unfazed, as the ordnance sailed toward its target. The engineer smiled grimly at the impact of the shot, watching through his spyglass as the shots kicked up great pillars of muck, swamp water, and sand around the Rebel forces, causing tremendous mischief in the ranks. He could almost hear the screams of the opposition as they were struck down and began to once more allow himself reluctant sympathy for his enemy. *Not all*

Rebels could possibly be as bad as Sergeant McFadden. He took note of his extreme swings of opinion on so grisly a topic. *Imprisonment appears to have jaded my perspective. I must fight this.*

Finch's thoughts were distracted by the call of a marine officer. "Soldiers, to the tenders. You are to make landfall at once." The British ground forces, comprised mostly of terrified new recruits—hastily trained replacements for casualties of the Seven Years' War—were shepherded off the ships of the line by their commanding officers toward their tenders, which set out toward dry land. Visibly shaken, some vomited over the sides of the vessels, some prayed, and others quavered like no tomorrow. They were joined by the veterans of past campaigns, who attempted to steady their comrades with a bracing pat on the back or words of encouragement.

After perhaps half an hour of bombardment, the far left of the Rebel force began to recede. The enemy, shaken for now, began to fall back to their encampments, located over the next ridge and out of range of the guns, leaving a few dead and wounded behind. *A close shave, but still a setback, however temporary, for the enemy*, Finch thought.

As the troops began to disembark and the smoky shroud created by the guns began to clear, Elway returned to Finch, having overseen the bombardment by supervising the aim of the gunners. Pointing to the king's colors still flying proudly overhead above town, the captain remarked dryly, "Seems Savannah will live to be besieged another day."

Finch took off his hat to wipe his brow, which had grown sweaty in the hot Southern sun. Well aware that the ships would soon set sail, he wished he felt sufficiently safe with the reinforcements with whom he was to land and whatever troops remained in Savannah. Unfortunately, the Rebels clearly numbered in the thousands, and he was very likely to be entering a heavy combat zone with little more than the city walls keeping the town from being overrun. He noticed the marines standing atop decks, scrambling about the vessel. Finch's face brightened, but then he shook his head. *We've asked for too much already . . . Perhaps it might be best to leave well enough alone. It is not my place to decide.*

And so Finch clambered aboard the next bateau and was lowered onto the choppy waters of southern Georgia. There was much jostling and cursing, along with some retching, as the British troops were crowded into the boats and rowed to shore. When blessed landfall was made, the redcoats took a moment to catch their breath, then began to file down the streets of Savannah, stretching out their sea legs and preparing themselves for another land campaign. A ragged cheer went up amongst the inhabitants. Finch found Cornwallis and smoothed down his uniform before walking up to his superior and nodding at him.

"Finch," Cornwallis responded by way of recognition. He looked about impassively as the town walls shook with artillery blasts and the inhabitants and soldiers scrambled for cover. Finch winced as a Rebel shell struck a nearby building, causing the top to collapse and land in the stables adjoining one of the town's taverns. Terrified whinnies filled the air.

Casually taking a passing grenadier sergeant by the shoulder, Cornwallis inquired, "Can you direct me to General Prévost?"

The elite soldier stiffened and pointed wordlessly in the direction of a beautifully built mansion near the battlements before hurrying away. Cornwallis briskly walked off in that direction. Finch was about to follow when he saw his family stepping off a newly landed boat.

"Go on ahead, General Cornwallis. I shall attend to matters in a moment," he said. Cornwallis grumbled, then sauntered off toward the mansion. Finch watched him go before turning to help his family ashore.

"Father, this is ever so frightening. What a ghastly little town we've landed in," Constance remarked, clutching her shawl about her as Finch helped her out of the boat.

"Never mind that right now, Constance. We must get you and the rest of the family to safety," Finch replied. He turned to his wife, who appeared as serious as he. "Adelaide, I am needed at headquarters to discuss the defense of the city. Please escort the children to yonder tavern." He pointed to a squat, ugly, but rather sturdy-looking structure a block down the street. "We shall meet again. Children, please be safe, and for God's sake listen to your mother."

"But Father," Caroline protested, "I wish to go with *you*."

Finch silenced her with a look. "I will be back anon." He hugged his family closely, then sent them off.

His fears for the most part now assuaged, Finch proceeded to the governor's mansion, which was serving as the British Army headquarters. As he passed through the cobbled streets, he noticed a great many people busying themselves with the defense of the town, whether putting out fires, stocking supplies, or patrolling the streets with all sorts of farming implements and other make-shift weapons, ready to take up the fight in the case of a breach. Doffing his hat to passersby and feeling slightly more inspired and hopeful with the knowledge that the town stood behind him, he nonetheless quickened his pace for fear of being struck by stray shot.

At length, he arrived at the governor's haunt, a formidable, well-fortified building that reminded him ever so slightly of Gage's home, and stepped inside to see Cornwallis talking with a haggard, wrinkly old man possessed of a strong Roman nose, attired in a powdered wig and the uniform of a major general. The two gentlemen followed the sound of the door's opening and glared in Finch's direction. Finch doffed his hat.

"Giles Finch, sir. Engineers. I was dispatched to help see to the defenses around town."

Cornwallis's opposite nodded politely, signs of strain clearly impressed upon his face. He spoke with a low Swiss accent. "Augustine Prévost, commander of the garrison here in Savannah. General Cornwallis and I were discussing plans for shoring up the defenses. Though we've plenty of supplies, we would not have been able to last long against the manpower that they throw at us. Your reinforcements bring us hope and a few more options with which to work. I thank God for your timely intercession."

Cornwallis smirked. "How did you lose so many men to begin with? I understand you had a reasonable-sized garrison drawn from many colonies at the beginning of the siege. And where is Colonel Haldimand?"

Prévost coughed uncomfortably. "After a botched sally, we lost a number of our regulars and local militiamen. Since then, we hadn't the numbers to drive the insurgents from the town's perimeter." His tone turned defensive. "We earlier had to divide our forces between here and the Ninety-Six District, you see."

Cornwallis groaned, palming his face. "Have you heard any news since then from the Ninety-Six District?"

"No, sir."

Cornwallis swore.

"General Prévost, sir! A word!"

Finch turned to see a bespectacled, dirt-streaked, rather short militiaman dash through the double doors of the mansion. He admired him his gall. He was wearing a bright red shirt to match his officer's sash, and at his waist was a rusty saber.

"Silverstein, look at you, man! What happened?"

The fleecy-haired fellow stammered a response. "The damned Rebels have occupied our cemetery just outside of town. They are using its prime position to place field artillery.

They're bracing their guns against our grave markers, marring them terribly."

The Swiss mercenary frowned, stroking his chin. "Let us look to the important things first, Silverstein. Are our battlements holding? Is there a means of securing additional labor to assist in the town's defense?"

Finch, content to hold his tongue up until this point, could not help but offer some advice. "Sir, I noticed many volunteers travel the streets of Savannah, helping to fight fires and protect the town from invaders, but that almost all of them are white. Does not your town have a sizable black population?"

Prévost looked at Finch suspiciously. "Mostly slaves, sir. Privately owned. Do you suggest we confiscate them for our usage? I do agree that the Negro laborer is a hardy worker, but I would not be so sure that the people of Savannah would wish to part with their slaves."

Silverstein shifted his weight. "Well, I think that we should spread the word that any slaveowner willing to contribute his bondsman will be compensated in coin, and the slave, in assisting in the defense of town against the onslaught of the Rebels, be rewarded with freedom. It would inspire the men to work harder than ever on this project. Such promises certainly brought many of Governor Murray's men to the fore."

Finch did not agree with what Lord Dunmore had done back in Virginia. *Better to simply free the slaves outright,* he thought, *without a requirement of military service in exchange. But I suppose sometimes one needs to take desperate matters into consideration.*

Prévost's eyes glinted with understanding. "Ah! That is an excellent idea," he said. Then his eyes suddenly narrowed. "I hope you do not mean to reenslave them after their usefulness is past, however. Back in Geneva, that would be seen as a most unworthy ploy."

Silverstein looked horrified. "No, sir," he cried, waving his hands vigorously, as though shaking them free of such a rank insinuation. "I meant it entirely in earnest. Why, it is a travesty of justice the barbaric practice continues to exist in our empire."

There was an awkward silence.

"That 'travesty of justice' keeps the financial and familial well-being of the families of the South afloat, Silverstein," Cornwallis replied. "What's more, we are under siege. Debating the merits of abolitionism at this moment seems most unproductive."

Finch cleared his throat and spoke in defense of his fellow abolitionist. "But at what *cost*?" he began. "With respect to the keeping afloat of the financial well-being of the South, that is," he hastily clarified at the look on Cornwallis's face. "Do you, a military man, truly value the luxury of a few aristocrats, who will not themselves do an honest day's work, over the very well-being of the black population, who have formed the bulwarks of our empire and have won their freedom several times over for their labor?"

"Shut it, Finch."

Finch complied.

"G-General Prévost?" Silverstein interjected hesitantly. "Permission to lead my contingent of militia to recapture our cemetery? At the moment there is but one battery present, guarded by what I understand is only a smattering of Rebel Continentals in support. Perhaps twenty men. We could chase them from the field."

Prévost, previously not even looking at the Loyalist, finally turned on the young man. "A very dangerous maneuver for a militia company by itself, Silverstein. I shall not have the good citizens of Chatham County risking their lives on a damned fool's errand, especially led by a journalist. I realize you seek glory about which to write epics, but you will find none here. This is reality now, sir. Not one of your God-be-damned faerie tales."

Silverstein persisted. "But sir, if we hold the cemetery, we shall have their flank! It—"

"Silence!" Prévost shouted, before quickly closing his mouth and awkwardly looking about.

Cornwallis's eyes narrowed, and he spoke: "That, General Prévost, is where you might be wrong." The newly arrived major general stooped a little to address the militia captain. "You want to save your cemetery, sir? You have joined the right army. However, you will not be going without supervision. You may retake your cemetery, and we shall provide lights in support."

"Why, General Cornwallis," Prévost said, "this is a shocking waste of—"

Cornwallis held up his hand and turned to Finch.

"Major Finch, convene a force of pioneers from amongst the men. Include your precious blackamoors if you must. You will aid in the restoration of the tombstones knocked over by the Rebel forces and any other damage they may have done besides."

Finch smiled, excited for a chance at valor.

"Silverstein," Cornwallis continued, "your company and the lights will retake the cemetery. We shall liberate the position by night, striking from the flank. Prévost?"

"We—we—we're sallying, General?"

Cornwallis attempted to silence him with a look, but Prévost pressed on. "But sir, our last sally led to the loss of Colonel Haldimand. We took numerous casualties in the previous engagement."

Cornwallis's response was swift. "We shall be pounded into the dust by yonder position if more guns are relegated there. Surely you must understand that we must retake the Jewish churchyard." He turned to Finch. "What are you waiting for? Gather your men, Colonel."

Finch snapped smartly to attention and set off to handpick his men.

Taking a cautious look around the town, Finch noted that Savannah was unlike any city he had been in before—a fraction of the size of the city of New York and full of blacks and Natives in addition to whites. He felt lost in this strange, relatively diverse racial culture, still steeped in superstition and religion, mostly Protestant, with a small meeting house for Jews.

Wandering the streets, having briefly lost his way, Finch finally made it to the Inn of the Smirking Sun with the guidance of the apprentice of a blacksmith in town who had been dispatched to personally escort Finch. A spindly black boy with enormous arms, Walter Kerr possessed considerable strength and nonchalantly hauled Finch's effects, stored in his sea chest, from the ship to the inn. It was there that Finch returned to his family, who had rented a quaint and hospitable-looking room of hickory. Upon carefully tipping Kerr, he wordlessly began unpacking and, after doing so, kissed his family goodnight.

"I am sorry, my loved ones—I shall be called to service soon. I must rest until evening."

This he did, snoring to the sound of the Rebel guns.

Not long after the artillery gradually abated for the night, Finch rose from his uneasy slumber. Looking out from the privy window on a whim, he saw a white flag of parley flying over the ramparts of Savannah. Slipping on his boots, Finch rushed toward the gates, accosting Cornwallis.

"As the ranking engineer in town, sir," he said, "I must beseech you, take me with you. I could be of service and wish to assist in these dealings."

Cornwallis sighed. "Colonel Finch, you may well have your uses, but diplomacy has not been one of them in the past. I shall take note of everything said and relay it to you at the meeting's end, but I see no reason for you to come along."

"I suppose he might be able to serve wine to us and our foes as an aide-de-camp," Prévost pondered aloud snidely. "Do you think you can handle that, Colonel Finch?"

"Of course. How hard could it be?"

"For you?" Cornwallis sighed. "I can only wonder, as it involves speaking only when spoken to."

Unfortunately, it was too late to dash for wine, as one of the guards spoke up from the ramparts of town. "They come, General! The Rebel envoy. Shall we open the gate?"

"Do so," Cornwallis replied.

Slowly, the town gates opened, and Finch and company stood forth to meet their guests.

"I am Brigadier General Lachlan McIntosh, Earl Cornwallis," Finch heard the Rebel general say. He was a gruff, serious-looking fellow with a wrinkled, weathered face and possessed a well-muscled physique. He spoke proudly, in a low, dusky Scottish accent. "I speak on behalf of my commanding officer, Major General Benjamin Lincoln. What is the meaning of this parley? Surely you don't mean to give up just yet?"

"Not at all, sir," Cornwallis replied with a smirk. "I mean to give *you* one last chance to withdraw from the field. Our newly landed force is one to be reckoned with. You will engage them at your own risk."

McIntosh smiled back at his entourage. "I'm sorry, General, but we would be quite content to face the wrath of the Lord Almighty Himself so long as it means we can take a crack at one of the last Loyalist enclaves remaining in the South. Nothing personal, but my men cannot live in harmony with yours so long as your fellows offer resistance."

Cornwallis appeared unfazed. "Then let it be known I take no pleasure from sweeping you from the field."

McIntosh grinned. "Worry not: our stout besieging force will give you what for." He gestured to Prévost as he remarked, "As General Prévost learned last time, a half-hearted sally will fail to dislodge us any day."

Prévost growled.

Cornwallis sighed. "We shall see."

As McIntosh and his men turned to leave, Cornwallis gestured his detachment back inside the walls of Savannah. "Now see here, gentlemen," he remarked smilingly, "Old Man McIntosh believes I am bluffing about sweeping him from the field. I can *tell* he *actually* believes I'll stay put until he assaults the town walls! Well, some lesser men might, but we are going to surprise these Rebels. I made a vow, both to McIntosh and to our very own Jewish militia captain, and I stick by my promises. But we are going to need manpower. Finch, recruit some additional pioneers from amongst the citizenry. We will need big, strong men—yes, regardless of race—to complement the grenadiers for the occasion. Prévost, rally the remnants of your original force. We're going to need them on watch duty. My own men will bear the brunt of this operation."

"What will your plan comprise?" Finch inquired.

"Patience, Colonel. You will see. Now go forth."

And so Finch set out to fulfill his orders.

Savannah Green, Savannah, Georgia

20 October 1776, 1:22 AM

Finding volunteers was not an easy task. Governor James Wright's strong leadership helped ensure that the South had a sizable Loyalist populace, but Finch still had a difficult time rallying them to fight for his cause.

"You're professional soldiers of the king," one remarked snidely in response to Finch's plea. "Shouldn't you be able to do the job yourself?"

"What do I care about the cemetery of a few Jews?" another replied.

Others were similarly inhospitable, some citing injuries they had sustained at the hands of the Rebellion and demanding reparation from the Crown. *This isn't working*, Finch thought. Then he thought of young Kerr, the blacksmith's apprentice. Stopping by the smithy, he offered the lad another shilling, "Go to, young man," Finch said. "Please hurry and, with your mates, gather some assistance from the dockyards. There is a war to be won!"

Soon, a small crowd of dockhands, drunks, thieves, and other people of the night made their way to the docks of Savannah, where Finch and his detachment of grenadier-pioneers were waiting for them. Taking a purse of his own wages, Finch turned to the hastily assembled mob.

"A bounty, sirs! We shall be going into a combat situation alongside the very people, your neighbors, whom the Rebels have slighted. The goal is to rout the Rebels from the Jewish cemetery, which they have fortified. As a service to these people of Israel, as well as to defend our own tactical position, we shall protect the sanctity of their tombs and restore them to proper order. For those who decide to join me on this expedition, to protect their homeland and neighbors, as well as not to die like fish in a barrel within their own homes, here is, in addition, a bag of monies from which I shall reward thirty pence to each soul involved."

I shall have to write my brother for money to compensate my losses, Finch thought before returning his attention to the crowd. "What's more, in the spirit of Governor John Murray, Lord Dunmore of Virginia, and in the name of the Marquess Sir Charles Cornwallis, major general in His Majesty's Crown Forces, I am authorized to emancipate any bondsman, regardless of race, who sees fit to join us in the defense of this town. I must say, I am aggrieved to note that this is an act of heroism that I see few free *white* men willing to partake in." He smiled at his final, cutting remark.

Many were taken aback by this sentiment and fell to murmuring mutinously amongst each other. Some white men walked away in a huff, but others, unfazed or otherwise willing to prove themselves to the Crown, stayed on to receive their payment in advance. Some free black men also joined in. Suspicious, but willing to jump at any opportunity for emancipation, numerous enslaved black men, a few white indentured servants, and a single gentleman who looked as though he may have been Native American fell in alongside the grenadiers.

When the ruckus in response to Finch's inflammatory speech had subsided, the colonel counted thirteen additional pioneers of various backgrounds, making a total of thirty-one laborers. "Now, give three cheers," Finch roared, "for His Majesty, as well as our own self-preservation!"

An awkward, somewhat forced three cheers were haphazardly given by the crowd until Finch silenced them with a raised palm. "We shall join with General Cornwallis in the town square. Kindly form two files and follow me."

Finch, now prepared to command these men to help restore the cemetery to its former glory, led his recruits to the center of town, where Silverstein's militia and Cornwallis's lights waited alongside several ox-drawn carts. It was these men, beasts, and supplies that would bear the brunt of the operation, whilst the frontline infantry, or hat companies, and remaining grenadiers of each regiment would remain behind in town, manning the defenses alongside a collection of guns.

Slowly, painstakingly, the gates were inched open, and over the next hour, detachment after detachment left the city by cover of darkness, attempting to make themselves scarce to the watch fires of the enemy. One step at a time, they approached their destination: the enemy artillery ensconced within the Jewish cemetery, protected in part by the low cemetery walls and braced against headstones and tombs to minimize recoil. Nearby, a select few Continental linemen stood, alert for any kind of activity.

The Rebel cannons were perched at an incline, as they were meant to hit targets at an angle and a distance off. Finch knew that the enemy would be unable to depress their guns well enough in order to strike targets almost directly below them. Finch's men plodded ahead slowly, burdened by the carts full of supplies, whilst, silent as a shadow, Cornwallis's men, deployed in a skirmish line and heavily spaced so as to decrease the impact of artillery, crept ahead, ever closer toward the artillerists.

As the lights, led by the major general, approached to about one hundred yards from the cemetery, the watchful eyes of a Rebel artillery spotter managed to detect the redcoats' advance. An alarm was sounded as the artillery rushed into action. Cornwallis, quick to note that his cover of darkness was broken, sounded the charge, drawing his blade and flourishing it at the enemy guns.

"Onward, Crown forces! Charge bayonets!"

The cries of surprise that ensued from behind the cemetery walls as the lights and Loyalist militia bore down upon the Rebel artillery and their guardians served only to push Earl Cornwallis further, as he, with loud shouts, encouraged his men onward. Eyes wide in terror, the Rebel artillerists, as well as a few of their line infantrymen, managed to hold their position, intent on delivering their dangerous payload.

At about fifteen yards, the field guns delivered a lethal blast of canister shot. A sizable tin's worth of small musket balls were blasted from the six-pounders arrayed within the cemetery.

Struck with this deadly wave of shot, several light infantrymen fell, and the gaps in the skirmish line grew larger. But even as the formation wavered, it held. The elite force converged upon the gunners mounting the walls with aplomb. The artillerists scattered, leaving their guns at the cemetery gates.

The Rebel browncoats fared little better, firing off a single volley before seeing through the smoke the true volume of soldiers rushing upon them and deciding to retire alongside the gunnery crews. Several threw down their muskets as they ran. Finch noted curiously that the muskets looked rather elegant. Were they foreign makes rather than the usual British Brown Bess? He vowed to take a closer look at them later.

Cornwallis grimaced as the enemy soldiers retreated. Doubling over, he took three deep breaths, straightened up, and turned to the men, forcing a smile.

"Never mind, lads. At least we have their guns. Lights, men of Chatham County, form outside the cemetery. Pioneers, enter as you see fit."

Outside the cemetery? Finch looked at him quizzically as the soldiers mumbled, eyeing the brush on the graveyard's outskirts. It did not provide the best of cover.

"We have liberated the Jewish churchyard, gentlemen," Cornwallis announced, resting an arm on a tree branch, which bent slightly. "It is time to rest and repair the headstones. I'll be damned if we besmirch this holy vessel with more blood, however. We must protect it from further enemy encroachments. Out of respect to the Jews, we shall do so from the outside. There is some protection from these trees, as well as the protection of the God of Abraham for preserving his son's cemetery."

Finch couldn't help but admire Cornwallis's consideration for his allies. Perhaps the engineer was wrong about him.

"Right!" Finch contributed, rising to the occasion. "You heard the good general. Pioneers, get these filthy guns out of the churchyard and into a position defending us from the Rebels' flank. We will need some men to deploy to the artillery, the better to operate it. It is not hard. The rest of you, restore these headstones to their original positions and fix this gate. Quickly, lads—with Mercury's touch."

"Yessir!" the pioneers shouted, apparently pleased to be behind the protective cover of the cemetery walls.

Jewish Cemetery, Savannah, Georgia

1 November 1776, 8:56 AM

The Rebels were suspiciously inactive as the Crown forces clambered up the hill to gain a toehold on the Rebel left, and Cornwallis and his men were given ample opportunity to dig in. Now safe behind the cover of trees and brush, the British troops and Loyalist militia waited as the pioneers scrambled to effect repairs to the cemetery.

In time, having finished with the headstones, Finch's crew began work on the collapsed cemetery gates. Made of wrought iron, they were supported by beams with a curvy superstructure, each topped with a well-crafted gargoyle—both of which, Finch noted to his disappointment, were missing pieces.

Just as he reached for his tools to follow after his crew, the general alarm was fired off. This was soon followed by another shot, and another, as scattered shots, both near and far, filled the air. Smoke and cries of agony accompanied the gunfire; Finch felt blinded and deafened but was intent on his work and on impressing Cornwallis and his fellow soldiers. He realized that it was time to be brave. He turned to his men, coughing away a hoarse voice.

"Steady on, lads. General Cornwallis would want us to continue our work here today. It is of foremost importance that we, as pioneers, service the citizenry before all others. Keep up the good work! We have our orders, and whether or not we are turning the cemetery over to the Rebels, I want it immaculate."

Some grumbled at this, then gave a collective shout of surprise as Cornwallis's newly captured artillery battery blasted a few rounds at the Rebel encampments below. To cheer the mood, Finch burst into the first verse of "Heart of Oak." The men were not impressed by his thin, reedy voice and chose not to join in. Work continued amidst shaky hands and nerves, and in time the job was done.

The gates creaked slightly but nonetheless remained sturdy in their reconstruction as Finch led his men out to reconvene with Cornwallis and his men. The general stood a short distance off from the front lines, surveying the carnage below. All manner of motley-attired Rebel corpses dotted the field and incline, with only one or two British lights and a few Loyalist militiamen fallen along a hastily erected entrenchment on the crest of the hill.

Silverstein waved to Finch. "All well along this front, sir. The men are holding fine!"

Despite their losses, the lights' conduct was beyond reproach, and even the militia seemed confident. Finch smiled. *Silverstein is doing a fine job keeping the men in tow.*

Looking through his spyglass, however, he recognized that though the detachment thrown at them had, indeed, been repulsed, it was but a small fraction of the enemy force.

The battle for Savannah was far from over.

CHAPTER 3

Humiliation at the Jewish Cemetery

Jewish Cemetery, Savannah, Georgia

1 NOVEMBER 1776, 4:21 PM

Earl Charles Cornwallis's expeditionary force was beginning to grow weary. Perched atop the high ground where the Jewish cemetery stood to the southwest of Savannah, the major general's small force of light infantry and militia had withstood the enemy's probing action. What was more, with the help of enfilade fire from Savannah's artillery batteries, two more Rebel assaults had been bogged down with heavy casualties.

But the Continentals and their militia allies had yet to give up on their objectives. To the south and east of Savannah (the north being only water), the Rebel general McIntosh's men had all but surrounded the town. It appeared that it had become a point of honor, in addition to a tactical boon, for Rebel command to retake the cemetery.

Through his spyglass, Finch could see the revolutionary officers consulting underneath a dining fly, many of the men wearing rather sullen expressions as they faced down the flailing arms of General McIntosh, his face reddened as he shouted at them. As the hours ticked by, Rebel troops slowly repositioned themselves,

37

ostensibly preparing for another attack. Finch hoped it would be another half-hearted, piecemeal assault that the Crown forces could once again throw back. So far, McIntosh and Lincoln's risk-averse technique had proven ruinous to the Rebel commander.

"Hold until relieved," Cornwallis had told his men. The battle had hunkered down to something of a stalemate, with the Rebels refusing any assault on their left flank by forming a line of their own parallel to the British protective line along the cemetery. Unfortunately, the batteries of siege guns bombarding Savannah also remained. Meanwhile, the skies had darkened and the wind was picking up, a welcome breath of fresh air for the embattled defenders, who were growing hot in their coats.

"Ah, so the Rebels have deployed some artillery toward us. Fascinating," Cornwallis said, smirking and pointing at a collection of guns that Rebel artillerists were rolling into position.

Finch noted that they were four-pounders. That struck him as odd, since the Crown rarely commissioned the use of such weapons on land. It was a wonder the Rebels had gotten hold of them.

"No matter!" Finch replied. "As we've captured the battery of six-pounders stationed here, we slightly outrange the opposition and can rain a holy hell upon the enemy." The colonel turned to the skeleton crew of gunners. "Let us pin the enemy down as they approach. What have we left for artillery ammunition, lads?"

"Two round shot and two canisters, sir. It appears the enemy was running low on ammunition when we took the position."

Finch was crestfallen but tried not to show it. "A-ehrm . . . a little lacking, perhaps, indeed. What say you, General Cornwallis?

Cornwallis pondered the situation. "How are our musket munitions looking?"

The lights murmured as they checked their cartridge boxes.

"I've got nine," one soldier replied, smiling uncertainly, his black lips and teeth showing the results of a hard and frenzied gunfight.

"Five."

"Seven."

"Three, sir."

Cornwallis raised an eyebrow.

"And I made every shot count!"

The general smiled.

"Sir!" cried Silverstein over the gusts, gesturing at a fourth body of enemy troops approaching.

"We're doomed," moaned a young private of the militia.

Cornwallis rolled his eyes.

Silverstein was quick to rush to his man's aid. "Do not be too hard on the men, Your Grace. These Rebels mean to kill us, and we have not much ammunition with which to defend the cemetery."

Cornwallis shook his head, a smirk playing at his lips once more. "That is just it, Silverstein. They *mean* to kill us. They *shall* not."

Silverstein nodded, turning to his body of men. "General Cornwallis is right, gentlemen. What—ehm—what he of course *means* to say is that we must exercise courage in the face of this oppression. Of course we may be frightened, but true bravery comes from the ability to stand against the terrors one already feels!"

"Perhaps . . . sooner bore your men . . . before we . . . Captain?" came a mocking cry from down the hill, barely audible over the screaming west wind. McIntosh had returned, his officers in tow, under a flag of truce. Though his exact words were garbled by the weather, Finch further made out, despite their twenty-five-yard distance, "Dine . . . Cornwallis. War . . . not always . . . vicious."

Cornwallis must have caught more than just that, however, because his face went red. "And yet, unless the men are afforded equally good treatment, I shall not take comfort in the luxuries of an enemy officer," he replied defiantly. "What is it you want,

McIntosh?" He and Finch stepped closer to hear the response more clearly.

"Why nothing, sir. Save our hill. Turn it over to us, and we will allow your men to return to Savannah unharmed."

Cornwallis grimaced. "And the cemetery?" the general asked after a few moments' pause. "What will become of it if we surrender the position?"

"Retaken, of course, but not defiled. The brave stand of you and your pet Jewry commands a sort of respect which cannot go unnoticed."

"No, sir! Do not give it to them!" Silverstein cried. Cornwallis silenced him with a glare. Whilst sympathetic to the poor Jewish journalist, Finch could not help but feel terrible for the major general. Cornwallis may have been cold and standoffish, but to Finch, he clearly had a good heart, and the conflict of interest the general faced now seemed a great challenge for him to reconcile.

After what seemed an eternity, Cornwallis spoke. "I see no need for bloodshed this day, Mister McIntosh. We shall withdraw under two conditions. First, that you do not occupy the cemetery. It has seen far too much combat as is."

"Aye, so it has. Many a good lad has laid down his life over a few yards of land, which is why you will surrender the cemetery to us. We shall safeguard it against further threats."

"That is not what I meant," Cornwallis responded.

"I understand that, Your Grace, but sometimes you are unable to barter for what you wish," McIntosh said, shrugging, before giving a sharp whistle. Suddenly Finch could hear a rapid shuffling of muffled footsteps as a number of figures appeared from behind them and to their flanks. He turned to see a body of men in frock coats positioned in a skirmish line displacing from previously hidden positions. It was a trap! In addition to being outnumbered and outgunned, the Crown forces had been surrounded all along. "Now, will you take what you can get or die like dogs?

Mister Marion, the commander of these fine gentlemen, is a very proficient partisan and has the most peculiar quirk of reveling in the hunt of his fellow man."

"Were I to fight this battle alone, sir, you know I would contest your men to my dying breath," Cornwallis snarled. "However, as I have a force to take care of, I shall be merciful to both our armies. You may have your flank, sir, as long as we might keep our weapons as we withdraw. Let us at least depart with our colors, arms, and dignity."

McIntosh sighed wearily. "You have my apologies, Charles, but surely you understand my plight. I mean to win this war, not prolong it. Whilst you agreed to hand over the hill, certain military protocol does still endure. You are surrendering a position. With it, at the very least, come all arms and equipment. Surely you Britons know your own codes of conduct in wartime. I hope you are not bitter that they are being used against you."

There was some scattered laughter from the Rebel ranks as Cornwallis let out a resigned sigh of defeat.

"I tire of this conversation, sir. Take our weapons, but leave the hill, or, by God, you shall know our wrath."

"An empty threat, Earl Charles." McIntosh waved his hand dismissively. "I'm surprised at you. Come, now. Stack your arms. Prepare for a march home in disgrace."

Earl Charles Cornwallis turned to the men. "Gentlemen, we return to Savannah unarmed."

As preparations were made to abandon the position, the enemy soldiers surrounding Cornwallis's men began to leave the shadows to seize the firearms and ammunition the British forces had surrendered. A giant of a man, the aforementioned Mister Marion smirked and tipped his hat mockingly as he ordered his minions to collect the assemblage of muskets, rifles, and ammunition. As Cornwallis and his men turned to go, they found a gauntlet of partisans leading back in the direction of Savannah's gates, about fifty men on each side. With a sigh, Finch began to walk in between the columns. Looking back, he noticed the eyes of the Rebel fighters were fixed hungrily on the African American recruits. They snickered mockingly as they passed and mooed at them like cows.

"I could kill you for disobeying your master," one hissed at one of the former slaves.

"You're no longer protected property anymore, Negro," another jeered. One fellow proceeded to kick Kerr in the shins as he passed. Kerr let out a cry of pain as a loud crunch echoed across the night sky. He grasped his offended appendage, backing up the line. Rather than fight back, however, he braced himself on a friend's shoulder and continued to hobble along. *Thank God it is only a short distance to safety*, Finch thought.

As they cleared the Rebel gauntlet and neared home, Cornwallis turned to Finch. "I am perplexed as to how you could not have seen those partisans' troops and did not warn us whilst we were fighting our battle, sir. The responsibility for the miserable outcome of this expedition rests entirely on your shoulders. Well done," he added sarcastically.

Finch nodded but remained silent. *Says the man whose armed troops were supposed to scout the area and engage the enemy*, he thought. *I would say my men were a little more busy than you seem to have thought, enacting the orders you gave us.*

A rain began to fall.

Governor Wright's Office, Savannah, Georgia
2 NOVEMBER 1776, 8:50 PM

It had been a humiliating march back to Savannah. Though Finch had perhaps felt the shame less than Cornwallis, embarrassment had still burnt in his cheeks as he strode through the gauntlet between the Rebel forces, each of whom seemed to smirk at their misfortune.

The Rebels were once more able to focus on a single body of enemies. Though they were situated within a fortified town, the Crown Forces—no longer even able to evacuate by ship, their navy having withdrawn the day before to assist the effort in the north—were trapped behind their battlements. The only positive outcomes Finch could see to all of this were that he was now behind more stout defenses and doctors could treat their casualties.

Bloody hell, he thought, still haunted by the injured as they trooped by. *If previous experiences were not enough, this surely has to be the defining incident: I am not cut out for field combat. When this war is over, prestigious or not, I'm retiring. I have no need to face the horrors of war head-on. I am here to build, not destroy.*

Constance and Adelaide helped tend the wounded with steady hands and brave, albeit forced, smiles. Many years earlier, Adelaide had been a handmaiden to Frederika Riedesel of Brunswick and had befriended the baroness's doctor, so Finch's wife knew something of the medical profession. She now passed it on to her daughter, who followed instructions as best she could, intent on aiding the cause. The two worked closely with the surgeons, preserving the lives of several wounded soldiers. Finch was proud of their ability to do their best to aid in the military's endeavors, and Constance suddenly found herself in the company of some very thankful gentlemen wounded in the last action. She was pleased with the praise and attentions they heaped on her and, in turn, took to treating their wounds with a caring touch.

Walter Kerr, the blacksmith's African American apprentice, was one such man. His leg injury was seen to with loving kindness. During his healing process, he, some of his friends amongst the off-duty soldiery, and Constance were inseparable. Though injured, he was still employed in His Majesty's Service, yet did what he could whilst off duty to assist Constance with her work. He was a gentle lad of sixteen, muscular and homely, but sweet, with a certain fascination with ribbons. When visiting the hospitals to check on his wife and daughter, Finch twice caught his daughter ponytailing Kerr's hair with at least three of them at a time, whilst the redcoats looked on approvingly. The young man would then on occasion play his fiddle, and Constance and their friends would dance to old English country tunes. Finch was initially unsure what to make of the fellow, who was rather young to be handling a musket, but these were desperate times, and another man on the field was a great luxury to be had. *What's more*, thought Finch, *he is a great comfort to my daughter.*

Meanwhile, he was aware that Cornwallis had had a difficult week and was sure to meet with a reprimand. Still, Finch did his best to keep his wits and humor about him as they faced down the military governor the next day.

Governor Wright's Office, Savannah, Georgia

3 November 1776, 8:07 AM

Lost in thought regarding the happenings of the past few days, Finch arrived late to the governor's mansion to discuss the future of the Crown forces in the South with Cornwallis and Prévost. As he approached the door to the governor's office, his hurried steps echoing down the hall, Finch could hear warning bells ringing in his head as he reached out to knock. He could hear stiff conversation in the room beyond. He raised a quavering fist and made his presence known. When a footman answered it, Finch could see the livid look on Prévost's face.

However, it was not in reaction to Finch's presence.

Finch looked on as the woebegone British-aligned Swiss mercenary scowled at Cornwallis. After taking a moment to check himself, Prévost proceeded to unravel under the stress of the situation.

"General Cornwallis," Prévost all but shrieked, "as the town is under my jurisdiction, I must protest the cavalier usurpation of my authority, regardless of your seniority. You have emancipated my slaves, appropriated my militia, sent both on a ludicrous mission bound to fail, and now give up our arms to the Rebel scum? This borders on the treasonous! Would you see the Crown undone, sir? Shall I make for England now to prepare her defenses against a Rebel assault?"

Cornwallis turned his attention from the open window, where he was looking down on the bustling population of Savannah, to Prévost, who still glared at him accusatorially, and smiled infuriatingly down at the Swiss soldier. He took his justly outraged subordinate's hands in his own.

"I share your concern, General Prévost, really I do, and am dutifully embarrassed by the disarmament of the men after the seeming fiasco of this expedition, but—"

"Seeming fiasco?" Prévost interrupted. "General Cornwallis, we lost over three hundred muskets today, and—"

"And through this prevented many deaths, and even gained the allegiance of the Jews, sir. Both muskets and men are replaceable, but I believe it better to lose one resource, especially a matériel one, than both. The men, even the Negroes, remain free of imprisonment and ready to serve. We must merely equip those we have. And I do not believe that will be a problem after the next few days have passed."

Cornwallis looked up to the heavens, which shook with thunder, the storm whipping the major general's coat about him.

Prévost sighed, finally managing to gather up his thoughts between heaving breaths. "Sir, with the deepest . . . respect, could you please speak more clearly? Why do you believe a storm could halt the Rebel siege for any significant period of time?"

As he spoke these words, a gust of wind pushed open, then slammed closed the windows to Prévost's office with a spine-chilling howl. Candles flickered and danced. Looking out the window, Finch noticed the weathervane atop the church spinning violently, and he smiled knowingly, the gist of Cornwallis's words coming to him at last.

"Gentlemen," Finch said softly, "with respect, it would be best if we all get to cover. That's no mere storm."

The Stockades, Savannah, Georgia

10 November 1776, 2:22 PM

The hurricane had lasted a good week before calming at last. Whilst the citizenry cowered in their basements and cellars, blockading their windows and doors, the weather wrought hell upon the town. The skies darkened and brought great thunder-claps and lightning to bear against Savannah. Raindrops pelted the town in waves. The wind whistled incessantly, kicking up sand from the beach and casting it about. Streets flooded, houses collapsed, and even the well-fortified governor's mansion suf-fered, with several windows cracking; the church's weathervane was sent flying. Fortunately, it was apparent that the locals had prepared themselves for hurricane season, and whilst no house-hold was spared the impact, the weather eventually abated before the town's supplies ran out.

The day the winds died down, Finch took what he deemed a calculated risk and poked his head from outside his shelter in

Savannah's stockade. The small explosions and holes in a few houses caused by the Rebels' attacks were nothing compared to the inundation of the Savannah River's banks. The combination of raging gales and tumultuous downpours had placed even the most seaworthy vessels belonging to the many prosperous merchants in town at great risk, as the docks and riverside residences were overrun by Neptune's mighty wrath. Still, it was over now.

Quickly, Finch sought out his family, who had stayed with him in the stockade. "Adelaide, children, it appears the worst of the storm is over, but I want you to tarry here awhile yet. I shall be sallying with my pioneers, and we will begin effecting repairs to the town. Please, stay safe and do not come out for another day or so." He turned to his pioneers, who had also sought shelter in the stockade, some with families of their own. "Alright, lads. Time to seek out your equipment and start patching up the town. We'll need some timber, though, so we shall have to slip out with a foraging party to fell some trees."

"No need to worry about that, sir!" came a cry from the battlements. "Looks like the devil's own farts have done some logging for us!"

Finch rushed atop the steps to the town walls, where he found one of the disarmed light infantrymen, a veteran from the cemetery fiasco, peering out to the lands beyond. A great many trees had been knocked to the ground by the strong winds, including many in the vicinity of the Rebel encampment.

Taking out his spyglass, Finch peered into the wreckage that was the Rebel headquarters. The encampment appeared to be abandoned. With the hurricane's passing, there might well be some matériel to salvage from the remains.

"Well spotted, Sergeant," came a grim voice behind the two men. Cornwallis was paler than usual, a shadow of his old self, as he made his appearance with his aides. "Finch, go out there with your pioneers. Salvage the timber and begin repairs."

"Shall we ransack the enemy camp?"

"That will be up to General Prévost," Cornwallis grumbled.

General Prévost's Office, Savannah, Georgia

10 November 1776, 4:00 PM

Finch cautiously stepped into Prévost's office as Prévost busied himself about his workplace. The engineer averted his eyes and approached as the Swiss man set to work writing dispatches and poring over maps.

"Can I help you, Colonel?" Prévost inquired in a low growl.

Finch, intimidated, stepped back a few paces. The general seemed in a foul mood, and Finch couldn't blame him. "I shall leave you be—I've no desire to bother."

Prévost laughed scornfully. "Well, you have already. What the devil do you want?"

"Your orders, sir. The Rebels have apparently vacated their headquarters. A look from the spyglass seems to indicate that the hurricane caused their retreat. Felled trees and derelict tents everywhere, sir."

"And Earl Cornwallis?"

"He's seen the wreckage from afar but awaits your orders."

"As he should. Let us marshal the men and take a closer look."

Prévost stepped out of the governor's mansion with Finch in tow. He cleared his throat. "Now see here, men of Britannia," he said. "I request that a reconnaissance party of rearmed lights be prepared for a quick foray into the territory once held by the Rebels. These men will be equipped with borrowed muskets from the line infantry and will make themselves scarce. We will try to recover all matériel we have lost but will not push the attack, at least not until we have reequipped the regulars."

And so the rearming of the lights began. The regulars called upon to give up their weapons were not pleased.

"One scratch on Betsy here, and it will be your head, light bob," a soldier grumpily warned a nearby light infantryman as he stacked his musket atop a neat pile of other such weapons, grunting as he did so.

"Well, it wasn't my decision to give up my own firelock," replied the skirmisher.

"Yah!" replied another light bob. "I noticed you gentlemen weren't even present at the fight. We could have used your assistance, you know." A fight nearly broke out between the two factions before Finch and Prévost stepped between them, promising each the expedient return of their arms. They arrayed the light infantry into columns, and the skirmishers hustled outside the town at a quick march. As Finch made to follow them, Prévost halted him with an outstretched palm.

"You have done enough damage, Colonel Finch. I hereby task you with repairs on the town and doing what light duties best suit you besides," Prévost remarked with a grim smile. "Why don't you confer with Cornwallis?" His tone turned sarcastic. "He might have some more *grand* ideas about rebuilding the town."

And so, like a good soldier, Finch sought out his superior.

"Naturally," Finch told Cornwallis as they strode along the main street, "the Rebels have wrought great mischief upon the city of Savannah, sir, and we are, in part, to blame for it by occupying the town and making it a target. It may not be the most strategically feasible idea, but if we were to win the hearts and minds of the populace, it would go a long way toward victory, or so Clinton always said."

Cornwallis nodded. "I am in accordance with you and Clinton on this occasion," he murmured. "Whilst Prévost might wish to protect us from the Rebels, he has no interest in the colonies, being Swiss and a mercenary. I do believe the best thing to do will be to make inroads with the community, thus protecting ourselves from a mutinous citizenry." He sighed. "I propose . . . I propose—though, of course, you are the final authority on this project—that we rebuild the houses and civilian buildings first. The Rebels are temporarily dispersed, and the hurricane has passed. Our soldiery may need rest, but the long-suffering citizenry deserve it more."

Finch scowled, deep in thought. "Is that an order, sir? Much as I'd like to help the citizenry, surely we should rebuild walls and fortifications in case the Rebels return in force. Perhaps it would even help the citizenry more to be protected from the Rebels than from the hurricanes and—"

Cornwallis cut him off. "It is an order. It is time to rebuild structures and relationships alike. Of course, you may do what you'd like with my suggestions; this is your project."

It was true, Finch had to admit. With the Rebels dispersed, now would be an excellent time to rebuild bridges between the population and the Crown. Upon returning to the Smirking Sun, he threw himself onto a chair with a sigh and scribbled out a hasty letter to his command. He passed the message on to his staffer, Major Simmons, a wild-haired, bumbling shrimp of a man with a strong mind for engineering, who stiffly saluted and quickly stepped out the door to rally the men.

Finch shook his head. He remembered his time as a major and his subsequent promotion, demotion, and promotion again. Competition in the British Army was petty and did not look kindly upon mistakes. Whilst it was clear the Rebellion was a foe to be defeated, many still desired personal glory. Simmons had been a rare exception to those officers prepared to endanger the Crown forces for their own ambitions.

Finch gathered the men together and briefly outlined the mission.

"Now see here, gentlemen: the people need our help. The elements have run the enemy off. We shall hopefully not hear from either anytime soon, and what will assist us most is not immediately preparing to do battle against either, but instead looking to the welfare of the terrorized citizenry. We are responsible for their discomfort. Let us put their minds at ease and rebuild their churches first, that they might congregate and plan projects of their own, as well as worship God. From there, we shall provide aid to those most in need. The waterfront housing first and foremost, I would say. We shall work with all civilian housing before we look to the town defenses. I know this means that rebuilding the barracks is later on our list of priorities, and that some of us might sleep under canvas tonight, but the citizenry are not as strong of will and body as we. Our comforts come secondary to theirs. I hope that is quite clear?"

"Yes, sir," was the chorused reply. It was not enthusiastic, and some of the fellows were quizzical, but the work conditions were passable, at the very least. It was a pleasant November afternoon in Georgia. Having returned after escaping the hurricane, birds sang in what trees remained.

Later that afternoon, Prévost's reconnaissance mission returned from their exploits. The shoes and gaiters of the soldiers were covered in muck. Major General Prévost looked pleased but exhausted.

"It appears fortune smiles upon us this day," he reported to Finch and Cornwallis. "Not only was the Rebel camp abandoned, but we managed to recapture several muskets and cartridge boxes of ammunition, some of which remain in miraculously good shape." He sighed. "We had to put up a devil of a fight for them, though, skirmishing briefly with some of those shadowy figures—perhaps the ones mentioned in your report, General Cornwallis. Led by that Frederick Marion?"

"Francis," Cornwallis groaned.

"Ah, yes, him. Apparently, he is known amongst the doodles as the Swamp Fox. He and his men put up a tremendous fight, so we gathered the muskets and left. They harried us like hornets from a hive and killed seven of our men, but our lights put up a strong rearguard action and surely felled a few of his as well. I may have counted three enemies fallen. It was a challenge to tell because he shrouded his men in the woods so well that we could rarely see more than one or two at a time, and only for seconds. In the end, we both withdrew in good order, I think. We heard some more skirmishing coming from another direction but did not stay and find out what happened. We had, after all, completed our objectives. Unfortunately, we were unable to salvage the Rebel cannon. They were rusted and crusted with dirt and weathering and wouldn't budge, even if they would have operated properly."

"You were lucky to have done so well in difficult terrain," Finch said. "General, I have been making progress on the home front. Come, look. Major Simmons, join us."

Prévost's visage brightened further still at these words, but then took a quick turn for the worse when he set out to examine Finch's handiwork. His face fell, and he glared angrily in the engineer's direction.

"Finch!" he snapped. "Where are our defenses? Why are you focusing on civilian structures?"

"Sir, you delegated to me the task of rebuilding the town, I felt it my duty to see to our citizens first, and—"

Finch stopped short before saying anything more, as Prévost shot him a look of pure venom. The Swiss mercenary took a deep breath to steady himself.

"This is not a philanthropic expedition. This is war. We won't be doing well by the citizenry if we get them all killed." Prévost turned to Major Simmons. "You are in temporary command of the rebuilding of our defenses, Major. Colonel Finch, you are relieved for today. Hopefully you will think upon your mistake and be more logical."

Logical? The word echoed through Finch's mind as Prévost strode off. Perhaps the superior officer had a point, but Finch had been promoted through merit, as was a requirement in the corps of engineers, whereas Prévost had bought his way through the ranks. Finch was unsure the Swiss man had the grounds to discuss ability with him. Perhaps Prévost had a degree of logic to his points, perhaps he hadn't, but Finch's project had been left to him, and he had done what he, a ranking engineer, was called upon to do, as it benefited the people. Was that not what the Crown was supposed to do? And if so, what would a mercenary, a Swiss one at that, know of befitting the people? *What's more*, Finch thought, *I was given a great deal of encouragement by another Briton, one of great seniority, to do as I did.*

He regarded the scene with a jaded eye. "Whilst I have the utmost trust in you, Mister Simmons, to facilitate matters for the day, I should like to request the opportunity to serve in the pioneer crews and be available for any questions you have."

Simmons gave him a steely look. "I can organize repair details myself, thank you, sir. You rest yourself. I need not be coddled."

Finch nodded, face red. "Good luck, Simmons."

Simmons acknowledged the well-wishing, then turned his back.

Finch returned to his family, woebegone and feeling decidedly betrayed by his until-now loyal junior officer.

"Welcome home, Father!" Caroline cried, embracing him.

Archibald looked up from a drawing he was penning on parchment and smiled uneasily. He then pointed at the ceiling. "There are rats up there, Father! They are most frightening!"

Finch smiled back at his son and ruffled his hair. "I shall find a cat at once, dear one. We cannot have rats disturbing your sleep and impacting your art." He chuckled. "How are you, Caroline? I must admit that it is always such a joy that I know I can depend upon those I care about to cheer me during some of my darker days."

Caroline scowled, her hands on her hips. "I'm glad you are feeling better, Father, but I am unhappy here. I miss Uncle Jacob and his creepy old mansion in Chelmsford. I loved exploring the attic and riding the horses. I even talked to sailors. You won't let me go out to see what's going on!"

Finch smiled inwardly but tried to look serious. "I understand, Caroline. I will see if I cannot secure you a small mount with which to trot around town. Surely that could be a start?"

Caroline crossed her arms. "We shall see."

Finch looked around. "Where is Constance?" he inquired.

Adelaide sat down next to him and took his hand in her own. "She is with a friend, husband. Enjoying herself, as we all should. Though I do worry—she is acclimating to her surroundings so quickly. What if she becomes too entrenched in Savannah? I must admit, life on the march will be difficult for the children."

"Of this I have no doubt," Finch said. "Perhaps we should invite this friend to dinner with us sometime. I'm sure it would be a good opportunity to evaluate Constance's taste in acquaintances."

Caroline stifled a giggle.

"Something you'd like to share with us?" Finch inquired with a smile.

Struggling to keep a straight face, Caroline blurted, "I walked in on them holding hands."

Archibald chuckled merrily as Finch stopped dead.

"Do you mean to tell me Constance has found a suitor?"

"Yes, Father."

"That's wonderful, dear." Finch grinned. "Who is it?"

"It's Private James Simmons!" Caroline blurted out, throwing herself into a stiff salute.

Adelaide turned beet red. "Darling, please remember to show restraint and reverence when you speak to your parents."

"Well, it's true!" she replied mischievously.

Finch blushed scarlet. *Constance, my perfect daughter, a woman of stature and high society, with the son of my replacement?* The engineer gathered his wits. "Ah? I see. His father works for me, you know. What regiment does he belong to? Was he injured at the cemetery?"

"Yes, dear," said Adelaide. "Now that I remember it, they did become rather friendly when he made his way back to town for treatment. He's one of young Walter Kerr's bosom friends."

"Did they seem . . . attracted to one another?"

"That is for them to tell, and you to—"

"Yes, Father. They admitted so to each other," Caroline piped up happily. Archibald burst out laughing, upending his inkwell.

Finch considered the situation. *I am taking the matter too critically. The lad has taken a blow for Britannia and appears to be one of virtue. Whether or not he was fathered by a disloyal man, Constance appears smitten with him. Perhaps I should talk to all involved and understand better the situation at hand.*

"Husband? Are you quite well?" Adelaide interrupted. "You have been standing silent quite some time."

"Oh, no, I am well, thank you. Merely some complications at the front." *The home front.* "One moment please." Finch tapped his head with a pudgy forefinger. He sighed and let a few moments pass as he expelled a series of bad thoughts from his head. Then he forced a smile. "I wonder, Adelaide." Finch looked into Adelaide's eyes as her brow furrowed. "What else can you tell me about young Master Simmons?"

"Well, whilst he was interned in our hospital, he appeared to be a bright lad, chipper and pleasantly minded. He dealt with pain well."

"Why, what happened to him? Specifically?"

"He was hit in the thigh by an unlucky musket ball. Whilst he was hobbling around on crutches, however, he was very good to Constance. He even attempted to help out around the hospital to repay us for our service. He seemed rather a gentle soul. He had a very good work ethic, dear."

"Aye, shame his father is a right bastard," Finch growled to himself. "You will forgive me if I remain deeply suspicious of this young man's motives. For all we know, he could be attempting merely to manipulate her for her money. The Simmonses have not had the fortunate background we have. We must be cautious."

"Giles Finch!" Adelaide responded crossly. "I'm surprised at you. Since when have you treated another based on their family's background?"

Finch did not back down. "When their father usurped my position over today's engineering assignments."

"That is no excuse, dear. Perhaps he usurped you because you made mistakes. You know what you must do when you err: you must rise above the blunders and put your troubles behind you as best you can."

"But my dear, I can never forget those poor imprisoned Ethiopians!" Finch reminded her, as horrid memories from his imprisonment alongside the Ethiopians in Easton once more came to the fore.

Adelaide sighed and replied softly, "Again, dear, you must honor them by learning from these mistakes. And remember how you just called for the emancipation of so many slaves here in Savannah? Let that be a start to further progress in their name." She shook her head and then smiled. "We are proceeding off topic. Think of it in this fashion: What if, by allowing Master Simmons to court Constance, you would force Major Simmons to be polite to you, the better to indulge his son and to help him marry upward in society? It would be yet another opportunity to see him at your mercy, even if you already outrank him and should not be embarrassed by a few individual blunders on your own part."

Seeing Finch was unconvinced, Adelaide continued, "Giles, I've worked with the child myself. His personality falls far from the tree as you describe it. Should you not at least allow the man to court your daughter? Grant him a chance? Do you not trust your own wife's sense of judgment?"

Finch hung his head. "Very well. We shall see the young man. You are sure the merits of this boy outstrip those of his father?"

"As sure as I can be, dear. And place yourself in Major Simmons's shoes, dear. Was he assigned the position, or did he grab it from you in a moment of weakness? Perhaps you need to be less sensitive."

"Hm."

Finch considered the situation. Father though he was, and thus able to make decisions for his daughter, he supposed that Constance knew herself well—and though love was a secondary matter in these partnerships, the engineer felt it best he take her thoughts into consideration as well. Father and daughter loved each other but had had little to bond over until now. Finch turned to Adelaide.

"Let us invite the lad and his family to dinner. It is important to meet with one's subordinates as people once in a while, and if their son is courting our daughter, surely we should ascertain whether he is a goodly individual and worthy of Constance's time." He turned to his younger daughter. "Caroline, please be on your best behavior. I appreciate your interest in your sister's romantic life, but you mustn't tease her about this. Romance is quite natural, and I hope you realize it yourself someday, should it be with someone you love. It surely worked out well between your mother and me. Despite our occasional differences, her calming presence and thoughtful mindset have been a great blessing. I would go mad without her."

"Yes, Father, I do believe you would," Caroline replied, a twinkle in her eye. Catching Finch's glare, however, she quickly put in with a quick bow, "I shall obey. Please take comfort in the fact that you shall never have to do the same for me as you do for Constance. I intend to devote myself to men's arts. Being a woman is stifling."

Finch chuckled. "Darling, surely, as a woman, you can sew, and coordinate a household, and . . ." His voice trailed off. That *did* sound boring. He turned to his son. "Come, Archibald, a game of chess?"

"No." Archibald gestured to his renewed drawing.

"I'll play, Father," volunteered Caroline.

"I'll help you," Adelaide offered.

Caroline smirked. "No thank you, Mother. I prefer to win by myself. Why not encourage Archibald?"

Adelaide laughed.

Midway through Finch and Caroline's match, Constance came home. Attempting to appear excited on her behalf, Finch rounded on her at once. As she made to kiss her father lightly on the cheek, he hugged her close.

"My child!" he shouted, perhaps a bit too energetically. "How was your rendezvous with young Master Simmons?"

Constance blanched. Wringing her hands together upon her release, she looked to the ground. "F-Father," she said, "I was going to tell you when time allowed, but you seemed so busy, and—well, how did you know?"

Caroline waved in Constance's direction, and immediately the young woman knew she had been betrayed.

"Caroline, you—" she began. She then caught a glimpse of her father's disapproving face and, quailing under his look, shakily responded with increasing panic.

"I know he is a common soldier, but who can help how they were born? I have very much enjoyed his company. He is sweet, well intentioned, and well read on Shakespeare. He quotes the sonnets to me. We've . . . we've held hands but a few times, though we have also exchanged sweet words and presents. I have come to dote on him so, such that treating his wounds has inspired me to wish to become an attending nurse to your men, that I might see him more."

Finch frowned mightily. *Quoting sonnets?* This did not bode well. "Do you love him?" he asked impulsively.

As the once-pallid Constance blushed scarlet, Adelaide mercifully interceded. "Now, now, dear, what does it matter if she cares for him in that fashion or not? Whether or not romance is involved in these meetings, she is enjoying the company of her contemporaries whilst serving on your campaign trail. This is an unexpected pleasure we must savor no matter what form it takes."

Finch thought on this logically, as any engineer should. *Archibald and the ladies are suffering through this war on my behalf,* he thought sadly. *Best to allow them some degree of joy in the process, allow them some company outside the family. Devastated though they may be if their new friends die, even that, too, may be ground for a life lesson.*

"You are quite right, Adelaide," he responded. He returned his gaze to Constance. "You may enjoy your time with Private Simmons when he is off duty, but do not distract him from his chores. I'm sure his business with the lights keeps him heavily occupied." Though hesitant, Finch managed to affect what he thought was a convincing smile. "Now run along and invite your friend and his father and mother for dinner sometime."

And so Private Kerr, consigned to crutches whilst his leg healed, was hired once more and dispatched with a hefty tip to invite the Simmonses to dinner for the next evening. Finch did not wish to embarrass Constance more than he already had and was nervous he might even make a fool of himself, but he couldn't help but smile to see his daughter grow up and possibly find a suitor of some virtue. The engineer did wonder whether the Simmonses could cater to her needs the way he could, as assisted by his bachelor brother: it occurred to Finch that neither Private Simmons nor, indeed, his father had purchased him any sort of commission at all.

Finch's fantasies in which things did not seem nearly so bad came to a jolting halt. *What if Simmons is using her to gain social status and money? Did she tell him about the wealth of her eccentric Uncle Jacob? I will try not to mind if my family's social status takes a blow based on their marital decisions, so long as it is what Constance truly desires, but I will not have her manipulated.* He sighed. *Perhaps it would have been better if I had left her in England, where she seemed to enjoy life, save for missing her father.*

He would have to wait and see.

The Hungry Peddler, Savannah, Georgia

11 NOVEMBER 1776, 5:07 PM

The next day, the Finches gathered at the Hungry Peddler, an eating house in the middle-class district of the town. Whilst Finch did not wish to skimp on this important dinner, he had no desire to show off the full extent of his wealth and risk manipulation. When the Simmons family failed to arrive on time, he began to get annoyed. *Not very genteel of them to keep a superior officer waiting*, he thought.

In time, Major Adam Simmons arrived, looking extremely uncomfortable. He nodded politely to the Finch family. "Colonel Finch," he said. "I hope you and your family are well. I am sorry for these past few unfortunate days. It was by no means my intent to replace you."

"Well met, Major Simmons," piped up Caroline, saluting the major before Finch could answer. "What is it like, working for my father? Where is your son?"

Simmons's eyes went wide. Then he chuckled darkly. He turned back to Finch. "So it is *your* daughter who is so fondly entertaining the company of my son, is it?"

"Yes, I am she," Constance responded, some iron in her voice for the first time Finch had heard in a while. Simmons turned to look at her, considering her, before softening slightly.

"Aye, well met, young one. I hope my son arrives soon." Simmons checked the handsome grandfather clock braced against the wall. "I am afraid he keeps better time with his music than he does with his pocket watch." He smiled apologetically.

Suddenly, the door crashed open as a young man in a red coat dashed forth, nearly knocking over a tavern wench as he fell into her. "Sorry!" he cried. He spotted the assembled company through a crowd and slipped his way through the masses to join them. When he arrived, Finch could see that he bore a striking resemblance to his father, if possessed of slightly more muscularity, which, with his overall academic look, could be considered handsome to some.

Though he was covered in scratches, some of which were bleeding, he offered Finch an honest smile. "Please forgive my tardiness, Colonel Finch. I was helping Old Missus Peterson coax her cat down from a tree." He looked in Constance's direction, and his face split into an even bigger grin as Finch's daughter blushed.

The young soldier crossed the table, stumbling slightly over his own feet, before taking Constance's hands in his own. As she pecked Simmons on the cheek, the engineer began to sputter, but, catching Adelaide's disapproving glare, he silenced himself.

"Are you quite well, my dear lady?" the younger Simmons inquired of Constance. "I have oft dreamed of seeing you once more."

"Yes, my good lord." Constance smiled. "And yet, it has been but a day since we last met! How could you dream of me so frequently when last we met so recently?"

"I must rest my wound from time to time, and when I do, I dream of you," the young man replied playfully.

Finch coughed, and Constance jumped at the interruption.

"Father, please meet James Simmons." She gazed lovingly at the soldier boy. "Simmons, my father, Colonel Giles Finch. James used to be an actor before he became a soldier. Now he's with the Forty-Seventh's lights."

"Why, ehm, well met, sir, I am sure," Finch said. Realizing he was seated, he quickly rose to take the young soldier's jauntily outstretched hand. *An actor? Oh, for a pistol to end it now.* "Why don't you tell me of your ambitions, young man? Also, do tell me:

how is life with the Cauliflowers? Does old Puffguts treat you with respect? Seems like rather a blustery fellow if you ask me." *Zounds,* Finch thought as he watched Simmons take a deep breath. *I may have opened Pandora's box.*

"Major Finch, you do me some honor to give your humble servant an audience," Simmons began.

Finch smiled patiently.

"Though I am, like my father, of low birth, educated by him in between performances, we of the Simmonses are honest folk of industrious stock. Unlike the fusty aristocrats to whom you may be attempting to marry off your Constance, you will find I will work hard to do my best to bring honor to you and to her and will wait on her as she will do me, protecting her, and showering her not only with gifts, but with services."

He coughed and smoothed his coat, and Finch caught himself smiling. "Fusty aristocrats. Ha!" Finch replied. *At least the man knows where he stands. He sounds a bit like my very own Caroline.*

"Speak on, Mister Simmons," Finch replied. "It is clear you wish to. You appear to be a man of opinions. Far be it from me to hold you back. You are amongst friends, none of whom are these aristocrats of which you speak."

Both Simmonses were taken aback. "Really? Well, ehm, of course!" the younger of the two said. "So you must understand the injustice and the lost opportunity there is in having an officer structure made up by only the moneyed. Though, as I understand it, the artillerists and engineers rise through the ranks by merit alone, rather than buying commissions as we do in the army, they still have to pay for engineering school when their work benefits the nation, and we may well be turning our backs on some of the nation's most talented."

As he went on, Finch stole a look at the elder Simmons, who was palming his face in shame. Finch was not surprised; many officers of the Crown would rebuff young Simmons for his tirade. Though he was astonished at the young man's idealism and ambition, he was pleased by it, as well as by his honest, if still somehow genteel, manner. Despite all the negativity that had dogged him the past few days, Finch found himself smiling. Before long, the entire table was eagerly engaged in active conversation regarding the politics of the age and comparing it to centuries past. Topics changed quickly, and even Archibald had his moment to contribute when the subject of Benjamin West, his favorite artist, was suddenly broached. He eagerly discussed the Christlike nature of General Wolfe's depiction in the piece *The Death of General Wolfe.*

As the evening wore on, a small band of musicians appeared on stage and played a rousing and chaotic tune that sounded, to Finch's imagination, like a somewhat transformed version of the old country dance "Dargason." Private Simmons held out his hand to Constance, who took it in her own. The two hurried out to the main floor and began to dance with the assembled crowd.

Caroline grinned gleefully. "You're not as stodgy as you let on, Constance," she called. "Come, Father, dance with me!"

Laughter ensued as Caroline led Finch to the dance floor and bowed to her father, taking the role of the gentleman. Finch, looking around carefully, shrugged his shoulders and curtsied in turn.

Even Simmons the Elder laughed at this unorthodox behavior. He then caught Adelaide looking at him and politely declined her request to dance. The two continued to chat.

After an hour of dancing and a pleasant repast of meat pies over which Constance and James declared mutual admiration for one another, the two families parted ways with new understanding of their comrades in arms.

All together, thought Finch, *this was a grand day for diplomacy, understanding, and Constance. That we found a new eatery of some quality cannot be undervalued, either.*

CHAPTER 4

Northward Push

29 NOVEMBER 1776, 2:10 PM

Giles Finch had suffered a series of setbacks of late.

Despite remaining a colonel and gaining the appreciation of Major Simmons, Finch still needed to regain favor with his commanding officers. As Cornwallis and Prévost had relieved him from duty, it was clear he no longer wielded much influence in their eyes. Depressed, Finch had asked his superiors for a few days' leave to overcome his emotional state, and this had only granted the generals more time to work with and acclimate to Simmons's command. He had then asked Simmons to stand aside, and though his subordinate had assented at once, it was a struggle getting anyone else to listen to him.

Early one afternoon, a messenger summoned Finch for a meeting with Cornwallis. As they stood along the mighty Savannah, watching the townsfolk busy themselves with the chores of the day, the sun beating down upon them, Cornwallis crossed his arms before speaking up.

"I understand we have had our difficulties with one another, Finch, but you are a good man. Let me offer some clearly

65

much-needed advice. You cannot have your major take power over your men. You have to fight for command and their respect. Having rank and seniority will only do so much to assist you. You must work your meritorious wonders and win them back. Why, look what happened with me and General Clinton. As he remarked, he has no societal status but still holds command over me because I thought my rank in society would ensure my position above him as an officer. It appears I must pay for my folly."

Finch laughed hollowly. "General Cornwallis, it appears that in the eyes of many, I have no merit. I was captured and imprisoned by the Rebellion and now am handily reprimanded by the Crown for these events of late. I do not believe I shall be trusted with another expedition anytime soon. Why do you even seek to comfort me?"

"Just you wait, old man." Cornwallis put a firm, bracing hand on Finch's shoulder. "You'll see action once more. Knowing your reputation, when high command orders a seemingly suicidal mission, they'll recall your bravery and deeds of derring-do and order you to the front. For better or worse, of course."

This statement did not assuage Finch's fears, but his cynicism soon turned to curiosity as he heard great shouts of joy from the other side of town. He and Cornwallis casually walked to the town gates, only to witness the sudden arrival of a breathless messenger.

"Victory at the front!" the courier cried. "Governor James Wright has done it: Augusta has been liberated! Having garrisoned the town, the governor now marches on your gates in the name of Britannia. He seeks to exchange pleasantries with the reinforcements to his fair colony."

"How excellent!" Cornwallis interjected. "You see, Finch? We are not defeated yet." He turned to a batman. "We must prepare for a feast. Let us treat the governor to all the comforts we can muster." He turned back to Finch. "Gather more pioneers and direct them to repair the district around the wealthier quarters. We must have some buildings look presentable for Governor Wright's arrival."

Along the Banks of the Savannah River, Savannah, Georgia

1 DECEMBER 1776, 4:22 PM

Two days later, as Finch and his men rushed to effect repairs to the town, they heard drums in the distance. Finch hurried to the battlements. A green-coated column of men swept over the storm-ravaged countryside. As they approached, he could see the colonial crest of Georgia imprinted onto a red field, with the King's Colors handsomely emblazoned into the top left corner. *Friendly troops, certainly, but who are these men in green uniforms? Rangers, perhaps?* Finch thought.

At the fore, he noted through his spyglass a blond, bright-eyed gentleman who seemed to bubble over with excitement. This man, Finch recalled from portraits in the mansion, was Governor James Wright, who, despite being some sixty years of age, did not look a day over forty, wearing a stylish mustard coat that might have come from John Hancock's wardrobe and clashed horribly with his men's green coats. Foppish as he looked, however, he confidently led his men to the gates of Savannah with an energetic, almost comical, loping gait. As they approached, Finch saw that whilst some of Wright's men were clad in green, others, trailing behind the greencoats, were the civilian-attired militia. There wasn't a redcoat in sight. These legions looked a little worse for wear but carried themselves with pride.

Upon reentering the gates of the capital, once again his domain to rule, Wright approached Cornwallis, who extended his hand in greeting, a forced smile on his face. *He must be positively scandalized by Loyalists doing what the redcoats could not,* Finch thought. Wright, oblivious to Cornwallis's attitude and clearly overjoyed by his victory, embraced Cornwallis as a brother, even as the major general recoiled.

"Praise God! We've done it, Earl Cornwallis! The Ninety-Six District: victory. Savannah: a successful defense. Augusta: a rousing rout of the foeman. They've all been purged of the Rebel rank and file, leaving only the niggling partisan! You held well, sir, you did. We actually have a small present for you. For keeping my city safe, don't you know." He gestured to a few mortified Rebel partisans as a band of Loyalists paraded them by. "A gaggle of troublemakers we happened to ambush as we made our way over to Savannah. With the help of some free-roaming Loyalist blackamoors, no less. I received word that these fellows here had given you a hard time, old boy, so we wanted to surprise you, offer you some vindication, wot wot. Think nothing of it."

Finch, who had accompanied his family to watch the provincials parade in, took a close look at the passing Rebels and was disappointed to see that none of them could be identified as the tall leader of the partisan fighters from before. *He must still be at large.*

". . . our combined coordination has allowed us to push back the enemy's many attacks and establish a staging ground from which to undo the foeman's villainous designs in the Southern territories!" Wright was continuing to babble excitedly. "From here, might I suggest I—"

"Steady on, Governor Wright," Prévost interrupted, elbowing and shouldering his way through the crowd that had developed around the other commanding officers, causing Wright to huff in indignation. "Your men must be exhausted with the conclusion of this campaign. The time has come to rest."

"My lads *are* very tired, General Prévost," Wright admitted, "but they are sure to do as asked. Especially with whatever support your men can render. I understand your lights and pioneers did all the hard work these past few days. Your line infantry have had plenty of time to rest, have they not?"

Prévost didn't answer but went pink. "Where are *yours*, for that matter, Governor?"

"Why, most are right here," Wright replied, gesturing to his greencoats. "A rustic militiaman may quail in the face of the enemy, but a *Royal Provincial*, also raised in the colonies but properly trained in the style of line infantry, equipped with the same Brown Bess and bayonet and held in esteem as an *equal* to a British redcoat, is sure to rise to the challenge. I came escorted by my Loyalists in the hopes of routing a Rebel contingent along the way to showcase this fact, as well as our force of will and strength, and have done so. The redcoats are currently garrisoning our bases of operation."

"Very well," Cornwallis replied. "What have you in mind with your band of Loyalist militia?"

"My *force* of Loyalist *provincials* is sizable, gentlemen," Wright continued. "Properly armed, we could drive the enemy clear from South Carolina and gather men along the way. I cannot do it alone in a timely manner, however, and require a man of military background to lead my soldiers to the fore. I am a civilian, fit only for leading a local garrison here in the capital and directing the affairs of the colony." He blushed. "It is only by the most damnable of poor fortune that I was the only man available to lead these men, and only by God's greatest blessing that we triumphed despite it. I know very well your regulars will neither respect nor attend my orders."

He looked at Cornwallis and Prévost, sizing them up.

"I know neither of you gentlemen to be particularly experienced in strategic operation, to be sure, mostly operating under a superior officer, but one of you will be leading our army before the day is out. Discuss it amongst yourselves."

"Sir, surely there must be another way," Finch protested. "There is no time for such gentility. The Rebel is on the run!"

"Then we must organize under one leader and give chase," was Prévost's condescending response.

"Aye," Finch conceded, "But perhaps we should defer to you once more. Though you are both major generals, you know the land better than Cornwallis here, and well, after what h—" he clasped his hands over his mouth.

Shite. That was not smart or kindly. He turned to Cornwallis. "Sir, I . . ."

But Finch had said too much. The slighted major general turned coldly to the engineer, smiling thinly before stalking from the town entryway and into the stockade, slamming the door behind him.

General Prévost's Stateroom, Savannah, Georgia

6 December 1776, 5:02 AM

Cornwallis did not speak to Finch for the next few days. In fact, much of his communication with anyone was limited to laconic grunts. Prévost, feeling sorry for Cornwallis after Finch's outrageous slip of the tongue, attempted to include him in the stratagems for his forces. With Savannah rebuilt, its walls once more able to repel the most determined attackers, Governor Wright returned to power at last, closely protected by Silverstein's Chatham County Militia and the green-coated provincials of the First Georgia Volunteers. That left the rest of the Crown forces to be divided up at Prévost's discretion.

It was to that end that Prévost called Cornwallis and Finch into his office to discuss plans for the rest of the southern campaign. With the sunrise still hours away, the gentlemen worked by torchlight, a map stretched across a table. Finch respectfully tried to let his superiors make the decisions whilst Cornwallis sulked at a distance. Only Prévost seemed invested.

"According to Wright's reports, the Ninety-Six District is protected by a star fort," Prévost remarked to Cornwallis. "That ought to provide a fair bit of protection for the men there. I'd say only a single regiment would be necessary to hold it, and yet it would make an excellent staging ground for our liberation of South Carolina, would you not agree?"

"*Hmph*," Cornwallis grunted, staring sorrowfully out the window.

Prévost carried on. "Let's order their local militia to hold the fort by themselves. They are likely to have gained some experience fighting the enemy for so long. They will be sure to hold to the last, as it is their homes that would be endangered."

"And Augusta?" inquired Finch. He still regretted his earlier words and now attempted to contribute to the discussion. His bright demeanor, however, only drew scowls from both generals.

"The Sixteenth Foot has been battered by combat from the late Colonel Haldimand's sally," Prévost replied icily. "Placing them there and advancing past them, they might take on replacements and supplies as they guard the town."

Cornwallis coughed. Prévost turned around expectantly.

"Do you have something to contribute, Charles?"

Cornwallis just glared.

"I do not know what he has to say on the matter," Finch began, "but I would certainly say—"

"Colonel Finch, you have said quite enough. You are dismissed from the room. Call in Major Simmons," Prévost replied.

Finch's face once again began to burn, but he decided that he had already served his punishment. The entire officer corps had snubbed him since his ill-chosen words. He would have apologized but felt the collective slights directed at him were too much. Taking a few deep breaths, he faced his commander. "I think, sir—"

"Do not think, Finch. Build. Thinking does not suit you."

"Whilst that may be true, sir, I am an engineer, and engineers think. More to the point, I would ask that you hear me out."

Prévost sighed, tapping the table. "What is it?"

"I do not believe your means of coping with circumstances is entirely fair. It seems most petty to offload such annoyance upon a fellow officer for pointing out the facts behind a failed excursion. I meant not to antagonize anyone, so much as to assist in a decision-making process. Whilst I wish I had chosen my words more carefully so as not to embarrass anyone, it was important to expedite the decision with respect to appointing an overall commander."

Prévost raised an eyebrow. "What are you trying to say, Finch?"

Cornwallis turned in Finch's direction.

"I mean to say . . ." Finch wavered a moment, unsure whether he should go forward with this line of thought. He was not sure he wished to blame others, much less incite the rage of Howe's protégé and his acquaintance. He also felt apologetic for his part in the conflict of late, but he had been on the receiving end for too long. It seemed as though everything had been made out to be his fault, and he did not appreciate it.

"Earl Cornwallis was responsible for both the nighttime assault on the Jewish cemetery and for advising me to rebuild Savannah's civilian structures first and foremost, sir. Whilst I understand you may disagree with my participation in both affairs, I'd thank you to not heap your cruelties upon me and to not raise the good earl, who is assuredly a fine man, on a pedestal."

Prévost turned to Cornwallis. "Is this true, sir?"

Cornwallis solemnly returned Prévost's gaze. "I apologize profusely for my conduct, sir. This is far more than Colonel Finch, who took my advice, has done."

Well said.

"Gentlemen, gentlemen, there is no need to fight," Prévost said. "All is forgiven." He turned to Finch, his eyes still smoldering. "Colonel Finch? Summon Major Simmons to the fore. Cornwallis and I will make use of his services as the campaign continues. That way, you may play counsel to Governor Wright."

Finch nodded, devastated.

"Dismissed."

The disgraced colonel turned on his heel and exited the room. Passing Simmons in the hall, Finch wordlessly jerked his head back toward the stateroom, gesturing the man forward.

Governor Wright's Office, Savannah, Georgia
6 December 1776, 7:30 AM

"Why, it's the controversial Colonel Finch. Do come in, do come in," Wright said with a smile, bowing floridly before drawing himself up to his gangly, five-foot-ten-inch height and looking dignified, if a little comical with his rustic charm, despite his efforts to be cosmopolitan.

"I am he," Finch replied, extending a hand, which the Georgian governor shook enthusiastically with both of his.

"A hero of the people you are, sir. Saving the cemetery, repairing our homes. Ohhh, I don't care what Cornwallis or Prévost say—we all feel you are quite the engineer, my boy."

Wright had still not let go of Finch's hands.

"Er . . . thank you, Governor Wright," Finch replied, at last extricating himself from the governor's crushing grip. "Thank you very much for your esteem. Now, sir, I understand from the earl that you have a role in mind for me?"

"Aye, sir, I do," the governor crowed, excitedly nodding his head. "Georgia, though a relatively new colony, anchors the flank of the thirteen in this vast continent. It is true that Florida is a newly captured fort unto herself, but I would not say we can proclaim any other territories to the west and south actual colonies in their own right yet."

"So you'd like me to fortify Georgia, now that it is largely liberated by the Crown?"

"Well, the large towns, at the very least," Wright clarified, clasping his hands.

Finch smiled, appreciating the respect he received from the governor. "Governor Wright, sir. I am at your service. You need only point me in the directions of the towns you wish fortified, and I shall sally forth at once." He bowed.

"Oh, wonderful!" Wright rubbed his hands together excitedly. "The next time we are hit by Rebel raiders, they'll see who gets the last laugh, they will. I shall provide for you the men of the First Georgia Volunteers. Peabody's boys, you see. They will protect and swell your corps of builders as you erect a fortress in Augusta. Take Silverstein and his lads, too. You know as well as I that journalist Jew is dead useful and a good man, as well. See if he cannot write a history of your victories, Finch."

The engineer was taken aback. "What about Savannah? Does that not leave the town virtually defenseless?"

"Worry not, Finch. I'll rouse the Tories round here to their proper sense of duty. They'll protect the capital." He smiled. "Now, as for towns to be fortified, since your pioneers have rebuilt Savannah, we have to build some fortifications around Augusta. It's one of the few other large towns in Georgia."

"Just Augusta?" Finch inquired, amused at the antics of the quirky governor. "You seemed to imply there would be more."

"There are not very many major settlements in Georgia, Colonel Finch," Wright said with a grin. "If any towns are settled during this bloody conflict, we shall let you know."

CHAPTER 5

The Construction of Fort Peabody

Loyalist Encampment, Augusta, Georgia

10 JANUARY 1777, 12:33 PM

As the day's sun beat down from the heavens above, Giles Finch nodded approvingly at the finishing touches on the construction of the last of the initial nine blockhouses guarding Augusta, Georgia. He wiped his brow free of sweat as he surveyed the deforested land nearby. *No less tragic than New Jersey, but now is not the time for mourning,* he thought. *At least the crash of timber has subsided.*

"Good show, gentlemen!" he declared, brandishing his baton, attempting to take a more energetic stance toward his command. Yet deep down inside, he could not help but miss Boston. The South had its charms, but several local matters, from the widespread practice of slavery to the adverse weather, galled him. The range of pleasantly cool to scorching-hot conditions that endured in the deep South meant that the war would be fought year-round, and such endless conflict would be sure to prove exhausting.

Already Finch's laborers and their escorts, the Chatham County Militia and the First Georgia Volunteers, had fought off two particularly vicious attacks on the fortifications as they were being built. The engineer could not help but wonder whether a vindictive Mister Marion was behind the desperate nature of the assaults.

Having gone from building to building and concluding his inspection, he had found all but one structure to his liking. Finch made a note of the offender, which was in the southwest sector. He poked at its moldy walls with his baton and turned to the ancient, rail-thin, and rather weaselly-looking Colonel Lysander Peabody, who led the construction crew responsible for the building of the blockhouse. "Do you see the mold growing on these planks of wood? This will not do. We must tear down this structure and rebuild it anew, sir."

As Peabody's face fell, Finch clapped him on the back. "Worry not. Your work will be done soon enough. Your men have assisted in building mostly solid fortifications so far. You are to be congratulated, Colonel Peabody. Please serve out rum rations and give them time to rest before starting again. For myself, I feel somewhat forlorn. My stomach rebels against me. I should like nothing more than to return to my family."

Peabody nodded at Finch. "Sah. You may do that, indeed, yet would you not like to partake in some lovely pipe smoke first?" He flashed a clay pipe. "Silverstein and I, along with some of the other lads, tend to partake after a hard day's work."

"It is most soothing, sir," Silverstein added meekly. "Eases my nerves so I can write about our exploits."

"Have you been writing about us, Captain?" Finch laughed.

"The *Georgia Gazette* finds the exploits of our boys most engaging, sir. We have quite a following, even though I have only embellished slightly on our tales of adventure. I am excited to see how many men we can rally to our cause."

"Is that so?" Peabody said with a laugh. "Well then, carry on." He turned to the engineer. "Finch? Are you joining us?"

Smiling at Peabody, the engineer replied, "No thank you, sir. I have other means of engagement, and my family is the only drug I need for my malady—that is, homesickness."

The firebrand Peabody was not to be denied so quickly, however. He threw a friendly arm around Finch's shoulder. "Come now, sir. I was a preacher before I raised this regiment, and I know that Jesus smiles upon all, including us poor sinners. We all sin in some way or form, and this would be a lesser sin compared to the killing of our fellow man. Come, join us. Know that God will forgive you. You may consider this an act of pressure from your doctor to be at ease with your troops and to fraternize awhile." He poked Finch in the belly with his index finger. "You seem lonely. When was the last time you spoke on even terms with someone you liked and trusted?"

Finch thought awhile. "I suppose it was most likely when I spent time in the company of Major Pitcairn in Rhode Island, when I was called upon to fortify Newport. I fear he was the last true friend I entertained the company of since the war's beginning. It feels like a decade ago, and yet it was but a year."

"That is still some time. You should reach out more to your fellow troops."

"I do wish to, but it is against regulations."

"Nobody will care. Light this pipe for me and chat awhile."

Finch did so, and followed Silverstein and the colonel to a secluded clearing. "There's a good lad," the provincial colonel growled. "Now sit."

The three officers seated themselves on logs and made themselves comfortable, as a few other soldiers milled about and smoked as well. Peabody took his pipe from Finch and inhaled deeply, closing his eyes before exhaling smoke rings into the sky.

"Now, how are things with your family?"

Finch smiled sadly. "They seem well, but I fear my children grow too old for me too quickly. I am no longer seen as a great hero in their eyes, and they begin to defy me, much as I try to support them. I am concerned, too, that I gain a bad reputation from having them with me—that my reputation will be jeopardized by their frivolous activity, especially because I approve of some of their madness."

"If they perform these activities, and you approve of it, then by God may it continue, sir. As an officer, you are beholden but to the rules of war and to your men. You need not stoop to the tenets of society. You are a man of action, a dog of war. And if dogs can be wild, so can you."

Finch had never thought of that. Though he led a life that strayed from the ordinary somewhat, he made every effort to act in a manner typically befitting his position, for fear of rejection. At Peabody's invitation, he now began to feel more at ease. He shakily inquired, "May I see your pipe?"

Peabody handed the pipe to Finch, and the engineer examined the vessel, turning it over in his hands. He found it to be a most agreeable and well-crafted construct.

"It is actually my pipe originally," Silverstein remarked. "I sold it to him at a fair price. I inherited my father's collection, but I whittled that one. For all the harsh punishments dealt out by Hashem, I do not fear the Lord's wrath over a little tobacco."

"*Har!*" Peabody cheered. "That's the spirit."

Peabody looked on approvingly as Finch, having taken a small sniff of the sweet tobacco, filled his lungs with smoke. As Finch coughed and gagged, his lungs burning, Peabody burst out laughing. "Don't be ashamed, Finch! There's a first time for everyone."

Finch proceeded to tell him about how his reputation amongst the men may have been besmirched by his capture and imprisonment, how he did not get along with his superiors, and how much he feared disembowelment by some of the more ferocious Southern partisans, most notably Francis Marion, the Swamp Fox. As he continued to puff on the tobacco, his ability to withstand coughing improved, and he began to grow relaxed. *Goodness, this is a powerful agent*, he thought. *I wonder if it is safe to continue to partake. Yet if Colonel Peabody smokes it, should tobacco really be considered a threat? He appears well, after all.*

After a long, comforting discussion, Finch noticed that it was dinnertime. Knowing that he shouldn't keep his family waiting, he turned to the two officers.

"It was an absolute delight, Colonel Peabody. I thank you both for the company. For now, I must attend to my family."

Silverstein nodded, whilst Peabody saluted him, returning to his professional military etiquette. "Sah," the fiery, red-haired man of God replied, green eyes piercing into Finch's soul. "Go with God, sah. I shall keep you in my prayers. Will I be seeing you Sunday at my encampment? After church?"

"I fear I am not a churchgoing man, Mister Peabody," Finch responded, "though I should be happy to see you, say, Saturday evenings, that we may continue this exploration of my mind. And, shall we say, yours too?"

"Very well, sah. Though you will find my mind to be quite simple. It is devoted to our God and to our king, who is to me an incarnation of Saint George the Farmer himself. Though in addition to slaying the dragon of famine, he is slaying the dragon which represents the disunion and dearth of patriotism in our empire!"

"I, ehm . . . I see."

What an eccentric.

Meanwhile, Finch had concluded that it would be unwise for the Loyalist forces to impinge upon the property of the town itself, no matter how loyal the population was, until they could erect fortifications that might protect them and improve relations. So he had ordered encampments erected around the town, with no quartering within. Though it pleased him that he was able to build structures and improve lives, he feared, as usual, for the well-being of his family, who had again insisted on accompanying him to the front.

"You are home early, husband. Welcome back," Adelaide called as Finch returned to the cramped officers' cabin. Then she wrinkled her nose. "What *is* that smell?"

"Why, it is tobacco, and aye, my good wife, I do return, feeling wondrous well, I might add." Finch gave her a kiss, from which she pulled away. "I gave the lads a half day because I felt ill at ease, and Colonel Peabody helped to assuage my maladies."

"Wonderful, Father!" Caroline replied, clapping her hands. "Now do something to assuage your breath!"

The room burst out laughing, and Finch blushed. "Perhaps pipe smoking was a poor idea, but the reverend's company was most agreeable. I should like to engage his company again."

"Certainly, husband," was Adelaide's reply. Smiling, she continued, "But mind you don't smoke so much, lest you would see us driven from your encampment."

"Very well, very well, I comprehend," Finch responded with a chuckle. "Indeed, even as I regret that you feel a need to follow me to war, your company has been endlessly helpful, and my love of each and every one of you is beyond words." Finch pulled his family into an embrace. This time they relented.

"Husband, you may have put several enemy regiments to flight in your day, but despite our jests, there is nothing you can do to force a withdrawal of your brood from our position. We are here for you until the end."

"That's right, Father. Don't you dare go on about wishing to send us back to Savannah," Caroline cried. "I was just getting to know the soldiers here. I fetched one of them some rum, and he let me fire a shot from his musket." She grinned. "I shall not tell you which soldier, though. He promised me a pie if I didn't tell, you see."

"See what you've done now?" Adelaide remarked to Finch. She turned to her daughter. "No, dear. Your father needs us too much to send us back to Governor Wright's. He just needs to be reminded of that sometimes."

"Good, because I like Governor Wright, but his cat is mean. She scratched me when I wanted to pet her kittens."

"Kittens?" Archibald piped up, having been heavily engaged in his latest artwork: what appeared to be a catalogue of the different uniforms of Crown troops he had encountered. He now seemed excited to meet the aforementioned felines.

"Back in Savannah, dear," Adelaide replied.

"Oh. Very well, then." Archibald returned to his artwork.

"Where is Constance?" Finch inquired. "Perhaps we might all have a picnic together on the town green. We could make sandwiches."

"Constance has been keeping to herself," Adelaide explained. "She has been somewhat moody since I instituted a curfew for her. She had been staying up far too late looking glassy-eyed into the moon."

"She was thinking about Private Simmons," Caroline interjected. Everyone nodded and chuckled.

"I was not!" came a cry outside the window. Constance poked her face through. It had gone scarlet. "Well, perhaps I was," she sighed dreamily. "I was writing letters to him under the light of the moon. The two of us have been exchanging pieces. He fancies himself quite the poet, with a most agreeable counterfeit."

Loyalist Encampment, Augusta, Georgia

20 January 1777, 3:55 PM

As Finch was reviewing the plans for his army's stay in Augusta in his office one afternoon, there was a sudden, resounding crash as a large leather ball flew into the room through a window, upsetting his mug of coffee. Picking up the irregular orb and stepping outside into the mild morning sun, Finch noted with irritation a quintet of youths anxiously watching him.

Looking them over a moment, he then realized that holding these children responsible over a broken mug, as expensive as it may be, was not the proper thing to do. Like Finch, they were only attempting to pass the time in between their menial tasks. He also noted to his delight that Archibald was amongst the boys. He was glad that his son, despite his shyness, had made friends. Finch waved at the boys, who appeared visibly relieved but regarded each other awkwardly.

"We're very sorry about your window, sir," one mumbled, clearly mortified.

Finch smiled and said, "No harm done, lad. I've had men shooting at me for just about two years almost nonstop. A football breaking the window is not the end of the world. Come! A brief game before we go our respective ways?"

Finch had never been much of an athlete, but huffing and puffing alongside the younger men, he felt a certain rush of joy, made only deeper as he watched his son skillfully block the shot of one of his companions.

Finch's family life was taking a turn for the better. He admitted to himself that he appreciated having the support of his wife and children despite the risks. They provided some relief from the stressors of the campaign; he spent the rest of his time in the company of petty politicians and bloodthirsty maniacs on both sides of the war.

With Private Simmons attached to Cornwallis's command and temporarily out of the picture, Constance took to pen and paper, writing to her beloved frequently, and in emulation of him also became a voracious reader, enjoying many of the classics Finch purchased in support of her education and discussing them at length in her letters. She spent much of the day in her room reading, and whilst Finch wished to see more of his daughter, he realized she was content and in love, and let the matter be.

His other children were a different matter, each tripping over the other to enjoy the company of their father. Oftentimes leaving Father Peabody to command the men for the day as they worked on the walls protecting Augusta, Finch, with an equally engaged Adelaide in tow, occasionally took the day off to play with Caroline and Archibald. A favored activity was teaching them the basics of swordsmanship and a few cardinal rules of soldiering.

"Parry four, riposte, prime, retreat, balestra, lunge!" he cried as he watched his children follow his instructions with sticks at the ready. "You must understand, children, that in order to win the day, it is important to know the enemy as well as you do yourself," Finch instructed, firmly but kindly. "If one can break the enemy's spirit without doing battle, as General Howe tried to do, then you need not battle, and many lives will be saved. However, if a fight must be joined, you will still do well to know how an enemy fights and maneuvers, so you can defeat them handily. Now try and hit me!"

He then listened patiently as they discussed their lives of late and played with dolls over tea. "So, Caroline, the lads of town have been mean to you again lately?" Finch inquired, sipping tea from a minuscule teacup intended for Caroline's poppets. "Have you sicced Reginald on them yet?" Caroline giggled as Finch gestured to her toy lion.

"Perhaps you can share your dolls with them, and they can tell that you mean no harm toward them," Archibald suggested. Finch smiled inwardly. *My boy the diplomat.*

"*RAWWWWWWWWWWWWWWWR!* A fine plan, my young sir!" Finch replied, imitating the voice of Reginald the Lion. "It is a wonderrrrrrrrrrrr Colonel Finch here got so far without your diplomatic guidance."

Though he knew that he could have spent more time around his loved ones, as "treatment" under Father Peabody continued, Finch concluded that perhaps he had been a bit curt with his family, the result of stressful days at work. In addition to being less short with his wife and children, Finch made it his goal to be a good father and spend more time with them, occasionally having another officer review the men in his stead.

As the days passed, his time spent in Augusta had become increasingly agreeable. Peabody's treatment plan worked wonders. Finch's cabin fever and outrage about being stationed behind the northward push slowly began to vanish. No longer did he grit his teeth and scowl in jealousy at the populace of Augusta as they went about their ways. He even began to offer help to the citizenry, encouraging those pioneers under his command to aid in preparing fields for a new year and calling upon his men to improve the irrigation canals along the bubbling Savannah River. The canals were then less likely to collapse. Entire fields of onions were planted quickly over the course of the mild southern winter.

With British popularity growing in town after the blockhouse construction project and the troops' work improving the local irrigation system, the engineer had turned his attention to drafting

plans for the next phase of Fort Peabody, so named out of gratitude for the old man's assistance.

Loyalist Encampment, Augusta, Georgia
27 JANUARY 1777, 10:37 AM

Peabody, always his philosophical self, was silently reading the
Bible in the officers' cabin, and Finch, fresh from a bath in a
nearby pond, was poring over maps from a chair of his own, each
by the light of small open windows and a flickering candle. A
knock sounded at the door.

"Enter," called Peabody in his calm voice.

The door slowly creaked open to reveal a Native American
warrior in full war paint. The ancient, relatively short fellow wore
a great many feathers in his long white hair. He was clad in buckskin trousers and a linen shirt that showed off a toned muscula-
ture; a crude trade musket that had seen many battles was slung
over his back, accompanied by a pair of knives in a belt strapped
to his waist. Finch could tell this man possessed great power and
energy, even at his apparent advanced age. He entered the room
purposefully. Trailing behind him were two companions.

Finch looked on in awe as Peabody and the war chief shook
hands across the table bearing a map of the surrounding territories. "Finch, this is Running Deer of the Cherokee Nation, a
close personal friend and convert to the Lord's will. Running
Deer, this is Giles Finch of His Majesty's Corps of Engineers."

With that brief introduction, Peabody returned his attention to
the chieftain and began discussing matters in the Native's tongue,
leaving Finch astounded. It was an elaborate language, gracefully
spoken by the war chief, even as Peabody seemed to struggle a

little, speaking haltingly and seeming to have to search for vocabulary. On occasion, the chieftain shot Finch a curious, appraising glance whilst speaking with the reverend, who used grand gestures in his speech whilst also looking in Finch's direction once in awhile. Finch hoped Peabody did not overstate his achievements. He didn't want to be expected to deliver in some grand way, for though he felt he had done the Crown some good in the past, his record overall was rather patchy.

Meanwhile, Running Deer's warriors stood behind their commander. Finch took it upon himself to be hospitable. He lifted himself from his chair and went to the warriors, who looked rather bored. Had they been through this repertoire before?

"Goood moor-ning," Finch began, speaking slowly. "I aaam—"

"Reverend Peabody has taught us well," replied one of the warriors, a slender woman with aggressive eyebrows and a single feather in her raven hair, who was attired in a simple buckskin dress. "You are Giles, a . . . erm . . . builder?"

A woman warrior, Finch thought, with a double take at her arsenal of knives and pistols. *Why, this is shocking. I hope Caroline and Adelaide never meet her.*

"Hm, what? A builder? . . . Errr . . . yes! An engineer," clarified Finch, his thoughts returning to the conversation.

"Yes. An engineer. In your King George's mighty warbands," the brave replied in slow, but steady, Georgian-accented English.

"Err . . ." Finch's face reddened. Trying again, he smiled. "Yes, I am. And you are?"

The other warrior, a striking fellow wearing naught but a loincloth and a belt of various implements of war, drew himself up proudly and replied, in slower, more halting English, "I am Jack Storm Crow." He smiled, looking proud of this announcement. He was not as well muscled as the war chief but certainly looked toned and deadly, with long, tanned legs and strong arms.

"Well met, Mister Storm Crow. Would you and your compatriot—"

"My name is She Who Laughs. I shall speak for Jack Storm Crow and myself."

"Err . . . yes. Would you, Jack Storm Crow, and you, madam . . . er . . . She Who Laughs, care for a spot of tea?"

Storm Crow smiled, and She Who Laughs grunted. "Thank you."

Finch turned to a batman, who had been hovering nearby. "Fetch the teacups, if you could, Perkins. We shall be having a little party for our Native allies."

Finch's slim, mustard-haired batman bowed and turned away to find the appropriate accessories.

"Have you had tea before, madam?" Finch inquired of She Who Laughs.

"Reverend Peabody has instructed us in your ceremonies and ways. I have never performed one outside our interactions with missionaries before, however," was the woman warrior's reply.

"Did you enjoy the experience?"

"Yes."

"Then by all means, let us partake," Finch replied with a smile.

As Father Peabody and Running Deer concluded their discussion, the entire company came together in the cramped, low-lit building. The map was furled, chairs and a spread were procured, biscuits gathered, and teacups nearly bubbling over with brew were served to all. It was a strong variety of tea, and Finch found himself reeling at its earthy taste. The Natives seemed used to it. Storm Crow smiled at Finch. "Do you like the tea?"

Finch tried to be diplomatic. "Is this the type that Father Peabody shares with you?"

Storm Crow nodded. "Yes. It is very . . . delicious, is it not?"

Finch nodded mutely.

After tea was polished off, the small group stepped out of the cabin to get some fresh air. There on Augusta Green they played ninepins awhile. The Natives delighted in the concept of this game of great skill, cheering raucously amongst themselves anytime anyone knocked pins down. As Finch looked around, he noted that the townsfolk had locked themselves indoors, afraid of the mischief the "savages" might make. Disappointed at the lack of hospitality from his own people, even as he realized that perhaps it was due to apprehension from past conflict, Finch threw himself into the game with a redoubled passion to take his mind off the matter.

As the small band of players looked on, Finch wound up, violently hurling the ball at the pins with an intense passion. He knocked seven flying in one fell swoop, skittering them in a matter most ungenteel across the pitch. Noticing the two pins remaining upright, he swore angrily as they swayed left, then swayed right, but did not go down. Looking from face to face, Finch realized his anger had concerned his fellow players. His frustration almost immediately melted away. "Sorry!" he said. "I shall collect them at once."

The meeting then continued as the warriors—Briton, Loyalist, and Native alike—gathered around a campfire outside the cabin, which itself was too small for all of them. Having chewed his biscuit politely, manners like to any Englishman, Running Deer spoke once more in his melodious accent. "Reverend Peabody, we must speak of strategies for the war ahead. My warriors await my orders, and our blood boils for combat. How would you lead us? Shall we merely raid the lands of your enemies, as is our wont? Or shall we lash back at them as they did to us, and raze their villages to the ground?" He smiled grimly. "I have also heard of tribes in the north kidnapping the children of those opposed to us and raising them as their own."

"Well," Peabody replied, appearing a little shaken at these suggestions, "for now we must show mercy and decency, as Jesus did for all." He took a deep breath. "What if you scouted for our own soldiers and ensured their safety by telling us what lies ahead, and by drawing the enemy into traps, when we might attack with more force?"

Before anyone could respond, a loud voice rang out from an enlisted man hurrying in their direction. "Sir! Courier approaching the front gates! White flag of truce!"

The reverend jumped up immediately, stomping off in the direction of the courier. Finch extended his spyglass, caught sight of the messenger, then gulped.

Francis Marion himself was at the gates of Augusta.

Finch turned to the Natives. "Francis Marion is at our doorstep. If he knows you to be in league with us, your people will bear the brunt of terrible punishment. We shall stall him and see what he wants. You should hide in the cabin."

A few minutes later, after the Native delegation had scrambled to conceal themselves, Peabody returned with the scarred, angry-looking giant of a man, who hulked over the priest's thin frame. Frock-coated and carrying at least three pistols and a fowler, as well as a pair of daggers and a tomahawk, the fellow was just as dangerous as Finch remembered. With a pronounced gulp, he could not help but harbor a sneaking suspicion that future conflict would be unavoidable. Attempting to be polite, Finch offered a hand to the towering partisan, which he did not take.

"My name is Francis Marion," the behemoth began in a pleasant enough manner as he sat by the fire, still as tall as Peabody, who had remained standing. He caught sight of Finch and nodded. "I believe we have met, Mister Finch."

Finch frowned anxiously, fiddling with a pipe he'd borrowed from Silverstein whilst trying to look brave. "Oh," he began, attempting to sound dismissive as he stumbled over his words. "Y-you're the commander of those local raiders who bullied my pioneers at the Jewish cemetery, were you not?" Marion glowered at him, and the engineer's resolve began to crumble. Finch continued, "It's a, well, ehm . . . here you are again."

Colonel Marion laughed bitterly at Finch's obvious fear of him. "We call ourselves freedom fighters, but yes, you may call us what you will. We did indeed give your men a hiding, and now we are back, here once more to harass you. Our next step will be to liberate the town you most cruelly occupy." He turned to Peabody. "You seem a nice enough sort, man of God that you are, so I shall cut you a deal. It would be a shame if civilians had to die just to uphold your misguided sense of honor. Leave the town, and nobody will be hurt. We can fight some other day."

Finch frowned, tapping his pipe against the log he used as his seat, as Reverend Peabody whittled a stick with a short blade. Marion sneered at them both, before Captain Silverstein stepped into the meeting, naked blade in hand, his face the picture of rage.

"W-we're not afraid of you, you scum!" Silverstein announced shakily, pointing his hanger blade at Marion's throat. "We may have ceded our cemetery to your men, but Adonai willing, we shall drive you from the field next time. In case you haven't noticed, we have fortified this town, where we shall make a stand until I see you and your followers dead at my feet!"

"You must forgive Captain Silverstein. "He is still . . . ahm . . . somewhat wroth with the past depredations of your . . . volunteers. But indeed I'm afraid your demands are quite impossible to meet, Mister Marion," Reverend Peabody said. "We have heard of your reputation as a villainous blackguard amongst the Natives and will not encourage your reign of terror. If you are looking for recruits or even passing support in Augusta, I feel you will not find much in the way of either. We have provided for the townsfolk in exchange for their hospitality, and they appear most content with our decency. Lord knows, perhaps they might even support *us* and welcome the security and resources we offer. In times of darkness, one must dig in deeper to defend what one holds dear. You, sir, will only force our defenders to be all the more stalwart in their efforts."

The Swamp Fox smirked. "Well, my force has grown since last we met. You will find yourself hard-pressed to defeat us. As for the Natives and their views . . . well, they're not like us. Why should they have their own land when they barely use it? Even if they were civilized, surely you don't think they'd leave us be after the war? You may think you are reforming them, Peabody, but know this: nothing can be made of their duplicity. Why, when settling the western frontier, my family ran afoul of a tribe and they killed my cousin! Abducted his wife and children! I am glad my overseers and I are so well equipped to protect ourselves and our slaves from such threats."

"Sorry, friend," Peabody snapped, "but we do not brook that kind of nonsense. It would be wrong to denounce an entire people for the actions of a few. Might I add that the local Natives are relatively peaceable and that many have become good Christians. Perhaps your cousin had encroached on that tribe's territory? If so, he was settling on land as delegated to the Natives by Britannia's treaties. The Natives would be defending themselves as such."

Marion grunted, and Finch realized the situation could turn foul very quickly.

"Indian lovers," Marion remarked, grinning a toothy, feral smile. "*And* Yids. Just my luck. See, I've tried to be patient, but I suppose you all will carry on with your absurd belief that Indian tribes should be treated with the respect of any nation, not to mention that the Hebrews can be trusted. Much as it would pain me, you realize I could kill you three right now. I suppose I would not mind killing the Yid, but it would dampen my spirits to slay you two, even as it would certainly put the fear of God into your men and your pet savages. I was no enemy to Britain until they began imposing their will on my rights over the Negroes and Natives."

"Kill us? Under a flag of truce?" Finch laughed, trying to sound braver than he felt. "Our men would have you subdued and killed at once. This war has been nothing but suffering for me since its infancy. I came into it with preparations made for my death. Have you? Do you not wish to live to massacre and pillage and plunder and rape another day? That is what you partisans do, do you not?"

The Fox scoffed. "You're a brave man, engineer. I respect that in a foe. I will make your death quick when it comes."

An idea came to Finch. His eyes flashed a second, and, shooting a quick look at Peabody, he smiled. "Though I have nothing to lose, I know many a promising man in our regiment who might die in the upcoming conflict. We cannot have that. If you allow us to withdraw our men, we shall evacuate posthaste."

"What?" Silverstein cried, horrified. "Sir, you cannot just abandon our position, so well fortified, to the enemy! It would undermine all we have worked for!"

Peabody nodded. *Excellent,* Finch thought. *He comprehends. And Silverstein's hysterics caused Marion to not question it.* The British engineer nodded to Marion. "Let us finalize the matter at hand by drawing out an agreement for the temporary cessation of hostilities back in the officers' cabin. Silverstein? Prepare the, ahem, biscuits."

Silverstein suddenly went quiet. "As you say, sir," he remarked at length with a dramatic sigh, glowering at the Fox. "We shall have ourselves a small reception." He turned and trotted off to the cabin.

The Swamp Fox appeared convinced by this lie. "You can stuff your cookies up your arse," he grumbled. "Just take me back to your cabin, and I'll sign the damned documents. I have my pistols trained on you, however. Cry for help, and it will be a waste of your life."

The Swamp Fox marched the two Crown colonels to the cabin, whilst Silverstein ran back toward the encampment. Onlookers gasped and pointed, but Finch urgently called them off before they could defend him.

Making their way to the cabin on the hill, Marion halted the Loyalist-British duo at its front door. "Open the door, and set foot inside," Marion crowed, "but if anyone is in there, you're dead."

"Fair enough," Finch opened the door into the dim light of the room. "After you, sir."

Marion curtsied sarcastically. "Oh, no, miladdo, I'm not so foolish as to turn my back on you. After *you*."

Finch shrugged and raised his voice ever so slightly. "So you want me to open the door, and you will follow Peabody and myself. Understood."

He opened the door and entered, holding it open for Peabody. Suddenly, Marion surged forward and knocked the aged preacher aside, attempting to sweep the room for antagonists with his pistols.

It happened in a flash. One moment Marion was clearing the room—then, to Finch's grim satisfaction, Marion was thrown to the ground in a flurry of wood, stone, and steel.

Crunch. A knobby oaken war club crushed his head, dashing his brains and fragments of his skull all over the floor.

Thunk. A wicked serrated scalping knife penetrated deep into the Fox's belly and was drawn across his stomach.

This done, She Who Laughs regarded the outfoxed partisan's body and smiled grimly. "It is done," she said.

Finch looked on in shock, as Peabody stood silent in front of Marion's form, which lay crumpled upon the ground, a bloodied mess.

At last gaining control of his nerves, Finch crossed over to his night table and shakily lit up his pipe, taking a long puff and coughing vigorously in an attempt to subdue his quavering nerves. He turned to the Natives. "W-well," he remarked. "We just murdered one of the Rebellion's best officers. We did what we must. This is sure to cause a frightful outrage, but it needed to be done."

"You are welcome," Storm Crow replied, nodding.

"Aye, aye, thank you all," Finch replied. "Whilst I worry what this may mean for your fellow Natives, regardless of nation, I am relieved we of the Crown have one less terrifying foe. Well done. At the very least, it will give us a few days to prepare a defense whilst the Rebels await his return. I only hope this action will not result in displeasure from those who would otherwise ally with us."

"Surely we will not receive too much difficulty for . . . this." Peabody gestured to the body. "From what I understand, the man was a slaveowner who treated his charges with great cruelty, and was a freelance Indian hunter as well. You see how our friends look on him with outrage."

Peabody's Native allies had crowded around the corpse and, as one, collectively spat upon it.

"I—I suppose so," Finch acknowledged. "I simply cannot expect our own authorities, least of all Cornwallis, will treat the Natives fairly for the murder of a Crown citizen, wicked or not."

"Nobody saw the act, and it was the killing of a monster who treated the Indians with scorn," Peabody assured him. "My interpretation of the Good Book says that whilst we must avoid bearing false witness, it may save a good man's life to omit certain details on occasion."

Finch thought awhile. "You are a preacher, so it is not my position to cite scripture to debate you," he decided at last. "But we had best prepare for a series of avenging strikes from the enemy." He turned to She Who Laughs. "Madam . . . Who Laughs, do you think you might take some men and bury the scum far from civilization? It will give us some time to determine our next action whilst we keep the Rebels wondering as to Mister Marion's whereabouts. Perhaps they won't act without his say-so." Looking back at Peabody, Finch inquired, "What are our numbers?"

"Well, I have two hundred men," Peabody remarked. "Silverstein's got fifty. That's not very many if we are to hold against a band of rabid partisan warriors. What's more, if the town is to be covered on all sides, we shall not have the manpower to protect every yard."

"Then we must even these numbers," said Running Deer, looking up from a silent meditation over Marion's dead body. "Surprise them."

"We?" Peabody inquired.

"Reverend Peabody, please understand you have our deepest appreciation for your assistance in protecting our lands. In learning to respect us, your King George has done well. He has our club in exchange for the troubles he put upon himself, including his acts of generosity in teaching us well the ways of your people and of your God. Some of us have found enlightenment in your Son King, Jesus. Others, they have chosen the path of our beloved ancestors. This is well, too. But despite the differences, you have kept us as one against the Rebel invader. You have shown me my way to heaven. Now let us together send our enemies to hell."

Reverend Peabody bowed humbly. "I thank you, my friends, for your kind offer of assistance. Let us prepare the blockhouses and get the citizenry to safety. Then we can speak of this surprise attack."

Fort Peabody's Foundations, Augusta, Georgia

30 JANUARY 1777, 12:33 PM

Spurred on by fears of a reprisal by the Rebels for the assassination of their leader, Finch's crew was able to quickly complete Fort Peabody. Finch, harrowed in his dreams by bloody ambushes and jumping at unexpected noises by day, laid out instructions to his pioneers and engineers with the lines on his face creased with concern. It had been two weeks since any sighting of the Swamp Fox's men, and yet their terror tactics seemed to be working. Finch's men, placed on high alert, were exhausted and on edge.

Unfortunately for the enemy, clumsy as the Loyalists' labor may have become, the constant fear of counterattack inspired them to work harder. Though the Swamp Fox had fallen, as Peabody had grimly remarked, this would only polarize the Rebels' disposition.

"Yes, gentlemen," Finch had hastily added to Peabody's words. "Marion was quite a threat, and his death, once it is known to the Rebels, will only serve to confuse our foes, making them more desperate. My understanding is that the enemy will almost certainly attack us in a frenzied vengeance, assuming their leader was captured. We must complete the fort." He pointed to a partially constructed wall. "Build that palisade."

And so the pioneers redoubled their efforts, hewing trees, cutting them to a proper length, fashioning them with tight-fitting notches, and ensuring there were small, concealed openings from which to discharge small arms. Situated in the center of town, the great blockhouse, at least twice as large as the others, would be able to cover the main streets and allow advancing armies on many sides to be harried. It could also be used to house the citizenry whilst the soldiery fought and rallied around the building.

As day turned to night, the men began to tire, and many pioneers drawn from the local Loyalist population began to grumble, having hoped to take the evening with their families. Tempers were wearing thin between the two commanders as the threat of Rebel assaults loomed.

"Dash it all, Finch, you needn't work the men this hard!" Peabody cried. "Marion was surely an aggressive and ruthless son of a whore, his men similarly terrifying, but surely they would attend awhile before striking? Would they not assume us to expect them to attack at once and thus keep us waiting and ill at ease? I imagine they would only harry those lads who go out to forage."

"I believe it is I who command the pioneers and engineers here in town, Reverend Peabody," Finch replied coldly, stressing the lack of military savviness he felt the colonel showed in this case. "The roof of the grand blockhouse still needs to be finished, per the orders of Governor Wright, and I remain concerned that the partisans will wish to attack before we are fully fortified. I shall lessen the numbers for the town watch, but for the civilians' sake, we must ensure the successful construction of this—"

A musket went off in the distance. Peabody's eyes widened.

"Alarm, lads!" the warrior-pastor cried. "From the south! Get the elderly, women, and children to the great blockhouse! Gentlemen, to arms!"

Finch grabbed a brace of pistols and a hatchet and ran for the nearest house, only to find its occupants already running toward him, screaming in terror and pointing to gouts of flame dancing about the houses to the south side of town, causing great destruction as weakening timbers collapsed under the weight of second stories.

Gesturing wildly toward the blockhouse, Finch urged the young and the women to sanctuary. "Here we go, ladies, young ones—hurry! Try to be brave. We'll see you to safety! You are under Crown protection now!"

Finch caught sight of Adelaide shepherding a band of children to safety, and his heart swelled with pride. Unfortunately, the elderly and infirm were slower as they struggled to make haste in their attempts to flee the Rebellion's incendiary handiwork. Finch was able to drag some of them to the blockhouse as the professionally trained Loyalist provincials swarmed past him, taking up positions to repel the Rebel invaders. There appeared to be no need, however, as the attackers melted into the night.

Well, that was strange, Finch thought, as he gestured to some men of the militia to come with him to retrieve large buckets of water from the well and fight the fires whilst the provincials watched for further enemy incursions. Splashing his bucket of water upon a blaze steadily peeling apart a once cheerily painted red house, one of his favorites in the neighborhood, Finch handed the bucket off to a young citizen before approaching a grim-faced Reverend Peabody.

Peabody faced him, biting his lip. "Seems you were right, Finch. My apologies. I've posted men on every entrance of town. We will fight this day and—"

"Make haste!" interrupted one of Peabody's staffers, a paunchy fellow named Somerville. "The enemy is upon us once more! They come in force from the north!"

"To arms, provincials!" cried Peabody. "Rally on me! Militia, take care of the fires!"

Chaos slowly gave way to order at the village square as the First Georgia divided into four lines, one for each main road. Not far off lay the partisans, taking scattered shots at the opposition from behind cover of barrels and fences. Though their individual shots were poorly aimed and largely ineffectual, a few lucky blasts rang true, and the odd greencoat fell to the ground, bleeding profusely. When the soldiers of the Crown forces attempted to return fire, they found the cover of the enemy difficult to overcome. At length, they fixed bayonets, in an attempt to overwhelm the enemy's position by sheer force. Finch looked on in horror as the late Swamp Fox's partisans proceeded to topple several provincials with a well-placed volley.

Wavering, the remaining provincials beat a hasty retreat. "Colonel, it's a slaughterhouse out there," a sergeant informed Finch and Peabody. "The enemy nearly wiped out my platoon. They will be a serious challenge to overrun."

"Steady, Sergeant," Peabody urged. "Finch, this is your call."

As the only British officer present, Finch, with his king's commission, had command. His engineer mind dashed through the possibilities. "Sergeant, you say the Rebels are firing volleys?"

The man nodded before whipping his head around Finch to observe the progress of the enemy.

Finch closed his eyes. *A skirmish line could nullify the volley fire but in turn lower the effectiveness of a melee attack, or even a volley of our own, decisively. . . . There has to be another way!*

He snapped his pudgy fingers together. "Sergeant, send word to all the company commanders. Street fire formation. I want ranks five men across, ten men deep by file. We shall hold this town."

It was not long before a formation of defenders was assembled. Finch saluted the captain of the company nearest him with his blade. "You are relieved, sir," he remarked. "I shall lead this company." He turned to a staffer. "Return to camp and inform my wife and children that they must assist the militia in keeping the fires contained."

The staffer nodded mutely and set off.

Finch now raised his voice. "Company commanders! Send your expedition down each cardinal direction from the center of town. I will have no ambushes or flanks of our force. Though they may have begun their march from the north, they could be anywhere now, and—"

"Yes! Yes! We understand!" Peabody interjected, having seized a command of his own. The officers sent their troops down the main roads toward the north, south, east, and west of town.

As the men marched off, Finch cried, "Fix bayonets!"

Whilst the men reached for their spearpoints with which to cap their firearms, Finch observed his forces. True to form, the front line of each comprised five men. As they advanced, the rest of the company marched behind them, benefiting from cover whilst loading their weapons. Those in front would fire a quick volley before retiring to the back of their ten-man column to load. Then the next front line would shoot and fall back to the end of the line themselves, as they all advanced on the opposition.

His company fired raggedly, as some troops were fatigued from helping build the fortifications and were not quite able to match the rate of their compatriots. But the men were fighting for their homes as much as any Rebel was, and when the engineer ordered them to surge ahead toward the opposition, they did so with the enthusiasm mixed with fear natural to a newly raised unit. Sensing inexperience, the Rebels opened fire, but when the smoke cleared, the partisans found their offensive capacities severely limited by the Crown formation. Though the provincials were close enough together for the partisans to hit, they were only exposed five men at a time to enemy fire.

Finch grimaced. "Very well, lads, we've taken their licks, and they've taken ours. Let us finish this! Charge . . . *bayonets!*"

"Huzzay!" the provincials roared, lowering their bayonet-fixed muskets.

When a Loyalist fell, another one was ready to take his place, each equipped with a shooting spear. This was too much for the partisans, whose commander suddenly called for a retreat. Quailing in the face of the bayonet, the partisans began to withdraw from the smoldering city that was Augusta, the provincials hot on their heels.

"*Halt!*" Finch ordered. "Return to Augusta at once. Our first duty is toward the citizenry." He noticed their crestfallen looks. Heartened to see them so engaged in the capture of their enemy, he smiled. "Worry not, men. They shall have their comeuppance."

Finch turned to Jack Storm Crow, who had snuck forth for a closer view. An awkward silence followed as the two watched the enemy disappear in the distance. Amongst the crackling of muskets, Finch noticed dark bodies of men scrambling about, as though harrying the partisans.

"Are those your men?" Finch inquired of the Cherokee warrior, who shook his head. *They don't appear to be provincials or militia, either.* "Tell Running Deer and She Who Laughs to send forth scouts to follow those partisans and whoever harries them. The enemy will likely attempt to lose their antagonists in the swamps. We shall seek them out and defeat them on our terms."

Fort Peabody's Foundations, Augusta, Georgia

31 January 1777, 3:02 AM

"Builder," came a harsh, hissed whisper into Finch's ear.

Or so Finch thought for a moment before dismissing it as the sighing of the breeze and turning over to sleep once more.

"*Builder,*" the voice hissed again, and harsh hands dragged him out of bed. With a yelp of surprise, Finch made to fight wildly but was humiliatingly dragged outdoors in only his shirt before being stood up. It was then that his abductors revealed themselves to be Running Deer, Jack Storm Crow, and She Who Laughs.

"We have found their encampment," Running Deer announced, smiling placidly.

Finch scoffed, "You could not have told me this later today?"

"No," Storm Crow responded.

Finch smiled, despite himself, at the candid answer. *At least we might be able to ambush them.*

"Where do they hide?" Finch gestured them inside and toward a map.

Heaving sighs of exasperation, the Natives followed Finch. Running Deer thrust his finger in the direction of a nearby swampland. Finch saw the danger at once. Swamp warfare was a serious challenge and slow going, with terrain heavily favoring the defender in the difficult wetlands. Of course, the Natives would want to enact a surprise attack with reinforcements.

"Shall I wake Father Peabody?" he asked the Natives. As one, the Natives shook their heads.

"He is protecting the town from any further revenge attacks," Running Deer explained. "We have discussed this plan with him already. Awaken but a few greenmen to assist our band and follow us."

As Finch put on his uniform, itchy and uncomfortable even in the January breeze, a thought came to him. *So the Rebels are ensconced in a swamp? They will be a challenge to defeat in such terrain. Could not my men surround their position, drain the water around their holdings, and launch the assault on more favorable ground?*

After slipping on his shoes, he reached for his tools and made his way over to the encampment where the enlisted soldiers slept under canvas. Worrying for a moment that perhaps he and his men were being led into a trap, Finch reminded himself of Father Peabody's amiable relationship with the Natives and the fact that he and they had an enemy in common. He decided to trust in his allies. Tripping through the night in his awkward, uncomfortable, crooked shoes, the engineer moved to rouse some select soldiers of Peabody's Georgia provincials. Grumbling, their hair matted, with stubble on their unshaven cheeks, the soldiers nonetheless dutifully moved at the word of the engineer, looking inspired more by fear than by hopes of valor.

"Lads, the Native allies have located the encampment of the Rebel cell that has been causing us such woe. Our engineering skills may be useful, so we are to bring as much kit as we can. The Natives will catch the enemy in the swamps and will help lay siege to their position. We will dig entrenchments to drain the swamp around the Rebel position. This will expose the enemy, and we will attack with help from the Cherokee."

No questions were asked, and, with only marginal grumbling, Finch and his small engineering detail gathered their effects and set off. Branches tore at their hats and hair as they flailed their way through vines and spiderwebs deep into the thick of the wilds. The Natives struggled, too, but appeared better prepared for the expedition, their attire more suitable, their knowledge of the terrain more accurate.

Soon Finch and his allies reached a clearing, where it appeared many more Cherokee warriors lay in wait. He again worried wildly that the occasion was a setup, but clutching his telescope and borrowed shovel tightly, his pistols holstered into a bandolier, the engineer now waited as his accompanying Natives talked to their fellows. In time, he counted at least one hundred warriors as they fell in alongside the pioneer-soldiers, with assuredly more melting in amongst the trees. In a few minutes, the expedition resumed at a fast clip—swifter than any British quick march. The pioneer-soldiers continued to curse and grumble as they tripped over the wilderness in the middle of the night. It was not long, however, before the Natives halted.

"There," She Who Laughs declared, pointing into the swamp, barely illuminated by the flicker of campfires not far off. "The ravagers encamp."

"Shall we engage, sir?" A sergeant of the First Georgia squinted into the early-morning darkness, trying to get a better view of the encampment.

"No," Finch said. "Not yet. The attack will be led by the Cherokee. They were victimized most by these partisans. Let them exact their revenge with our assistance. We shall surround the foemen, then drain the swamp, before we strike."

Wordlessly, he and his men began their unenviable task, digging great trenches to channel the water away from the swampland around the Rebel positions. As they worked, they took great care not to approach too closely to the encampment. Hours passed as the work of the pioneers, closely guarded by Native allies, slowly began to take shape, and the swamp began to seep into the trenches. This exposed a great many plants and animals, the latter of whom scrambled out of the way of the pioneers, who, on edge, jumped at the sight of the various frogs, turtles, and flies.

All the while, Finch could have sworn he was being watched. By what or whom, he wasn't sure, but after hearing some rustling in the trees, he decided to double the number of men-at-arms to diggers as they cut their way through the swamp, unsure of what they would see. Though no Rebels showed themselves, the continued gentle rustling of the brush put Finch on edge. But he knew sending men to flush the brush would attract attention and be of no good.

The Crown forces stumbling about failed to elicit any initial reaction from the Rebel forces, who had apparently not posted guards this far out, but the mosquitoes were present in force. As they buzzed about the king's men and their Native allies, there appeared to be no end to their blood-sucking evils, not to mention the itchiness that followed.

As the sun began to rise over the slowly draining wetlands, Finch sent word to call his men to arms. "Stay sharp, men. The Rebels will be taking notice of our handiwork any minute now."

"Perhaps it would be—be—behoove us to take cover amongst the trees," Running Deer advised, his spirits high despite scratching several insect bites.

"A splendid idea, Chieftain. Let us dig just a little more first."

Not much time later, as the swampland continued to drain, revealing great patches of wet mud in its wake, Finch noticed the rustling of movement coming from the brush where the Rebels were encamped. Gesturing for his men to take cover, he and his lads hid behind some enormous ferns.

As they did so, a single partisan soldier climbed out of the brush. Surveying the lands around him, he almost immediately caught sight of the swamp draining into the trenches and turned around with a loud swear, raising others to various states of alarm. "The swamp's gone, sir! What the blazes is going on?"

An officer clambered over to the soldier's position. "What the blazes *is* going on here? Who did thi—"

Krak!

Running Deer's battered trade rifle sang, catching the officer in the throat, and the older man gargled for breath. The first partisan who had spoken dove for cover.

As if commanded by the rifle's bullet, or perhaps some unspoken words, the Cherokee rose from their hiding places. Brandishing their tomahawks, clubs, and knives, they surged from the trees and fell upon the Rebel colonials from all sides. Watching their compatriots commence their attack without so much as an order, the Loyalists, realizing the time had come to fight, quickly fixed bayonets and followed their comrades in arms with a cry of "For the king!"

With their defenses trickling into the trenches, exposing their encampment and no longer providing as much of an obstacle to their foes, the Rebels were now threatened on all sides. As they had no more training than Silverstein's militia, save in ambush tactics, they found themselves entirely outmatched by the Cherokee warriors and Peabody's provincials. Dispersed and disorganized, they returned fire in ragged, single shots, each partisan firing at will, without accuracy or discipline.

But they had numbers.

With their base under fire, the Rebel troops swarmed from their disadvantaged position in an effort to break out. Gathering into one enormous body of men, they pushed hard against the approach of the Loyalists and Natives from the north, trying to free themselves and run to safety. Formed in a thin circle around the Rebels, the Crown forces struck hard, rattling the enemy with shots from all sides. The partisans fell in droves, but the hand-to-hand combat was fierce, as the Rebel partisans' sheer manpower opened breaches in the Crown lines, and they began to make a break for the wilderness, where Finch was commanding the troops from afar.

Now, as the Rebels turned their eyes upon him, catching sight of the engineer behind some brush, Finch once more found himself in mortal danger. Fumbling with his brace of pistols, he drew them both and waited for the front line to come within twenty meters. He aimed at two separate onrushing soldiers, then fired.

Blam!

Blaham!

Two Rebels, struck in the stomach and in the gullet at close range by .65-caliber ball and shot, fell to the earth, clasping their wounds.

Lucky shots.

The engineer's inward grin at his good fortune soon faded as the rest of the force, temporarily shaken, regained their composure and continued to plunge after him.

Finch turned and ran. "To me, men! We must capture these rascals!" he cried before gracelessly tripping on a root and falling to the ground. As his pistols skittered away, Finch clambered to his feet and went for his blade, prepared to die after stalling the partisans as best he could.

As he did so, he found himself face to face with an onrush of rough, burly fellows. The lead man in the pack flashed him an ugly grin, raising a pistol of his own to bear on Finch and preparing to shoot. Realizing this could be the end but still caught up in the heat of the moment, Finch glared at him in challenge.

Krak!

The lead man fell.

Krakkrakkrak!

One after another, single shots felled enemy soldiers, cleanly and efficiently laying waste to their line of battle. Having caught his breath, Finch whirled around to see a band of redcoats.

Light infantry!

"Greetings, Colonel Finch!" came a gentle, familiar voice.

Simmons the Younger!

The young light infantryman and several of his compatriots popped up from behind some brush and began to shred the evacuating Rebels with punishing fire. Realizing they were beaten, several partisans laid down their weapons and raised their arms in surrender, expecting to be treated in the genteel manner agreed upon in European rules of wartime conduct. Leaving their fates to the Cherokee, as it was their expedition, Finch approached the light infantry with a jovial gait, nodding to their captain before striking up a conversation with the son of his protégé and former rival.

"Why, Simmons!" Finch replied, catching his breath. "What brings you here?"

Simmons doffed his hat to wipe the sweat from his brow. "Gaining your favor, sir! Cornwallis heard about the attack your lads fended off at Augusta and elected to send reinforcement in hunting down the partisans. I was overjoyed at the prospect of seeing Constance again, sir, and volunteered to join a small company to offer assistance. Captain Cutty here came along to oversee my abilities. When we arrived, we were informed by Colonel Peabody as to where you went."

"And assistance you did lend, young man. Thank you for the aid of your light bobs!"

"Silverstein and his coterie came along too, sir. Militia or no, Chatham County never backs down from a fight, or so he says."

"God bless that mad Jew. Now, rejoin your men. Your platoon is waiting. There will be time for pleasantries later. You will help escort these poor ruffians back to the Cherokee encampment. Process the enemy as our Indian allies see fit, for it is they who suffered most under their tyranny. Then report back to Augusta for further orders."

If Simmons harbored any reservations about the wisdom of Finch's orders, he kept them to himself. As the private stepped back into formation, Finch nodded to Captain Cutty, a short, slim fellow with swarthy skin. "Thank you for overseeing this action, Captain. Keep up the good work mentoring Simmons."

As Finch stepped forward to join the Natives in accepting the surrender of the partisans, the remainder of the Crown force stationed around the rest of the perimeter caught up to the sallying partisans and, misunderstanding the situation, opened fire in a resounding volley. Militia and provincials alike all volleyed with a thunderous roar.

KRABAM!

At least seven men who had already surrendered fell, nursing crushed ribs and other shattered bones.

"*No!* We are under parley!" cried Finch angrily. "Parley! Let us cease our hostilities!"

The Loyalists stood down, their eyes nonetheless burning with hatred toward their treasonous neighbors. The partisans followed suit, lowering their longarms with a similar vitriol.

This did not stop some of the Natives, however. Hearing the fire and misinterpreting the orders, spoken in English as they were, they moved to mete out a horrible revenge against the enemy partisans with wild war cries.

Killing these men would mean a world of safety in the short run but would justify many an atrocity against us and our Native friends in the future, Finch thought. *This is not right.* He looked out upon the mewling, terrorized partisans and felt a twinge of guilt poking its way through his veneer of vengeful rage. These combatants were cowards and terrorists but no longer posed a threat and were themselves endangered.

"Stop fighting!" Finch yelled, trying to wrench a tomahawk from Running Deer's hand. The wizened warrior looked up at Finch in shock but shouted something that seemed to calm his men at last.

"I hope you know what you are doing, Colonel," She Who Laughs said calmly, even mournfully, as the fighting ground to a halt. "These men, they burned our villages, killed the very livestock they traded to us, cheated us of our lands, forced us to worship their god. The only thing they peddled for free was disease."

"Peace," Running Deer insisted. "What they did to us was terrible, but further acts of cruelty will come, and in greater intensity, if we meet action with action. We must turn to their authorities to seek their comeuppance and to champion our safety. Their authorities are right here." He pointed to Finch. "What shall be done with them?" he asked the engineer. "Though they have been captured by us, we will not risk the wrath of those white men who wish to ally with us in exchange for petty vengeance."

Finch paused for a moment in thought and then spoke. "They were captured by you, though on our land, and it was against you that they committed the majority of their crimes. Whilst I am sure the Crown will dislike me delivering Crown citizens into the hands of your kind, I shall make it clear to high command that you offered them to me first and will take full responsibility for their fate. I would ask, however, that you treat them as prisoners of war and let them live. Perhaps the disgrace of defeat and the mercy you show them will temper their fighting spirit."

"Please! I have a family!" one partisan pleaded, before being thrown to the ground with a resounding groan by She Who Laughs.

"Silence, fool!" the warrior woman glowered down out him. "So did we. Where do you think they are now?"

"We're sorry! My God! We are so sorry," cried another, grasping at the Cherokee warriors, pleading for mercy. "Don't kill us! I shan't encroach on your grounds again!"

"I'm a merchant by trade outside of the war!" cried a third. "I can get you anything! A musket, a sword! Even a pretty floral bonnet for you, miss!" He smiled uneasily at She Who Laughs, who growled at him gutturally.

"All we want is to be left alone," Storm Crow responded. "But since you have taken us to war, we must see it through. Today, however, because our allies have pled for your lives, you will follow us back to Augusta and into the blockhouse. They will make you *their* prisoners. Let it not be said we were merciless."

CHAPTER 6

The Advance through the Carolinas

Augusta Green, Augusta, Georgia

15 FEBRUARY 1777, 7:03 PM

> *To Colonel Finch, Commander of the Pioneers of Governor Wright's Expedition*
>
> *Dear Sir,*
>
> *Having heard of the sterling work done by the men under your command toward pacifying the wayward partisans, General Howe has sent me with reinforcements to bolster the forces present in the South. After doing so, he abruptly resigned, citing an inability to take arms against his friends in the colonies any longer. Ever the sentimental coward, I fear.*
>
> *After much begging and pleading from Horse Guards, I have been called upon to serve in his stead. Grabbed myself a knighthood in the bargain, and so I now do style myself Sir Henry Clinton.*
>
> *Now, to business. As you may have heard, HM the King has called upon German allies from Hesse-Kassel, Waldeck, Ansbach-Bayreuth, Braunschweig-Lüneburg, and many*

113

other principalities to assist us in quelling this insurrection, and it is my duty to conduct them southernly to partake in the conflict. Meanwhile, General John Burgoyne, newly returned in force to the colonies, prepares to march in a secret and ambitious winter action on the Rebel capital in Philadelphia from our headquarters in New York City, hoping to strike a severe blow that might finish the uprising once and for all.

I understand that sniveling worm Cornwallis has replaced you with another as commander of the engineers for his detachment. No matter. I am sure you are the better officer of the two, and almost certainly the better personality, and you may tell him I said so. Unfortunately, he is within his rights to choose his staff, and if he replaced you, I would be overstepping my boundaries to place you back in the role of chief engineer in the South.

Since you are free of his direct command, however, I would have you join me in Charleston, in the colony of South Carolina, a time. Cornwallis, Prévost, and I captured it, along with its fortress, Fort Moultrie, in a protracted and destructive, if relatively bloodless, siege. Though Charles and Augustine must continue to thrust northward into the heartlands of the Carolinas, because of my recent appointment, I have decided that I shall direct the war from a readily accessible headquarters and surround myself with strong fighters and a good support staff.

In the face of petty political squabbling, I should like to request of you your assistance in winning the town over with works of engineering, your insights in handling Native and Negro affairs, and most of all, your friendship and moral support once more. I shall require as much of each as I may get and therefore order you, your family, and your band of Native allies here with all possible haste. Though we shall have only so much time to rest and enjoy one another's company, it would be good to see you again.

Name a local commander for your forces in Augusta and move at once. I have pressing business to attend with you. Pray, don't fumble it up.

With fond regards, I am &c.,
CLINTON, Sir Henry

Finch consulted the letter a fourth time before turning to address his assembled troops.

"Gentlemen, you all have done well. As we have completed a palisade around the town's limits, strategically placing blockhouses as we have seen fit for the protection of her populace, I hereby deem this small settlement fortified. We have shown great valor in combat and chivalry in our treatment of civilians and foes, but now we must part ways. I have been redeployed to Charleston to counsel and staff General Clinton. Please continue to uphold the honor and glory of the force we have assembled, trained, and fought for together. Do your work bravely in garrisoning this town, and we will meet again. I thank you for all you have done and wish you well. Peabody? Take care of these fellows."

"Sah." Peabody saluted stiffly, very unlike the more casual self he was around Finch in private.

Finch then turned to Running Deer. "Chieftain, I welcome you on behalf of the people of Augusta to settle in their fair city, though I would additionally value greatly your assistance on the warpath. We can use all the help we might receive against the Sons of Liberty. Captain Silverstein, though it is out of your jurisdiction, I would be honored to have your assistance, too. I should very much like to engage your services as Royal Provincials for the time being, rather than militia. God knows you fought just as hard in the swamps as they did at Fort Peabody, where your men did well combatting the fires."

"Of course, sir," Silverstein replied, doffing his hat in a dramatic bow. "My lads are humbled to be at your service. We shall keep you and your family safe."

"And you, Captain Cutty?" Finch inquired of the commander of the company to which Simmons was attached. "Have you any wish to join us on our march to Charleston? I'm sure General Clinton would find your services invaluable."

Cutty frowned. "Alas, sir, we were given orders to march on Camden and rejoin our battalion not three hours ago." He extended a hand. "We shall meet again, however, and you can tell your daughter I shall take good care of her beloved."

City Gates, Charleston, South Carolina

25 February 1777, 9:50 PM

"Who goes?" called the Charleston sentinel amidst the chirping of crickets, a torch in his hand.

It was nighttime when Finch and his troops reached the coastal city. Their challenger, a Loyalist soldier, the flames from the torch casting strange lights on his lean, clever face, was revealed to be quite nervous at the sight of the force arrayed before him.

Though the First Georgia Volunteers were under orders to stay in Augusta, Finch had Loyalists of his own at his command. Silverstein's onetime Chatham County Militia, now Third Battalion, Georgia Volunteers, accompanied Finch and his party as an escort to Charleston, having received their first stipend of pay and uniforms. Running Deer's warband, deprived of a home following Francis Marion's earlier atrocities, had also accompanied them.

This motley crew stood behind Finch as he replied, "Friends and soldiers of the king. Colonel Finch, at your service." He extended the letter from Clinton. "These are my orders."

The guard frowned as he extended a hand and took the paper from Finch. After taking a moment to read the letter from Clinton, he opened the gates with a resounding screech, a frigid scowl upon his face. Finch's family and Silverstein's provincials entered without further issue, but upon the attempted entrance of the Cherokee through the gate, the guard whistled loudly.

"Not you!" he cried at the warriors, who, misunderstanding, continued to troop into Charleston. The sentinel ran for the alarm bell. As he rang it vigorously, a number of additional militiamen came to the fore, weapons at the ready.

"Hold hand, Sergeant!" Finch ordered. "These men come as allies. Surely you would let them stay as guests?"

"They are savages, sir, and have no understanding of our culture. For all we know, they would murder us at the drop of a hat. They have done so before."

In his time in the South, Finch had seen a lot of unsurety around the Natives and by now had grown exasperated at their treatment by townsfolk, Rebel or Loyalist. He turned to the militiaman guarding the gates. "These *men*, Sergeant, are heroes from earlier battles. They know to respect comrades in arms."

"We will sleep outside," She Who Laughs said. She was not happy with the long march and clearly wished to retire for the evening. As the sentinel looked on hawkishly, she spoke sharply to her warriors. Grumbling, they began to march away from the gates.

The sentinel was not finished, however. "Your weapons, please. Can't have armed Indians on the outskirts of our town. Won't be safe for any of us." Catching Finch glaring at him, the militia sentinel frowned back at him. "This is our town, Colonel Finch. Just because you are a ranking officer does not mean you can override our laws. There will be no Natives allowed within Charleston, save as traders. Such has been the law of our establishment since its infancy."

"Built on land that was once *theirs*," Finch retorted, as the Natives obligingly began to surrender their weapons in neat piles, frowns on their faces. "What's more, these particular fellows are without a land of their own after our wayward citizens destroyed their homes."

The guard raised a hand. "Apologies, sir, but such are the rules, instituted by those wiser, to be sure, than me. If you wish to appeal your point, you may do so, should they see you, to Governor Campbell or General Clinton in the morning." He smiled scathingly, and Finch hated him for it.

"Very well. Until then, I shall take my stand out here as well," Finch declared, and motioned Silverstein forward. "Inform the men that we shall set up camp in yonder forest." The soldier nodded.

"Finch? Is that you?" a familiar and welcome voice thundered from the darkness. The brawny Sir Henry Clinton, likely having heard the ruckus, had appeared on the scene with his red-coated retinue, hungry for drama as always. He turned to the militia sentinel. "What seems to be the problem, soldier? There had better be an excellent reason as to why you are causing my good man Finch such delay."

The private, saluting deferentially to the general, then gestured to the collection of trade muskets he had confiscated. "I was protecting the town, sir. Colonel Finch wishes to keep armed savages in and around Charleston, you see. That is against our laws!"

Clinton stiffened. Drawing himself up to full height, he towered over the portly soldier. *The general is a bully with a heart of gold,* Finch thought as the general worked his magic.

"Young man," Clinton began, his eyes smoldering. "We are at war. Presently, it is due to the fact that we are treating the *Natives* so well that they have deigned to side with our king and country. They are our allies. Allies aid one another in battle. Your antiquated, rustic laws were meant for times past, during peace, when *Natives* were looked upon with disdain. We can no longer afford to be so mistrustful and must embrace what soldiers we can raise. I do not, after all, see as many Loyalists as Rebels racing to enlist!"

The private scowled. Stepping up to the nearest warrior, he offered one a patronizing smile. "For-give me, O—"

"They speak better English than you do Cherokee, Private. No need to condescend," Finch remarked with a chuckle.

The private grumbled something under his breath before turning to his musket stockpile. Picking up the chieftain's beautifully carved trade rifle, he turned to its ancient owner. "I apologize, great chieftain, and return to you your rifle." The ancient chieftain graciously took the weapon back, clearly taking the moral high ground with it.

Sir Henry Clinton's Headquarters, Governor William Campbell's Mansion, Charleston, South Carolina

26 FEBRUARY 1777, 7:15 AM

"You have done a damn fine job, Colonel Finch, surviving this war."

In the sitting room of Governor Campbell's mansion, Clinton smiled down at the seated engineer. It had been a silent walk the previous night to the British headquarters, a beautiful manor house with all the charms the South had to offer, but now the general's exuberance showed through. He was in one of his good moods. Standing at attention behind General Clinton were a trio of officers.

Finch made a show of modesty, embellishing only lightly on his actual feelings. "I did my best, Sir Henry. There were some serious setbacks over the course of this campaign, however. What with Cornwallis and Prévost and—"

"And you did damn well attempting to combat their shite. Can't be helped that you served under those dunderheads—that Howe-boy Cornwallis and that fellow Prévost, whose brain is like to Jarlsberg."

Finch was taken aback. "Well, thank you for your confidence, General Clinton. What have I done to earn it?"

"Why, Finch, you have shown all the traits an officer should show," Clinton replied. "A decent hand in combat, an inspiring command of our language, an ability to amiably cooperate with our allies . . . Well, you tried there, at least. And a freethinking mind. You know the difference between risk and suicide, wot wot!" Clinton chortled at his own remark.

Finch blushed, but Clinton was not finished.

"Not only are you possessed of all these traits, but you seem to use them best on the field of combat, rather than when engineering defenses and infrastructure. Whilst you are strong at both, we have a serious dearth of freethinkers amongst the light infantry, where they are needed."

Finch's mouth fell open. He looked Sir Henry in the eye. "W-what do you mean to say, General Clinton?"

"I mean to say that I am offering you a brigade, Finch," Clinton said. "You've fought enemy partisans a few times. Now you will be equipped for it. You've bloody well earned it."

"Christ!" Finch swore, before blushing madly. "Sir Henry, are you quite sure?"

"Indeed," the general replied, "but you are right to be unsure of yourself. A good seventy-five percent of military success is instinct. But the other twenty-five percent is discipline and knowledge. One can never be too well educated on the topic of the role they play. The German school of soldiering took me far, by the wounds of God! I did not do it alone. I hereby assign you, Finch, to read up on the role of light infantry and learn how to put the theories into practice with the assistance of your officers."

Finch sat up straight in his chair and nodded.

"What commanders will I be working alongside, Sir Henry?"

"Ah yes, the details," Clinton replied with his fingers steepled. "Your command, *Brigadier* Finch, will be an interesting exercise in diplomacy." He gestured to the men behind him. "Loyalists, Germans, Britons, and Indians. The Indians elected to remain in the forest for the time being—forgive their absence. A light brigade, to be sure, but one that will work together on all manner of missions. *Now*," Sir Henry continued sharply, swatting his baton against the gentleman officer on the far left. "This Thomas Browne fellow is far from easy on the eyes, but a hell of a fighter. His mounted rangers and Indians, hailing from Florida, the Carolinas, Georgia, the South over, have done sterling work this past year and need a good commander to attach to."

Lanky and weedy, like an overgrown spider, the man called Browne may have already looked homely without his many battle injuries. *But good God*, thought Finch, *what has he been through?* He sported a broken nose and several deep, only recently stitched lacerations, as well as old scars, beneath both eyes and one across the mouth. A patch covered what Finch assumed was a blinded eye. The engineer could only wonder what other injuries had been dealt to the man, as a regulation Loyalist ranger uniform covered the remainder of his body.

Browne, upon noticing Finch's horrified stare, grinned crookedly, removing his wide-brimmed hat and revealing a grievous and only partially healed hatchet wound. "They made me walk the coals for my loyalty to the Crown as well, sir," he remarked casually in a voice of wealth and privilege. "Nearly tarred and feathered me." He smirked. "But I learned them. All I wanted was to tend to my newly founded settlement in peace, but they got me angry." He glared at Finch, "Don't get me angry."

"Really now, Thomas," Clinton tutted. "Finch is a friend. And your commander. You would do well to treat him as such."

Browne gave another crooked grin. "As you wish."

Clinton nodded his thanks. "Now, Browne, I saved him from Cornwallis because I hate the man, and Prévost because their personalities would conflict, but he has just the right amount of derring-do and, dare I say it, dash to be your man. Put him on your flank, sir. He will be the best commander you have. His mounted rangers and Native allies aren't bad, either. Good scouts."

Finch made a mental note. He then gestured to the next fellow. "And who is this, may I ask?"

Bewigged, medal-studded, and with a slight paunch, the officer to Browne's left jumped at being indicated. A nervous, high-pitched, academic voice issued from his mouth. "Ludwig von Wurmb, sir. I humbly anticipate subservience to your seniority, mein Herr. I command a most valiant band of mounted Feldjaegers—that is to say . . . ehm . . . ah! Hunters, woodsmen, rangers. We pave the way to battle with naked short sword and blazing rifle. We were gamekeepers of our homeland of Hesse-Kassel. Our marksmanship with our longarms is without peer."

Hearing this claim, the fellow to von Wurmb's left stifled a snicker.

Von Wurmb's face contorted into a look of rage Finch could not have imagined possible from the fellow. "Ha! Ferguson!" he screeched. "Your men are no better than mine. That you have been granted special rifles has clearly inflated your head!"

There was an awkward silence. The man named Ferguson stepped forward. He was a relatively unremarkable-looking fellow with green eyes and a nose like a hawk's. Apart from a feathered tricorn hat, he wore a green uniform similar to a ranger's. "Captain Patrick Ferguson," came the Scottish brogue of the offending gentleman. "I most humbly apologize to our German compatriots and to the general company for the ruckus."

"That's all very well," Finch replied, "but why does a captain stand before me alongside these colonels?"

Ferguson grinned. "I command but a paltry fifty men, yet my fellows and their devices are the jewels in the crown of our brigade. Like von Wurmb's men, they are sharpshooters to the highest degree, but they are gifted with weapons that supersede the jaeger rifles of years past if not in looks, than in operation." With a flourish, he unslung his longarm and placed it on the table in front of Finch.

"One of my patented Ferguson rifles," the captain said proudly. "The first breech-loading weapon to be produced en masse for any army."

Finch looked at it curiously. It was stubby and short, with numerous new mechanisms he had not seen on a firearm before. His engineering mind fast at work, he ascertained its workings.

"Fascinating! I see that rather than be loaded muzzle down, the ammunition is fed from the rear? That ought to improve its rate of fire significantly."

"And don't forget the bayonet lug, too," Ferguson added, unsheathing his own and flourishing it about as the rest of the company shied away. "It's long enough to make up for the shorter longarm itself. Would you like to see me fire it at a rate of *four* rounds per minute? Despite its rifling?"

"*Hmph!*" was all von Wurmb could say.

Finch stole a look at Sir Henry, who coughed dramatically.

"Perhaps later, Mister Ferguson." Clinton said, smiling. "There is still business to attend to."

"As you wish."

Finch turned to Sir Henry. "So these fellows and their regiments, plus some Indians from my establishment and that of Browne's, yes?"

"Quite right."

Just then, a batman entered, placing a letter on the table as he did so. "A dispatch from General Burgoyne, sir. Its messenger appeared quite haggard and desperate."

"What could that dandy want now? Did he not just set off for Philadelphia?" Clinton pondered aloud.

Whatever the news was did not bode well for the Crown forces, as Clinton's face fell.

"Confound it!" He gnashed his teeth as he threw the letter to the ground.

Finch looked on, attempting to appear professional as Clinton swore like a sailor for the next minute. As Clinton's rage abated, he looked past Finch and gestured the batman forward.

"Are you quite well, General?" Finch inquired as the batman returned to Clinton's desk.

"Absolutely not." The general cast a withering look in Finch's direction. "New York is under threat from Philadelphia. The Rebels wore out General Burgoyne's force. They managed to capture his supply train. Eventually they surrounded his troops as they marched on Princeton. They forced his surrender. *Surrender!* We have lost in excess of five thousand men in one stroke. *The fool!*"

"My God!" Finch cried. "That is a terrible defeat. Who commands the defenses of New York City? Do we have the manpower to protect it? Should we send reinforcements from the South?"

Clinton sighed. "We must not let Charleston fall into Rebel hands yet again. The establishment from Braunschweig und Lüneburg, under General Riedesel, is likely only days away from New Scotland and can ship out almost immediately from there to

New York City. I will send out a dispatch to them at once. Their presence, alongside that of the forces of Sir Charles Grey and the local Loyalists, will be enough to deter any enemy advances. I shall hold here with the locals and what redcoats we have shipped south. Finch, you're a man of letters and learning. You saw our rangers in action in the last war. You know what a skirmish line looks like. According to your dispatches, you even knew how to lead a force in a street-fire formation. Whilst these desperate engagements rage in the north, I must ask you to go forth as you are now."

"Yes, sir, but—"

"Report to Camden at the earliest possibility. Cornwallis is stationed there, and you must work in concert with him if we are to win this war. You can rely on your books and Colonel Browne to teach you irregular tactics on the road. Though he is a gentleman, he is a rough man of experience, too, who knows how to work with the Indians."

Finch nodded reluctantly. "What are my orders then?"

Clinton cleared his throat as he gently picked up the letter and sat down, opening the drawer to his desk and finding some paper inside. Scribbling out a note with a quill pen, he responded, "In brief, I will need you, sir, to roam the Southern Colonies. You will fight in support of Cornwallis when needed but otherwise commit what mischief you can to undermine the Rebellion. I want you to fight a hit-and-fade war. Partisan-style, you see. But you will also have to be available to fight a general engagement, for who knows when Cornwallis and Prévost may need you? We still have the towns of Charlotte, Hillsborough, and Wilmington to take before we have secured the major towns of the deep South. I shall need your help embarrassing those addlepates by occupying these Rebel held towns before them, but you will simultaneously contribute to their success on my terms."

He pushed the piece of paper toward Finch. "Present this to General Cornwallis with my, ehm . . . compliments. Make me proud, would you?"

"I shall do my best, sir," Finch promised. He thought a moment. "May I entrust my family to your protection here in Charleston as I tend to these goals?"

"You may not," Clinton replied. "Family, Finch. Remember what I said of family: never leave them again, if possible. Mine died of disease far too young, and I'd hate to see that happen to yours before you could spend quality time with them."

What if they die in battle? Finch asked himself.

Nevertheless, the engineer sighed and nodded.

Augustine Prévost's Headquarters, Camden, South Carolina
17 March 1777, 12:25 PM

Finch had reviewed his troops and liked what he had seen. Each unit made a display of its skills in a series of war-gaming tourneys and competitions, and Finch was delighted to see such a disciplined body of men. Though it made him uneasy to be in command of them, he was determined not to let Sir Henry down. The better to facilitate closer relations between him and those under his command, as well as the men of each unit with men of other units, Finch invited each of the commanding officers to tea regularly, sometimes individually, sometimes as a group.

In doing so, he noticed that some men tended to gravitate toward each other, whilst others were more the loner type. Thomas Browne and Sandsnake, of the King's Carolina Rangers and their Creek Native allies, whilst loyal to the Crown, seemed somewhat distrusting of their compatriots, consciously forming a protective clique amongst themselves and not discussing matters, regardless of importance, with anyone but themselves and Finch.

The distrust the Creek harbored was especially pronounced in the face of their fellow Natives, the Cherokee.

Warriors of the two indigenous factions were often seen arguing with each other, neither side taking responsibility when Finch inquired as to what caused such difficulties, nor did they have good answers for how to remedy matters. Jack Storm Crow, She Who Laughs, and Running Deer were equally ineffectual, Storm Crow frequently trying and failing to calm both sides down whilst Running Deer and She Who Laughs would placidly puff on their pipes off to the side of the argument.

Patrick Ferguson and the Hessian commander, Ludwig von Wurmb, also tended to feud with one another. *It is a damned shame,* Finch thought. Though Ferguson was a jovial, outspoken, confident Scotsman and von Wurmb was a shy Hessian aristocrat of great intellect, his nose always in a book, Finch had gleaned from separate interactions that the two had similar interests in engineering and astronomy. Unfortunately, "Bitter" Wurmb's temper never failed to make a fool of the colonel when Captain Ferguson made a joke at his expense. As these jokes were frequently mean-spirited and cruel, Finch could not help but pity the Hessian, though he felt it rude to intercede on his behalf. The man outranked Ferguson, after all. That being said, it sometimes distracted from meetings, and Finch was sure that one day it would go too far.

The soldiers of the light infantry had proven a largely competent lot. Well trained in their art, they had, after all, been drawn from some of the hardiest survivors and best marksmen of British, Loyalist, and German stock. Meanwhile, the Native Americans, having lived much less indulged lives than their European compatriots, proved equally strong survivors. Whilst not as well trained with their inferior-quality trade muskets and rifles, they nonetheless made for effective skirmishers and were second to none in the usage of their clubs, tomahawks, and knives.

No matter how talented these men were, however, their reception was a cold one when Simmons the Elder, whom Finch warmly greeted to a surprised and embarrassed response, saw Finch and Browne into Prévost's tent, where an outraged Cornwallis made his opinion known.

"*Finch!*" Cornwallis shouted as Prévost's eyes went wide. "What the blazes are you doing here? Return to Savannah at once!"

"Special orders from General Clinton himself, sir." Finch said with a smile, amused by the hubbub. He placed his orders on a folding table over some maps Prévost was reading, saluting before continuing. "I am to march alongside your men and rejoin the offensive. I come bearing reinforcements, in fact. A light brigade of various elements bridging our alliances."

"A light brigade, hm?" Prévost said, cutting into Cornwallis's response, having glanced at the letter. "Very well. It says here you will scout for us and fight alongside us in an irregular capacity. It is clear General Clinton wants you around, so you must be good for something besides causing drama." The general frowned. "You had best do good work."

Finch nodded, and Prévost's manner softened. "Relax a time, Finch. You must be exhausted. You will find that when you earn my good graces, I shall treat you well. We will break camp in the next few weeks but are taking on supplies and resting here awhile, as Simmons builds us a fort."

"Your servant, sir." Finch bowed, turned on his heel, and marched off, whilst Browne backed out, refusing to take his eye off Cornwallis until he had exited the tent.

"Je-sus," remarked Browne, the aristocrat ranger. "If ever there was a cold welcoming, sir, that would be it. Cornwallis there looked angry enough to kill, if you'll permit me to say so."

"Granted, as always, Colonel Browne," was Finch's calm reply. "It is refreshing to hear the voice of honesty, rather than pandering from the ranks."

They returned to the brigade. The Natives and rangers, close to the wild and sensitive to the desires of the townsfolk, had encamped in the woods. To his dismay, Finch noted that Colonel Browne's Creek allies continued to keep a significant distance from the Cherokee. Warriors on both sides had posted watches, presumably almost as much to ensure the other faction did not cause a ruckus as to look out for the Rebels.

On the brighter side, at least the riflemen under Ferguson had guardedly joined the jaegers in town, pitching tents on the green, the officers staying in inns and taverns and dining together. *Well, if not together, at least in the same town,* Finch thought. *Perhaps sufficient immersion might make allies of these men. But I really must speak to the Cherokee and Creek about this feud.*

Browne must have read Finch's intent, however, for having seen the newly appointed brigadier make his way toward the Creek encampment, he dashed after him.

"Uhm, *no,* sir. That is *not* a good idea," the ranger remarked candidly as he caught up to Finch, huffing and puffing.

"Uniting our allies? Why not?" Finch inquired.

"It is lucky enough that we all seem able to march as a cohesive unit. The Cherokee and Creek hate each other. It would be unwise to stoke the fires of that animosity."

"But I was only going to encourage a bit of courtliness between them. We are all on the same side, after all," Finch said, proceeding down the path.

"That is true, General, but friends are brought together in their own time, of their own volition," said von Wurmb, who had stepped out of his tent, the better to hear the conversation. His face was half shaved, and Ferguson appeared about to make a joke regarding it until he caught Finch's stony expression.

"Gentlemen, you two are with me. We are talking to Sandsnake."

Von Wurmb shrugged. "Have you made out a will, Captain?" he inquired of Ferguson.

Ferguson laughed and clapped von Wurmb on the back; the latter winced. "Funny, Colonel. If a tad grim."

There were some murmurs amongst the Creek warriors as Finch and his compatriots stepped purposefully over to their encampment to deal in the affairs of the Natives. Nonetheless, as Finch approached their war chief's encampment, Finch could feel his courage ebbing away.

"N-now, Sandsnake," Finch began hesitantly, addressing the war chief of the Creek band, a towering, lean, heavily painted fellow, as he, von Wurmb, and Ferguson stood before him. "I understand you and your followers have misgivings with our Cherokee allies. What is this all about?"

"The Cherokee have no honor, Gen-er-al," Sandsnake spoke slowly, stumbling over Finch's rank. "We have always had to fight them when they trespassed on our grounds, and it was not long ago that many signed a treaty with your defiant colonials when they were defeated in combat. Now that you and your many soldiers are winning the war, the Cherokee will fight alongside you, but this was not always so, whilst we have always fought alongside you. Be cautious with him!"

'Sblood. "Hold that thought, friend," Finch said. "Gather ten of your warriors and come with me. No weapons. Trust in me."

Leading Sandsnake into the Cherokee encampment, Finch was unnerved to see several Cherokee warriors reach for their armaments. Running Deer stood amongst them.

"I understand what you are trying to do, Giles Finch, but these men are not our friends. The Earth is meant to be shared, yet they cut us down for foraging her wonders."

"It was land given to us through right of conquest!" Sandsnake exclaimed heatedly. "We fought people of other nations and died for it, and you had no right to take from it whilst it was under our rule. You should not have come, nor should you have ignored our demands that you leave."

"Perhaps we would have listened if you did not tell us with arrows and tomahawks."

"Enough!"

She Who Laughs had poked her head outside of her tent. She appeared to choose her words carefully.

"The Old Ways will come to an end if we do nothing to protect them. No longer can we afford to fight amongst ourselves. If we do not work together, we will all be subject to the white man's dominion. Even now we are fighting only to stall what may become the inevitable if we do not come to see each other as brothers. Sandsnake, we may not have come from the same nations and tribes, but we are brother and sister in spirit. I beg you, put aside the past. It will only cost you your independence in the future."

She turned to Running Deer. "Father, though the Earth belongs to all, these men are proud warriors whose ways are different from ours. Let us, in the future, pay them the respect their formidable campaigns have merited them. The lands will not flourish with many people, disunited, picking at them."

Sandsnake smiled. "You speak well, She Who Laughs. I shall accept any apology offered by Running Deer."

"You will *receive* no such thing," Running Deer growled, his voice rumbling like thunder.

"Halt!" Jack Storm Crow snapped. "I shall be silent no longer. It is clear speaking kindly will get us nowhere. We are at war, my brothers and sisters. We must work together or we shall die." He turned to Finch. "When my brethren—and this includes Sandsnake—when we, native to this land, lead our warriors into battle next time, I will promise you this: that no one will tell Creek from Cherokee. We shall be intertwined and united like the branches of a tree, together in brother- and sisterhood. We will train together, eat together, sleep together, fight together, and, if need be, die together."

Finch smiled inside but didn't want to be too open with his feelings. "This is what I like to hear," he said, nodding.

Sandsnake smiled and lowered his drawn tomahawk. "You speak well, Jack Storm Crow. Your words appeal to me, too. Enemies though our peoples may be, there are more pressing concerns for us both to address. Our own petty feuds can wait."

Finch allowed himself a relieved grin. At least *this* crisis was averted.

Augustine Prévost's Headquarters, Camden, South Carolina
17 MARCH 1777, 2:52 PM

Later that day, Finch's family dispersed about the town, with Archibald playing amongst the trees in the nearby forest with a few newfound friends as Adelaide and a begrudging Caroline darned holes in socks for the soldiery. Constance joined in but spent most of her time longingly watching the newly promoted Corporal Simmons drilling the men delegated to him.

In the meantime, Finch and his officers took lunch, polishing off some pork and bread provided for them by a nearby eatery. As he was savoring the final bites, Finch heard footfalls along the cobblestones as Cornwallis strode leisurely toward the encampment. Browne made to slow his pace, standing in front of the engineer. Cornwallis hesitated, intimidated, but persevered, attempting to push past him. Finch waved Browne aside, and the brigadier and major general stood face-to-face.

"Well, well. General Cornwallis. How may I assist you?"

"Brigadier General Finch, now, is it?" the major general replied coldly.

"At your service," Finch said, bowing.

The major general scoffed.

"This is for you. Compliments of Prévost." Cornwallis thrust a letter into Finch's hand and stood back. "See to it you don't blunder about like a dullard, and please pick up what waste your Native friends leave behind."

Finch was left to wonder why Cornwallis insisted upon being so obnoxious. Had the engineer not proven himself a better man than he had been before? Was it not obvious that the past was a mistake? He smiled sadly to himself and took the letter from Cornwallis's hand, breaking its seal.

Brigadier General Finch,

Hillsborough is under occupation by the Rebel. Diplomatic dealings between them and the local mayor, who is well respected by the surrounding population, are under way. I suspect that they desire the mayor's blessing before initiating a sizable recruiting drive to replace the men lost in past campaigns.

You are under orders to march ahead of our column, bound for North Carolina, and scout the enemy positions in force, reporting back to us their numbers and disposition as we advance to Charlotte. From there, duly advised, we shall move on Hillsborough with your forces in support.

This is your first time in command of so large a body of men. Conduct yourself with caution and do not seek armed conflict.

Respectfully yours,
Augustine Prévost

Finch flinched as memories of the foiled Connecticut expedition came swimming into his mind's eye. His imprisonment, torture, and remorse stemming from the ambush he walked into dealt him and his psyche a harsh blow.

"Finch? Are you quite alright?" Cornwallis inquired only somewhat sincerely. "If this mission proves too much for you, I am sure we can find a replacement. You need only say the word."

Finch snapped to attention. "No, sir. My men will be ready by dawn tomorrow." He turned to Browne. "Colonel, assemble the troops on the outskirts of town."

"Aye, sir." Browne chuckled. "I wonder what the other officers would make of this. Shall I call them together for a meeting?"

"Do so," Finch replied, doffing his hat to scratch his head.

Augustine Prévost's Headquarters, Camden, South Carolina
17 MARCH 1777, 4:47 PM

As evening began to fall, Finch, Browne, von Wurmb, Running Deer, Sandsnake, and Ferguson met upon Hobkirk's Hill. Finch relayed Prévost's orders to the assembled soldiery, pipe in hand.

"So we are to be scouts for the main force?" the cocky Ferguson cut in. "Excellent! I look forward to the fight. My tactics and elite soldiers will prove the mettle of my patented weaponry. We will show you all how the Experimental Rifle Corps fights!"

"Shut it, Ferguson," Browne cut in. "This will be a challenging engagement. No need to brag about the value of one unit over another. We must work in support of one another, as my lads and the Creek always did. However, we are not to carry the fight to the enemy just yet, anyway. We must scout the lines and return to be briefed on our role."

"Gentlemen, I know not," von Wurmb replied uneasily. "It seems as though we may be used for our scouting abilities, but when the time for glorious battle is upon us, we shall be put aside and left to do menial tasks. General Finch, I beg you, remember that Cornwallis does not like you. If you wish to win glory for us all, you must make wise decisions of your own and not play into his hands entirely, for he would surely see you undone. In doing so, you may want to consider the well-being of your family as well."

"Why, what do you mean, Colonel?" Finch inquired.

Ludwig von Wurmb saluted stiffly. "What I mean to say, sir, is that your incessant placement of your family in danger may see them killed. Can you at least tell your little Fräulein to stay away from my feldjaegers? She distracts them with her incessant words, which is most pleasant, ja, but for a woman to take an interest in fighting is unladylike, whilst the child that should learn to defend himself and others, your son, Archibald, runs at the sight of conflict, more womanly than the women of your house."

Von Wurmb then paused when, as though summoned, young Archibald Finch poked his head from behind a tree. "It appears he spies on others, too, sir," von Wurmb continued with venom. "Thank God he is on our side."

Archibald gasped and ducked back behind the tree.

"I believe he was actually playing with sticks," Finch replied testily.

"Lord, friend! Why such hostility?" Ferguson remarked. "The Finches have ever been most pleasant to us all. I beg you remember that though you may have a high rank amongst us, there is no reason to treat General Finch with such acrimony!"

Von Wurmb sighed. "I apologize, sir. I only wish the best for the brigade and worry about the success of my men, who are strangers not only to these lands. We have a reputation in warfare to defend, too, so when my superior officer harbors children in his ranks as we fight a partisan war, I grow frightened for all involved. They will slow us down and will give away our position with their frolics. I suggest we pass your children off here in Camden, where we know we have sympathizers amongst us."

"My friends," Running Deer said, a patient smile on his face as he reached out to his brothers-in-arms. "I beseech you, we should all be calm. Yes, the situation is unlike one I have seen, and yes, no child should be in a camp of soldiers, but we must adapt, like a willow tree on the breeze, for when we are divided, the Rebels grow stronger. General Finch's family are only attempting to help support their patriarch, and he them."

"I . . . agree with Running Deer," Sandsnake contributed reluctantly.

"Colonel von Wurmb," Finch said patiently, "your concerns as to my family shall be taken under due consideration, and I am sure your men will fare admirably on the field of combat. My only worry is that you prove yourself overly opinionated and curmudgeonly off the field."

To this, von Wurmb only huffed and puffed, but then he nodded, the lines on his face fading slightly. He smiled. "If you take into consideration my thoughts, I shall ease my humors somewhat."

"Splendid. I look forward to seeing you and Captain Ferguson interacting more pleasantly in the future," Finch replied. Finch relayed Prévost's orders to the assembled soldiery, pipe in hand, which he had secreted past Adelaide, and steadied himself. He was surely stressed by the disagreements of his officers and by his own insecurities, but fortunately there was tobacco to balance his humors and maintain his calm.

"What say you, General?" came von Wurmb's voice as Finch shut his eyes, savoring the pipe smoke. A quiet moment passed. At length, the engineer's eyes snapped open.

"Gentlemen, gather your men," he said. "We shall inform Prévost of our departure at once."

"Surely we shall not need an entire brigade for a scouting

mission," von Wurmb shrilled. Ferguson again gently attempted to calm him, yet he continued: "Sending a force so moderate in size, unsupported, to do the bidding of General Prévost seems unnecessary. It would be too small to last in a large-scale engagement and may yet alert the enemy to our presence with its size. I have read reports about you in the past, sir, and you are known by the officer class to be impulsive and reckless. I beseech you, sir, use caution. Scout with a small force, unseen, ascertain their defenses, then call in the large-scale support that is the rest of the brigade and Prévost's division."

Finch took a puff on his pipe and looked upon his subordinate officer with confidence. "You are quite right about the need for stealth and subtlety. We will all travel together for safety until we reach Salem, which we will occupy with as little bloodshed and as much gentility as possible. From there Ferguson's rifles will be the ones to scout the enemy positions ahead. I do believe the Natives will appear out of place, whilst any horse would be easily spotted. I also promise you I will not prevail upon Ferguson to baby-mind my children as he scouts. They will be in Salem, savoring the delicacies of North Carolina, where the rest of us will also lie in wait until the heavies arrive. At this point, we will all go in together and put an end to the Rebellion's mischief."

Running Deer, Sandsnake, and Browne smiled. Ferguson nodded. Even "Bitter" Wurmb seemed satisfied.

"I understand, sir," he answered.

As the officers left, Finch went over to Archibald's hiding place and took the sniffling child into his arms. "Now then, young one. No need to worry. Von Wurmb will not get his way. You will remain with your mother, but know that none of us truly think ill of you. You are beloved by those who truly know you."

The boy wiped a tear from his eye. "Am I really a woman for not wishing to be a soldier, Papa?"

"By no means, my son. It was wrong of him to deride you for who you are, and even if you were a woman, do not your mother and sister work very hard in their own way? There are many ways besides soldiering to aid the war effort. I am sorry that my role as an officer influences you so."

Finch paused, considering. "I further think that perhaps the reason von Wurmb felt as he did was because he saw you were handy in the arts. He may deem these skills unnecessary, but that is more a commentary on his ignorance than on your usefulness. Do not his men's jaeger rifles rely on exquisite German crafts-manship to be made? This is your preferred course in life. Your skills at painting, drawing, and sewing are unimpeachable. I am proud of you, my son."

CHAPTER 7

The Battle for North Carolina

Guilford Courthouse, North Carolina

3 APRIL 1777, 8:15 PM

After a great many days' march, Finch's men had reached Guilford Courthouse, North Carolina. There the soldiers under his command pitched camp for the evening. Much to Finch's surprise, the townsfolk treated them with great hospitality. Some gathered to provide food and drink from taverns, whilst others sought blankets from the supplies of many households.

"I do not understand," Finch remarked in passing to Ferguson, von Wurmb, and Browne. "I have been told in briefings that Guilford largely thinks ill of its Loyalist population and the Crown forces therewith. *Especially* Natives and Germans! Why do they reward us so?"

"Well, we have marched many miles to liberate these towns," von Wurmb began cautiously, but Ferguson shook his head.

"I fear it doesn't work that way, my dear professor. Do you really believe they would care about our labors to protect them from the Rebellion? They hate us, alright. I just wonder whether they are trying to buy our mercy or are luring us into a trap."

139

Browne smiled darkly. "The latter is a distinct possibility, Ferguson. We should keep a sharp eye for militia ambushes, true, but look to these so-called presents, as well. I've called on my men to refuse all gifts from the locals. They might distract us from an enemy creeping up on us."

Finch raised an eyebrow. "Surely you don't think they'd poison their own food and drink just to spite us."

Browne shook his head. "All I know is that this distribution of blankets seems awfully suspicious. Keep a sharp eye for trouble, and check anyone who comes into our camp."

"Why, we are trained elites!" von Wurmb cried in surprise. "They wouldn't dare attack us directly, would they? And killing us in our sleep? Poisoning us? Surely they wouldn't dare!"

"Wartime makes monsters of us all," Ferguson replied simply.

"Then it appears we are agreed," Finch remarked sadly. "It is tragic the locals may well not trust us, but what must be done must be done. Let us thank them prettily for the gifts, but abstain from their food and drink, whilst we return the blankets immediately before any more potential damage can be done. In the meantime, let us send our nonessential personnel back to Charleston, where the main force lies."

Finch returned to his tent, where his family awaited him with dinner.

"My darlings, an urgent matter has come up, and we must separate the soldiery from the nonessential staffers of the force at hand," he said.

Adelaide shot up from her chair, but before she could speak, Finch continued. "Yes, Adelaide, you and the children will be included in this order to abandon the main force. I will send a few of Browne's rangers to accompany you to Charleston, where you will seek the company of Earl Cornwallis's force. His men will eventually catch up to us, but we must lessen the exposure of our women and children to an ambuscade. Allow yourself to be led southernly, my darlings. I will see you soon."

"Yes, husband," Adelaide replied with an uneasy smile.

It is good to see the two of us see eye to eye on this dangerous matter. Finch was relieved at her obedience.

"You take care of yourself, beloved," she continued. "I shall never forgive you if we must bury you after an act of suicidal bravery. Honor we can easily do without, so long as we have your love. Without your love as well?" she shrugged. "We'll still survive, however unhappily."

Caroline suddenly rushed over to her father and enveloped him. "Don't let them eat you, Father!"

"Caroline! The Rebels are citizens like you and me. They will not eat Father," Constance scoffed.

"That's not what Captain Cutty said!"

Archibald tearfully waved goodbye before hugging his father. Finch ruffled his hair. "Paint broadly and creatively," he said. He then gathered everyone together in an embrace.

Guilford Courthouse, North Carolina
4 April 1777, 9:20 AM

Removed from his family, Finch had not rested well, and the rest of his men had fared little better as the cool April breezes made them all shiver. Early the next day, a thunder and lightning storm hampered progress for any sort of advance toward Hillsborough, so the tents remained pitched, and Finch declared a period of rest to wait out the rainfall and storm bolts. He hoped the Rebels would not use the squall to cover any rash movements of their own.

As hours passed, Finch had begun to worry about the well-being of his army. The arms, formerly stacked outside of the tents, had been brought inside, along with the powder and provisions, but he could not help thinking something was off. Finch wandered the encampment.

It was too quiet.

Zounds, Finch thought. *I do not wish to engineer the capture of some of the finest troops in the British Army. Oh God, and not just the men, but the matériel, too! Losing those breech-loading rifles would make me the laughingstock of the army. Clinton would roast me alive!*

As he pondered these horrible thoughts, he reached for his pipe, plugging it with tobacco, before halting and furtively looking around for Adelaide. Then he remembered she had returned to Charleston. Sighing, knowing he would be better off pursuing a healthier coping mechanism, he began counting the feathers artfully arranged in the hair of the Creek and Cherokee warriors waiting alongside the rest of his men. This earned Finch numerous confused looks from the warriors.

"Are you quite well, General?" Browne inquired, as Finch reached the seventy-third feather amongst the warriors of Sandsnake's Creek. "You seem a mite worried."

"Do you not worry for the fate of your men on missions?" Finch snapped, on edge.

"Well yes, but the men tend to like a commander who is above worry for their well-being. Worry less, sir. Smile more. It will inspire them."

Finch nevertheless persisted in counting the feathers of his allies. However, as he did so, he made sure to force a bracing smile at his men.

Finch had come close to counting the entirety of not just the Creek warriors but that of the Cherokee allies when, suddenly, von Wurmb came trotting up to him on his horse.

"Sir, pickets report a body of British light foot approaching. Perhaps they are reinforcements?"

That would be heartening, Finch thought. *More men to assist us in the early action.* He turned to von Wurmb. "Come, let us meet our compatriots."

Guilford Courthouse, North Carolina

4 APRIL 1777, 10:07 AM

A dripping-wet Colonel James Grant was not pleased to see Finch, and the feeling was quite obviously mutual. There was fire in the eyes of the wrinkled, squinting colonel as he opened his mouth to speak.

"Colonel Grant," Finch interrupted coldly. "Welcome back to the colonies."

"By God, sir," Grant said with a surprising bit of restraint. "I asked for the commanding officer of the lights, not some snotty, upstart engineer! Where the blazes is the leader of this brigade?"

"You are looking at him," Finch replied with a smirk. "Brigadier General Giles Finch, at your service."

Grant's eyes bulged at this announcement, but he did not say anything untoward. Clearly his time abroad had cooled his temper a bit. "I see . . . General." He sniffed contemptuously. "I come bearing reinforcements for the light infantry brigade arrayed here in Guilford Courthouse. Allow me to fall in alongside your other . . ."—he looked from the British to the Native to the German and, at length, the Loyalist troops arrayed with him—"skirmishers."

"You are welcome, of course, Colonel Grant. I must ask, however: How did you manage to find your way back to the colonies? Were you not exiled by General Howe?"

Grant snorted. "By Howe, maybe, but Clinton knows a good officer when he can find one. He brought me back from the

Jamaican garrison because he knows my tactical acumen is second only to that of Sir Charles Grey himself." He smiled confidently.

Finch was unnerved. "And the fact that you nearly burned Concord to the ground? Has high command forgiven you for the acts related to that incident?"

Grant reddened slightly but remembered he was talking to his superior officer. "Cleared by Sir Henry Clinton, sir! He needs aggressive officers, and I am willing to offer my services toward his ends. Some of these ends, however, are most peculiar."

Finch raised an eyebrow.

"Ah, yes, you've been on the march for a time," Grant continued. "Since Clinton took command, he's been very ambitious in terms of winning the hearts and minds of the people. Well, *some* of the people, at least."

"How do you mean?" Finch wondered.

"Sir Henry has been courting the Negroes, sir. The Papists as well. Jews and Indians, too, as you know, and sometimes former prisoners, the better to gain the advantage on the Rebels. He feels that with the help of the unwashed and uncared for, coupled of course with their white sympathizers, he may win the war at only the cost of making them our equals."

Finch labored to contain his excitement. "So what has he done to follow up in the fashion of his beliefs?"

Grant grinned before reaching into his coat for a dispatch, which he offered to Finch. "See for yourself, sir. It's a right mess in Horse Guards right now. Delightful, I say! We're really shaking those old crows up!"

Finch took the dispatch and began to read.

To General Giles Finch, Commander of the Light Brigade

I, Sir Henry Clinton, do hereby empower you to restructure your army based around the newly written Charleston

Proclamation I have instituted throughout the colonies. So as not to take too much of your time with formalities and pleasantries, I shall discuss the bare-boned basics of this new approach to our war:

FIRST: That all Negro or Mulatto slaves (hereafter referred to as "Negro") and indentured servants of all races previously owned by rebelliously inclined masters may be confiscated and liberated.

SECOND: That any Negro, be he freed or slave, whether indentured or otherwise, be allowed to enter service as smith, or teamster, or cook, &c: any position as camp follower in which he proves himself useful, including at arms as a guard. On the field, he may serve as a musician or in the militia but may not don the red coat of a Crown regular. Regardless of position, he will be paid and monied as a white man would. His family may follow with him.

THIRD: That any slave owned by a Royalist who would masquerade as a Rebel-owned slave and who escapes his master before seeking freedom at the hands of the Crown forces must be returned to his master, though he will be so under promise of no retaliation by the master's hand. Should a Crown officer wish to, he may purchase the slave off the hands of his Royalist master at an agreed-upon price and free him thereafter.

FOURTH: That any Negro may be authorized to raise and command partisan and militia forces comprised of those willing to serve under him, provided they find their own equipment.

Let it be further said that all white persons, be they Jew or Papist or proper Christian, enjoy the same rights and regulations as one another in the eyes of His Majesty's Army.

I hope this dispatch finds you well, and that your efforts in the northward push are met with success.

> *GSTK*
> *Yours sincerely, &c.*
> *Clinton*

Good God, Finch thought. *He's really done it. Clinton has challenged the status quo and taken several steps toward liberty for slaves. Whilst I am sure he wished he could do more, Parliament has probably tied his hands.* Finch turned to Grant. "I am proud of the man and can only hope to improve the rights of the Negro from here," he said before scratching his head. The flies were out in force.

Grant nodded and said, "Clinton did well. My time abroad alongside the Negroes in Kingston got me to thinking that not only was Howe wrong to send me back to England for my strategies, but he was wrong about a great many other things, too. As I had said from the beginning, I would not be wroth to see more Negroes following us. I was merely nervous, considering the damage it would do to our relations with the colonies, about which I was also correct. Charleston is in an uproar."

Finch took a deep breath. He worried for his family, though he imagined they had not yet arrived. "Fighting in the streets?"

Grant shrugged. "Some scattered riots. That said, our lads lost precious time seizing the town, I am told, and will not cede it without a fight. The men have forestalled the gathering storm well, and for a good enough cause. Some have seen the light and expressed sympathy for Sir Henry's proclamation. Others remain coldly neutral. And many are heavily opposed to the act, but their combined outrage is nothing the men cannot handle, and nothing the Rebels can support."

He stretched his arms over his head and smiled. Finch exhaled in relief. *Sir Henry will protect the family.* "Lovely day. I'm very glad you encouraged Sir Henry toward this proclamation. The chaos that will reign as a result will herald a most gratifying return to the front."

"Now see here, Grant. You are under my command and will do nothing untoward to the Rebels . . ." He paused. *Was not freeing Rebel-owned slaves untoward to them?* Grant was smirking at him. " . . . within reason, I suppose. And believe you me, however *inconvenient* for the Sons of Liberty freeing their slaves may be, it is not untoward in the same way *enslaving* them would be, as they have done our subjects."

"As you wish, of course, sir," Grant gave a curt half bow.

"I might add, Colonel Grant," Finch continued, "that I hardly encouraged Sir Henry toward following up on his goal. He merely mentioned his desire to abolish slavery one day, and I may have simply suggested he evolve the idea slowl—oh dear," he mumbled as Grant roared with laughter.

"Worry not, General," Grant remarked. "You were a tool in creating a proclamation that is unprecedented in scope for what it will achieve, and what it will achieve is *good*, sir. You say you have seen Negroes fight and die on your watch? You say they *do* stand as good a man as any? Now we shall *all* find out, by God! For surely they will be possessed of a zeal for freedom far more real and reasoned than anything the Rebels can field as they fight for their conflicting, inconsistent, and petty demands."

"Well, I wouldn't speak that ill of them, Colonel Grant," Finch replied. "They fight well."

Grant snorted. "Let us hope not, sir, lest we lose the war and be branded criminals to history. Following this coup by Sir Henry, we will all be seen as monsters."

Finch shuddered at the thought.

Guilford Courthouse, North Carolina

4 April 1777, 3:43 PM

As the day wore on, Finch joined von Wurmb, Grant, and Browne in a traditional forty-deal game of quadrille.

Whilst the Native war chiefs looked on, admiring the elaborate artwork on the deck of cards, Finch, making excellent usage of his swift engineer's mind and command of statistics, played competitively against von Wurmb, a fellow intellectual, and the two raced ambitiously neck and neck to win tricks, leaving the others in the dust.

The game came to a close after a brief twenty minutes of play with von Wurmb, beaten, clamoring for more, whilst Finch, noticing the boredom of the other players, suggested a spot of tea. This was agreed upon by all, and the cards were given to the war chiefs, who had caught on to the rules quickly enough to play amongst themselves.

If only Archibald were here, Finch thought. *He would take this unusual moment to draw their likenesses as they played.* He sighed, looking around the encampment. *Constance would spend the time cavorting once more with young Mister Simmons, I'd imagine. How disappointed she'd be to know his company has been converged into Grant's detachment of lights and is with us here, not with her. Meanwhile, Caroline would be playing quadrille with the Natives, and Adelaide . . . well . . . I wish she were here with me.*

Orange County, North Carolina

6 April 1777, 3:43 PM

As the column of light infantry, riflemen, mounted rangers, mounted jaegers, and warbands neared Hillsborough, Finch took his leave of the men and went ahead with Ferguson's rifles to scout with strict orders to have the rest of his force follow suit two hours after the initial force set off.

Finding his spyglass missing, he decided, under the pressure of time, to forge on without the implement and borrow Browne's. Before he set out from his tent, Adelaide burst in from under the flap, Constance and Archibald in tow. Caroline was notably absent.

"Husband," she hissed, as quietly as she could, making Finch jump. "It appears Caroline has left my care."

Having recovered his wits and deciding not to press the point that his wife had secreted herself back into Finch's camp against his request, Finch nodded, growing pale. "And you're sure she's not out wrestling with the Indian warriors again?"

"Yes, dear."

"And she's not taking marksmanship lessons from Ferguson's rifles?"

"No, dear. I checked."

Hrm . . . Finch frowned. "This indeed poses a problem."

Ferguson now entered the tent. His eyebrows twitched as he noticed Adelaide.

"Sir?" Ferguson interrupted. "We really must be off."

Finch nodded, a frown on his face. "Go ahead. I'll be right with you."

Ferguson saluted and took off.

Adelaide shook her head. "It's alright, Giles. The war waits for no man. You may join him if you must."

Finch looked down. "I apologize, Adelaide. You know I love her, but I also have my duty to attend to, and—"

"And she shouldn't have run away, I agree. No, Giles, your duty is important here. It is your child's well-being as opposed to that of over a thousand men. I shall attempt to hunt her down myself. She is a tricky one, but you will find I have some wits of my own!"

Giles kissed his wife on the lips. "Good hunting."

Orange County, North Carolina

6 April 1777, 8:21 PM

As night began to fall, the rifles and their commanding officers reached the tree line near town. Before they could reach their destination, however, a small, impish figure came running in their direction. *Shite*, Finch thought. *If she sees us, the mission will be imperiled.* Then Finch took a second look and swore under his breath. He would know that little gremlin anywhere.

Finch poked his head from out of cover. "Caroline, take cover at once!" he hissed, fearing the worst. Caroline obediently did so, giggling. This ceased when she saw the look on her father's face.

"What do you think you are doing?"

"Scouting, Papa!" she replied excitedly.

Finch rounded on his daughter, his voice deadly soft. "Return to the safety of the column at once, Caroline, but believe you me, we will speak on this matter soon."

"But, Father, you must listen! You're in danger!"

Finch stopped short. "What's that?"

"The Rebels are waiting for you there! You must be careful! Please, Papa!"

"You . . . you saw them?"

Caroline nodded vigorously, handing over her father's spyglass. Finch snatched it away from her before gesturing impatiently to his daughter to continue.

"They are out in force, sir. There *were* just two groups of maybe two hundred men, just men with firelocks, in the center of town. It looked like they were training. But as I was leaving, I saw two more groups of *soldiers* present, positioned on the outskirts of town, near those plantation houses. I even saw cannon! I walked into town to buy some milk and saw some strange men haggling over them, like something at a market. They spoke with funny voices."

"How is the terrain for a surprise attack?" Ferguson inquired, despite himself.

Caroline blushed and replied thoughtfully. "Well, Captain Ferguson, there are some lovely woods near the town that we could hide in for a time. Oh! And those beautiful plantation houses on the outskirts will help, too!"

There was a silence before Finch spoke up again. "These plantation houses," he said. "Have they . . . laborers we might be able to rescue from their unenviable tasks?"

Caroline grinned. "Indeed they have, sir, and mighty fine big brown men they are, too."

Finch could not help but smile back at Caroline's observations. "Thank you, child. You have been very . . . helpful."

Caroline curtsied.

"Now return to the back of the column and find your way to your mother. We were both worried sick about you. Seek safety within the column at once!"

But Finch's daughter was not quite ready to leave yet. "Be careful, Father! The townsfolk spoke of another large army coming from the north!"

As Finch watched his daughter trundle off, he couldn't help but smile sadly. He would never have expected the utility of his own daughter as a scout, but stranger things had happened in times of war. And she had done a fine job, too.

As the rest of Finch's column converged on his position, he gathered his officers together. "I have something to say to everyone before we begin our maneuvers today."

As the soldiers of the Crown and their followers came together at the outskirts of town, Finch cleared his throat and began to speak. "Gentlemen, as you may know, Sir Henry Clinton has passed an act granting new powers and rights to the Negro in the colonies. Today is a special day, for though we advance on Hillsborough to the beat of our old drum—that of defeating the Rebellion—we shall temper it with a new tune, one of liberty to slaves. For too long has the Negro withered away under the heel of taskmasters both Loyalist and Rebel aligned. Now do we have a chance to play a role, however small, in liberating many of these poor souls. Whether to strike a blow for justice in a dark time or merely to disrupt the fortunes of our enemy, may almighty God smile down upon our endeavors and deliver justice and the King's Law for all, regardless of their color."

"Hear, hear!" cried Ferguson, as Grant nodded. The force began to prepare themselves for the march eastward. As Finch waited for his groomsman to saddle his horse, Browne appeared in the makeshift stables prepared for the officers.

"Greetings, General," Browne said. "A rousing speech you gave this morning. I hope we can back our promises with our actions."

"Indeed, Colonel," Finch replied. "So do I. I have never been one for empty promises."

"Without a doubt. I just sincerely hope you know exactly what you are doing. Freeing the slaves is a kindly concept in theory, but when the war is over, even if we prevail, where will they turn for housing? For food? For capital? I previously owned such men back in Brownesville, but I understand they have long since escaped since my apparent death. I bear them no ill will, and hope to God they have prospered since then, but it is a challenging world for a black man, slave or free. I hope you think on what comes of this. Though fighting alongside Indians has taught me the equal value of what so many others call 'lesser men,' we must be careful to ensure we can deliver on our word."

Finch took Browne's hands in his own. "Thomas, on my word as a gentleman, I will do everything in my power to provide for these poor souls. Not only will they prosper in our ranks, but if I must, I shall break down the very doors to Parliament to campaign for the equal rights of these men, women, and children."

"Then I am for you."

Vicinity of Hillsborough, North Carolina

7 April 1777, 1:15 AM

"Very well then, gentlefolk," Finch addressed the assembled officers gathering in the forest. They had just marched a short distance and had heard the church bells of Hillsborough on the hour.

"Here is the plan. After due consideration, I have decided that the best way to engage the enemy will be to take the town swiftly, before our own reinforcements come up, so the enemy will not be afforded a chance to entrench. The rangers and jaegers will ride into town to skirmish with and attract the attention of the enemy forces. Then, whilst the jaegers exchange shots with the forces arranged against them, the rangers will break through to the far side of Hillsborough and draw some of the foemen after them.

"Because these forces will then be split, we can hope and presume the Rebels will believe these men to be the entirety of the force sent after them, and this will cause the Rebels to deploy their entire force after what they may assume will be a raiding party, thinking it the only threat. With luck, we can even get them to deploy their artillery. After some amount of skirmishing, it will be at that point that we will attack in force with our infantry, smashing the enemy garrison pinned down by our skirmishers and putting them to flight. We will occupy the plantation houses surrounding town and set up field hospitals with our camp followers there. With luck, we shall capture their guns as well. Perhaps when the fighting is over, we can ascertain the politics of the plantation owners and free the slaves!" He paused. "Does everyone understand?"

There were some murmurs of assent.

"Then get you to your soldiery and apprise them of their roles. We *will* carry the day."

And so the rangers and jaegers set out. Not long after they rode into the distance, Finch heard shots being exchanged between both sides of the pickets and hoped for the safety of his men. He planned to give them one hour and then start his infantry marching. Attempting to display an air of self-confidence and ease and keeping the tree line in front of him, he strode amongst his men, taking time to clap one on the shoulder or offer one some cheese and crackers from his earlier tea.

"Take heart, gentlemen. We will soon be breaking our fast in town, alongside the citizens of Hillsborough," Finch remarked jovially, a forced smile on his face, to a few of Ferguson's riflemen. "Keep your distance and your rifles firing, and we will prevail. You may only number fifty, but with your covering fire, our opportunities to create mischief are endless!" The riflemen shared in some of his laughter, but the engineer could tell they were tense about the encounter ahead.

From there Finch made his rounds, attempting to ascertain which unit seemed most in need of additional moral support. Ferguson's riflemen, despite their training and discipline, had not seen much action yet, and their leader, though competent, was especially aggressive. The warbands, on the other hand, had made their peace with one another, were well led, and would chafe, Finch imagined, at being encouraged onward to battle by a white man.

As his two mounted units had taken to the front and were already conducting battle with the enemy—evidenced by the occasional volley—all that Finch could do now was improve morale amidst the light infantry Grant commanded. Stepping up to Grant, he nodded to his subordinate.

"May I join you in the fight this day?" he asked. Mutely, Grant nodded, gesturing to his right. Finch stepped into position alongside the skirmishers.

"Lads, let us go forth now, whilst the enemy is distracted. Ferguson and his company will first occupy the plantation house directly in front of us, taking up firing positions to cover the town. Meanwhile, the Natives will run roughshod over the enemy, who should still be caught in the confusion of the firefight with our horse. The lights will keep up the advance and take the enemy's flank. We will catch the enemy as they try to fight off the raiding detail we sent earlier. We *will* win this town without the reinforcement Cornwallis will give. Now go!"

The plan took shape quickly, as the riflemen dashed into position at the plantation house. Finch was not immediately able to witness what had come to pass, having stayed back with the light infantry, but from the sounds of cursing, crashing silver, and yowling cats and barking dogs, much chaos had ensued.

Before long, a pair of green-coated riflemen trooped an octet of roughly dressed, bruised, and beaten overseers into temporary captivity. Ferguson and Finch stepped forward to receive the prisoners. "What would you like us to do with them, sir?" one of the riflemen asked.

"Best to give them a taste of their own medicine, Captain. Imprison them with the slaves until we can figure out on which side the master of the house lies," Finch replied with a grin that surprised even himself.

He noted with a hint of pride that the riflemen followed suit at once, locking the overseers, despite their intense protestations, into the slaves' quarters. The slaves were delighted with the new company and, with whoops of laughter, proceeded to rain additional blows down upon their bullies with a great many jeers. *Even if we may fail to free these poor souls,* Finch thought, *at least we may give the Negroes a crack at their oppressors.* He could not help but laugh as he and the lights passed Ferguson, bowing pleasantly to the slaves.

"Enjoy your new roommates, laddies!" Ferguson called. "We'll be back to sort things out soon. Please remain calm." He then saluted Finch as the light infantry and Natives passed him and his men, making their way into town.

Hillsborough was in shambles. It was clear the Rebels had preyed heavily upon the hospitality of the citizenry and had effectively torn the town apart for their pleasure. Livestock roamed the streets, which were littered with wine bottles and debris. Doors hung off hinges, and even the town fountain was beheaded. As an engineer, Finch was appalled, but as a soldier, he realized more important matters were at hand.

Gesturing his men behind cover, he took a look about. Out of the corner of his eye, he saw a musket-wielding soldier rise up from behind cover not far off and give fire. Finch twisted out of the way and the shot went wide, but he found himself confused. *Was that Rebel militia? Surely they were needed to defeat the cavalry we sent to attack the far flanks of the enemy.* He turned to his men. "My fellow warriors, it appears we are being opposed by a more oblivious, or perchance more confident, force than we initially imagined. This bodes suspiciously poorly for the fate of our cavalry. We must see to their safety, an—"

"Charge!" Grant interrupted with exasperation, haphazardly brandishing a saber and gesturing his men to draw their melee weapons. The Natives followed suit, and Finch sighed.

"Yes!" he shouted after them. "That is what I meant!"

As the Crown forces advanced, however, the militia anticipated their actions and committed to a long battle line the length of the main street, where they had set up a number of small wagons of hay in a line across the road to hinder the Anglo-Native advance. Firing from behind this position, Finch noticed his troops, deployed in an orderly line themselves, beginning to waver.

"Come, lads!" Finch cried. "They are only militia! Surely they are a lively bunch, but we will take their position!"

His cries were answered by an undisciplined volley from the Rebels' Orange County Militia, which struck down several Cherokee. This, in turn, was responded to by concentrated fire from Ferguson's riflemen on the rooftops, resulting in cries of agony as some of the militia, previously fancying themselves safely behind cover, were gunned down. Finch's men drew ever nearer as the Rebels struggled to reload. His heart began to pound as he advanced toward the barricades, when the Rebels, having finished loading, began to fire once more. Finch briefly closed his eyes, expecting a wall of lead in his direction, but found no more than a few scattered shots flying at his men. Inexperienced and exposed to their shot from above, some militiamen had begun firing to little avail at the far-off riflemen.

Finch flourished his blade forward as he looked back at his troops. "We've got them, lads! Keep up the advance! Stead— *oompf!*"

Having neglected to watch where he was going, Finch had run face-first into a wagon carrying a great many bales of hay. As he fell to the ground, the wagon, having tipped slightly, deposited some hay on top of him. Flustered, Finch crawled his way out from under the straw, spitting and stammering, just in time to watch a militia officer toss a torch onto the bales that remained on the wagon, causing a column of flame to shoot up and slowing the Crown advance. Other minutemen dashed amongst the various bales on other wagons, lighting flames to form a barrier and slow the Crown forces before they themselves fell back.

Whilst the light infantry fired shots through the inferno at the retreating backs of the militia, Finch turned to Sandsnake and Running Deer. "Gentlemen, your time has come. Head for the outskirts of town once more and swing around the flames. Break off from our force and operate independently. Try to defeat the militia once and for all. My men will try to help the horse. You must overrun the Rebels and ensure they fail to fall back to a more defensive position. Try your best not to tear the town in twain as you do so."

Both men looked at Finch quizzically, but then nodded. They turned to their warriors and barked orders in their languages over the firestorm. Responding at once, the Natives slowed their attack on the currently impassable Rebel center and launched themselves into an all-out run along the side streets of town, attempting to cut off their quarry.

Grant sidled up to Finch and watched as the Natives dispersed themselves along the adjoining roads. His face was a picture of concern. "Damme, Finch! Why let the Indians have all the fun? Firing at this distance will render my lights and rifles ineffectual! You are cheating my men of glory, sah!"

Finch sighed. "Colonel, let us rally Ferguson's rifles. We, along with your men and his rifles, will assist the Creek in attacking the Rebel right flank whilst the Cherokee push the left. We must find out what happened to Browne's rangers and the jaegers."

Grant saluted gleefully. "Yes, sah!" He dashed along the battle lines of his battalion as they primed and loaded their weapons. "Come, lads! It is high time we cause some mischief." He looked up contemptuously at the Experimental Rifles, still taking pot-shots at the Rebel militia. "Are you coming, Ferguson? Finch has ordered us to move out!"

"Sorry?" Ferguson cried from a window, cupping a hand to his ear.

Finch cleared his throat. "Kindly direct your men forward down the street and continue to occupy buildings to set up additional bases of fire!"

"Oh! I see! That I can do!" Ferguson shouted back. "Alright, you lovely bastards," he roared to his men, his Scottish brogue piercing the night. "The brass want to kill off every last bugger amongst us, so what are we waiting for? Onward!"

Finch stared at Ferguson before nodding and smiling. "Onward, lights and rifles!" he shouted. "Follow the Natives!"

Stumbling down the staircases of the plantation house and vaulting over the fences surrounding them, the rifles joined Grant's light bobs, and the band surged after the Natives. As the Creek came swimming back into view through the smoke, flames, and entropy of combat, Finch and his British allies found the Natives heavily engaged.

The militia had formed into square formations of fifty men each and were fending off both the Creek and Cherokee with some success, the Natives finding themselves unable to flank the militia units on any side. Meanwhile, in the distance, loud artillery blasts could be heard, punctuated by the sound of small arms. *Good*, Finch thought. *At least our mounted forces are holding. Let us pray they can sustain themselves just a bit longer.* He turned to Ferguson and Grant.

"Alright, fellows. Our horse have seen enough combat today. It's high time we relieve them or at least use them to turn the enemy flank. So the enemy militia are in a square? That means they will be slow to react to our movement. We will rush past them and attack the rear of the Continental force where they attack our horse at the city limits. If we can seize the enemy guns firing from that position, too, we will do well. Meanwhile, the militia will be unable to follow us, lest they be attacked by the Indians."

A collection of shots from the Native forces suddenly rocked the nearest militia square. It now appeared the Natives had withdrawn behind cover and were exchanging lead evenly with the enemy. Though he was aware they could not hear him, Finch shouted out to his allies, "Good show, lads! Pin them down!"

He turned back to his lights and rifles. "Now, lads, let us engage those Continentals yonder. They are already attacking our horse and expect their militia to guard their rear. We can slip in behind and pin them down, perhaps forcing their surrender. If we do so, their artillery will soon become ours. Stay low!"

Grant nodded but did not seem pleased as Finch primed a pistol, just in case, and trotted after the bounding steps of the light foot soldiers. "Sir, are you sure you are up for this battle?" Grant inquired. "It would not do to lose you!"

"I thank you for your concern, Grant, but I believe I know my limits," Finch replied. He nodded at the colonel. "Good luck."

Grant smiled sourly. "And you."

As the men closed on the rear of the enemy Continentals, Finch noticed Browne and von Wurmb's cavalry had dismounted, their horses safely out of the way, as they deployed in a defensive skirmish line. *Good lads.* "Alright, lights!" Finch bawled. "Form on me and discharge your weapons. Then prime, load, and fire at will!"

The Continentals jumped at the sound of Finch's voice, and some, whirling around, began shifting their position to cover the rear of their fellows. Chuckling at the surprise he had caused them, though taken aback at the enemy's cohesive training, Finch heard Ferguson's voice ring out.

"Commence firing!"

As the riflemen began sniping at the enemy troops from a collection of prone positions, Grant pushed the advance to get his light infantry into range with their muskets. As the British lights came within range to fire their muskets, they were met with a small shower of musketry from their antagonists. Fortunately, between the small force facing them, the losses said enemy had taken from the riflemen, and the skirmish line in which the lights were deployed, the Rebels were unable to inflict many losses with their attack. The light infantry's trained, steady response ripped through their lines.

As Finch looked on, he observed, to some relief, the Continentals clumsily attempting to swerve around, feed, and fire a collection of field pieces. *These guns must be the ones they just bought,* he thought, remembering Caroline's report. *I imagine they have had no training in using them.*

He fell to a prone position as a counterattack swept across Grant's position. As the lights took cover, pinned down, the Rebels began fixing their bayonets. The lights returned fire, blasting many to the earth, but it appeared the Continental regiment was not to be stalled. They began to march swiftly in the direction of the British light bobs with cries of "Down with the king!"

"Light infantry, never surrender!" Grant declared, pulling out his blade. "Shoot them all to Hades!"

And so, as the Rebels advanced, the lights did their utmost to strike them down with a series of quick volleys. The Rebel line wavered but did not break. Finch closed his eyes and prayed for the best before drawing his blade and kissing its handle. As the Rebels advanced, however, he saw movement in the horizon and heard the guns blast another volley.

Good Lord, he thought. *They come!*

A deafening hunting horn ripped through the night sky as the jaegers, once more mounted, charged down the enemy position. Their allies, the rangers, were hot on their heels, each regiment's horses pounding the ground and rocking the earth as sounds of snorts and whinnies followed in their wake. As the Rebel gunners, both longarm and artillery, struggled to reload, a bruised but far-from-beaten 230 head of horse smashed into them and put them to flight in a flurry of steel. Their allies overrun, the Rebel line closing on the lights saw the danger ahead and broke off in many directions, routed from the field.

With a loud cheer, the jaegers and rangers rode after their beaten foes, exacting a terrible vengeance for the punishment they had suffered earlier. Without wasting a moment, Finch turned to Grant.

"Colonel, you will leave the Continentals to the horse. Instruct your lights to man the artillery and bring them to bear on the militia guarding the town and fighting the Indians. Their squares should make much more appropriate targets than a gaggle of routing men!"

Grant saluted and turned to his redcoats. "By God, sirs!" he bellowed. "Man the guns, and be quick about it. Blow those rabble to the dickens, then roll the cannon into a defensible position in town!"

Finch nodded at the men as they rushed to fulfill his orders, then strode up to the riflemen. "Excellent job, Ferguson. First-rate fire coverage!"

Ferguson bowed. "Your servant, sir."

"Now get you and your men back to the rooftops. Once up there, assist the Natives and Grant in forcing the surrender of the militia."

Ferguson wordlessly slipped away to do Finch's bidding. Now unattached to any unit, Finch stepped forward toward the guns to inspect them. As with the Rebel cannon at Savannah, they were four-pounders.

Then he saw them. Words that struck terror into his heart.

Ultima ratio regum. A seal and inscription atop each of the guns. Latin, but a phrase infamous for its ties to the French king Louis XIV.

Damme. So that's it, then. The Rebels have been soliciting arms from the French.

Finch decided that now was not the time to report his findings to his allies. Instead, he watched with grim satisfaction as the surrounding light infantry loaded and fired the artillery. Looking through his spyglass, he followed the blasts as they broke up the square formations, the balls sending the militia flying like nine-pins. He could hear their cries of agony as, with the core of their defensive positions broken, the Rebels fell prey to the tomahawks and knives of the seasoned Native warriors, who surged forth with terrifying ululations of their own. Seeing the melee joined, Finch turned to the lights firing the cannons.

"Silence the guns, lads. We don't want to hit any of our own."

He extended his spyglass. Despite outnumbering the Natives and fighting for their lives, the militia, exhausted and devastated by the artillery barrage, looked all but beaten. Finch, fearing for their lives, dashed toward the Creek and Cherokee position, waving his arms.

"Spare them!" Finch cried. "They have done little wrong! Let them surrender if they wish!"

Sandsnake and Running Deer heard the order and ordered their men back, as some Rebels began to lay down their arms and stopped fighting themselves. One Rebel militia captain fighting under the banner of Orange County, his face streaked with blood and sweat, made his way through the dead bodies and thicket of men to surrender his blade to Running Deer, and his men were taken without further conflict. Sandsnake's Creek faced more significant opposition.

"Can you not see you are beaten?" Sandsnake shouted over the clash of arms as the Rebels he faced refused to surrender. "Stand down! If you fight on, you will die no more a hero than you would have already lived!"

"Damn your savages to hell, coward!" The face of the captain of the Guilford County Militia was set in a defiant sneer as he cleaved through another Native warrior with a basket-hilted broadsword. "I shall not stand surrender and will slice through as many of you as I can, that I may make heaven with a clear consci—"

The captain stopped short and fell to his knees, gargling, as blood rushed from his mouth. He then collapsed to the ground, impaled by a pair of daggers wielded by She Who Laughs.

"He talks too much."

Witnessing the death of one of their captains, the men of Guilford County fell silent, unsure of their next move. Finch, though equally horrified, decided that it would be poor form to chastise the warrior woman at this time. Instead, he spoke up.

"Gentlemen, some of the finest men the Crown forces command stand before you. You stand no chance. You may surrender, or you may die foolishly, victim to your own pride."

Another captain, this one of Beaufort County, nodded wearily. "Alright, men, our jig is up." He took a look at his hanger, now dripping in blood, and said to it, "It was a pleasure. I will be lucky if I ever again find a sword as worthy as you."

With a sigh, he sheathed the blade and laid it respectfully upon the cobblestones of Hillsborough. He then looked to his men, who lowered their weapons in accordance with their commanding officer.

Finch was overjoyed. The town was his! *However,* he quickly reminded himself, *Caroline spoke of Rebel reinforcements. If she is right, we will not be long for the world if we are caught out of place.*

The engineer turned to his men. "Gentlemen," he addressed the forces arrayed before him, "we have won the opening skirmish of what may be a greater battle on our hands. Prepare yourselves and take cover. The fight is far from won."

There were some general murmurs of assent, followed by a great deal of whispering within the ranks. Finch couldn't blame them and was glad he had not announced the presence of the French cannon.

As the soldiers spoke amongst themselves, he beckoned Grant, Ferguson, and the Native war chiefs together.

"I daresay the enemy militia did a reasonably strong job protecting their sector of the town today," Finch said. "It is a damned shame we cannot emulate some of their tactics, but I imagine there isn't a bale of hay left in town."

"We cannot," Ferguson affirmed. "But my rifles, though yearning for some rest, will be able to surprise the enemy with some rifle fire as they close in."

"This is good. Thank you, Patrick." Finch smiled. "I am sure we can find a skeleton crew to continue to work the French four-pounders we found, as well."

The officers started. "French four-pounders?" Grant exclaimed.

Finch nodded. "Surely their capture will get the enemy's dander up. The revolutionaries are short on guns, and Washington will be in a fearsome rage to hear that they lost a battery of them right after their purchase. We will place the cannon so as to overlook the main road north, and when the Rebels come, we will make a considerable show of force."

"And what of us?" Grant gestured to the lights, who had preemptively begun fortifying the low walls surrounding town.

"Ah, excellent course of action, Colonel Grant," Finch agreed. "Keep up the good work with your men. See if we cannot find ways to funnel the enemy's attack through crowded passages, that we might strike them down as they come. As for our Native troops, they have suffered considerably at the hands of the enemy. Let us swell their ranks once more."

"You don't mean to offer up townsfolk to the command of Indians?" Grant asked, his face flushed.

"What is it to you if I do?" replied Finch. "You have no love for the colonials, and besides, this will allow our allies to assist those in favor of our designs to lock down the town."

"Aye, that is so," Grant admitted. "But I fear we will not have many volunteers."

"What of the slaves?" Ferguson inquired. "We counted at least twenty in the serving quarters of the plantation house we occupied. I am sure we can find many more equally able-bodied men who are willing, besides."

"Well done, Ferguson!" Finch nodded enthusiastically. He turned to Grant. "Get your men to gather them together, emancipate those who are bondsmen, teach them what you can about firearms, and arm them with whatever they can find, even if it is just a dagger. We need all hands on board for this endeavor."

"It again does not matter to me, of course," Grant replied, grimaced, "but what if these slaves belong to Loyalists?"

"Then the liberation of the slaves is their just reward for fighting and dying to protect their masters," Finch replied with a furtive smile. "What better way to serve?"

"So we will defy Sir Henry's express orders, no matter how progressive and merciful they already were?"

Finch glared in Grant's direction. "Strange words coming from a man who threatened to burn down a town."

Grant stiffened up, a frown crossing his features. "I—I care not either way. I merely—"

Finch drew himself up proudly and to his full height, looking at Grant hawkishly. "Colonel Grant, know this. It has become my goal to see the slaves of America freed. This is almost assuredly the case for Sir Henry as well, though, as he is bound by his role of commander-in-chief, it will be much harder for him to enact this deed. He has done well working alongside a relatively removed government overseeing the war. Now it is my turn to work behind the scenes to ensure greater rights for our allies. Grant, you will free those men, then train them in weapon usage, before turning them over to swell the ranks of the Natives. Or by God I will have you dismissed again for disobeying orders. Is this clear?"

Grant spluttered before saluting. "Very much so."

As Finch issued his orders, a sort of uneasy excitement began to occupy his thoughts. *It is only necessary to hold this position against a counterattack,* he thought. *With the assistance of the slaves, I can do just that. I've worked with their type before. With Sir Henry's policy firmly in place, they will work with me again.*

He marched downtown to where Grant's men were escorting the now-freed men to safety in British lines. Their former masters looked on with horror as their erstwhile servants were then given the equipment of the fallen militiamen and Natives. Powerless to stop the onrush of new recruits into the Crown forces, however, they remained silent, if absolutely mutinous, their glares of rage boring into Finch's soul as they stood by, clutching their children and wives for safety.

"I see you will stop at nothing to grind us under your heel again, General," a distinguished-looking gentleman remarked angrily, kicking the dirt road. "Curse you and your men! I was looking out for the best interests of myself and my family, and you have ruined my very livelihood!"

Finch gave a bitter snort of laughter. "And how many livelihoods did you have to ruin to achieve that sort of security? What about the well-being of these poor fellows?"

"I fail to recall when the Crown, in the past, cared about the Negroes. Did not she encourage the slave trade in the past? Who is to say that this is not just a propaganda stunt, an economic ploy?"

That stung. Finch had wondered a tad about such a possibility himself, and to hear another voice such suspicions was terrifying. Drawing himself up, however, he replied curtly, "Though the Crown has not been and never will be perfect, it is a work in progress. Though the Negro may have been freed for the purposes you mentioned, remember: England's abolition of slavery came earlier than this vile insurgency. So did advances in Native relations and other, less sizable demographics in the colonies, such as the Papists. We are becoming a more progressive and noble empire. Far more, at least, than that of your Rebellion."

The man's face turned scarlet. *"I was a bloody Tory!"* he screeched, stomping about helplessly whilst his family looked on in embarrassment.

Finch sighed. "Then you will lend your men to the conflict. The Crown will reimburse you for your lost slaves. Perhaps, by then, you may see the decency of our reasoning and allow me to purchase the freedom of the rest."

The plantation owner took a deep breath and recovered his nerves. "Very well then, sir. Take your men at five pounds each. Fight your battle, but know that in the name of my ancestors, I, James MacAfee, will be out for blood."

"If you value them so much for your own ends, perhaps you should liberate them and retain their labor as equal citizens," Finch retorted, turning on his heel and leaving the slaveowner to ponder his folly. Then he remembered to pay for his men. Reaching into his purse, he found a paltry ten-pound note. "You may have this, and my word of honor that Sir Henry will pay for the rest, should you ask him," Finch remarked shortly. "We will take these twenty men at a five percent interest, which you can, again, receive from General Clinton." He then left the man stammering for words as he went over to inspect the other four large plantation houses that dominated the outskirts of town.

Though the owner of the MacAfee estate had turned out to be disagreeable despite his Loyalty to the Crown, the other three estate owners were Rebel aligned, which thankfully allowed Finch to do what he wished with the terrified families within. Still, the engineer turned lights officer did his utmost to keep matters peaceful with these plantation owners. "You do realize," he remarked, "how much damage the Rebellion did to your homes and the town in which you live, and in what low regard they hold your livelihood? Your militia and regulars have been put to flight by our men, and if they were to return, they would ravish your town all over again. We ask only for hospitality and reinforcement. We shall not even demand the help of your own family members, but only from those men you have trapped in bondage. An expensive proposal, I am aware, but it is either them or your very own family. Either, based on the state of Hillsborough, would be a mercy compared to what the Rebels have done to pillage your village as is, and they are likely to do it again."

Finch repeated this speech three times, at three different houses, and three times was rejected. With a melancholic sigh, he ordered the light infantry to storm the slaves' quarters of each house, holding each outraged family at a hatchet's blade. *By God,* Finch thought. *What have we become?*

Freedom fighters, he assured himself. *We are an army out to set men free and doing much less damage in the process than many would.* He sent a runner to fetch Captain Ferguson. When the Scottish rifleman arrived, panting slightly from his run across town, Finch said, "Captain, take the Natives to the outskirts of town to reinforce your rifles' position. See if you can recall what's left of our horse, too, to hold the line here. Take most of the lights, too, but leave a good ten men to train these Negroes with what little time we have before the Rebel counterattack."

"Deploy your lights. Give us the muskets, and we shall train them," called a familiar voice from behind Finch. Finch whirled about.

The words had come from a nondescript black fellow, average in height, dressed all but in rags, with scars scoring his face. Though he had seen him in better days, Finch had misjudged this fellow before and knew his identity at once.

"By God, Titus!" Finch cried, clapping the man on the shoulder. "Good to see you again. I could have sworn you were reenslaved in—" Finch caught himself. "That is to say, I am very glad to see we liberated you! I am merely surprised to see you. Goodness. There is so much to discuss. I am so sorry about my inability to effect your rescue—"

"It wasn't your fault, General. You gave it your best attempt, more than most would have, and failed. At least you keep trying to learn in the face of your failures."

"Ah," Finch replied, then brightened. "I see you have rather a body of men with you. The sla—fellows we rescued, no doubt."

Titus shook his head. "We weren't amongst the Negroes you rescued." He smiled before waving behind him. "You should consider watching your rear. This has been the third time my men have harried an enemy force in your vicinity."

"You mean you followed us?" Finch inquired, blushing.

Titus gave a sharp whistle. Out of the shadows came a few dozen more men, black, white, and Native, each armed with some combination of salvaged longarm and melee weapon.

"My Black Brigade, sir," Titus said. "At your service."

Finch was impressed. The men were ill equipped but carried themselves well, clearly proud to have fought their partisan war in support of the Crown. "How did you raise these men, Titus? Did these white fellows really consent to serve at the behest of a . . . well . . ."

"Of a Negro?" Titus finished for him. "Yes. These men represent the black slaves and freedmen I was able to liberate from the oppression of the Rebels, coupled with the idealistic abolitionists I could attract. As you can see, we picked up a few Shawnee along the way. They rescued me from imprisonment in a raid on Rebel lands, and I then aided in their successes along the way and earned their respect." He saluted Finch. "I am Captain Titus once more."

Finch smiled. He unsheathed his hanger blade and saluted Titus. "Take command of and train these fine men we just liberated here, and I can all but assure you it will be *Colonel* Titus before the day is out, sir. Well deserved, too."

Titus nodded. "Your offer is fair, sir. Consider it accepted." He turned on his heel and strode off purposefully toward the freedmen arranged nearby by the light infantry. Finch called out to the lights, "Leave the Negroes in the care of Captain Titus, gentlemen. Go off and find your brethren."

Now to find some local white militia to complement Colonel Titus's force, he thought. Taking a bit of time to look around his surroundings, he noticed an inn nearby. "The Pegasus," he read aloud to himself, before shrugging. *It may well be worthwhile to sway them in the fashion of William Howe.* Ensuring none of his men followed him, he entered the tavern.

In more pleasant times, the Pegasus would have been a luxurious dining hall. As Finch entered, he noticed a long, winding bar protecting a kitchen behind which several barkeeps could serve a thirsty populace, ready to discuss the news of the day. Long benches, with tables made of strong mahogany, stretched across the center of the room, with small booths built along the walls. A stage where musicians could play protruded from the bar. The walls were studded with framed pictures as well as pleasant upholstery, and Finch felt he could have made himself at home rather easily, were it not for the thirty-odd people brandishing various improvised weapons and glaring at him from behind the cover of overturned tables set up as barricades. He tried not to show fear as several firelocks were cocked and pointed in his direction.

"What the blazes are you doing here, ye lobsterback?" one man shouted, flailing an arming sword defensively. The others roared their support, clanging their assortment of sharp implements against dishware or on tables. Cries of "Leave at once!" and "Get out of 'ere!" resounded through the room. Finch gestured for their silence. This did not assuage them, as they continued to harass him, tossing dishware perilously close to his head as he made his way to the podium.

The erstwhile engineer paced awhile, head held high, attempting to look professional before addressing the crowd of townsfolk assembled here. "Now see here, you gentlemen of Hillsborough," Finch began. "My name is General Giles Finch. I realize you to be . . . undecided regarding the conflict at this time, but I urge you to dance to our tune. You may be rewarded if you do so, and whilst neutrality will avail you no ill will, misbehavior will see you summarily hanged."

He paused, hoping his bluff would work, and a few of the locals blanched. Finch sighed in relief as no more glassware was thrown in his direction. "With the Rebels run off, our van—well . . . ahem, very well, yes, our vanguard will hold until support arrives, at which point you will be well protected. Then there will be no further need to risk your lives for an insurrection, much less one that has caused your fair city such harm. I am more than willing to make some concessions to see to it that you remain safe whilst we are in command. To earn your goodwill, I will instill no curfew and will let you assemble freely, as long as you give me reason to believe you will not attempt to rise up against the reign of Governor Martin and myself. If you help form a small body of men to assist us in policing the town and perhaps in foiling any attempted Rebel counterattacks, matters will improve all the more."

Finch's audience began to murmur amongst themselves.

"Take time in your deliberations, gentlemen. My men did not want to leave their homes and families to come here to kill their fellow citizens. We only wish to see to the safety of our brethren under the Crown. You can disagree with us—hell, even write about it, as God knows Lord North's foes in Parliament enjoy hearing of the opposition to our cause. But there is no need for violence, and such actions will only result in more death and despair."

A general buzz followed as the citizens talked amongst themselves. Finch took this as a good sign.

"We will occupy this town a time, take on supplies, and, in due time, leave only a small force to supplement any Tories who might volunteer to guard you. From there, I will send word to high command that you are to remain unmolested."

More muttering.

One man spoke up. He was short and slim but well toned, if a little tired from a day's work. "Hiram Watts here," he said, scratching his nose. "That is very good of you, General Finch." He turned to the assembled company. "I say we give His Majesty's soldiers a chance. I have been a supporter of the Revolution. Indeed, the rabble his soldiers ran off broke into my mill and ransacked my flour. When I complained to their commander, he told me to bill Congress. Goddamn them for the bandits that they are!" He shook his head before addressing Finch again. "Many amongst us tire of their depredations. Let us work with the Crown and see it can do us a better turn."

Finch bowed his thanks to Watts. As he did so, a prosperous-looking farmer came to the fore. Finch recognized him as a local plantation owner. "My name is Smith," he roared, flourishing an ebony cane topped with a silver dove. "And you must forgive me if I voice some considerable suspicion. The Revolution knows what's best for us, Watts. The Crown does not think of us as equal, merely separate, and goes out of its way to torture us with cruel and unjust methods. For God's sake, they were not only content to steal our money but also stole my slaves! Smirk if you'd like, but I am prepared to fight for independence with every fiber of my existence. Had the Crown truly wished us well, it wouldn't have stirred up the militias and local battalions in the first place. If that were so, this town would have remained pristine."

This seemed to divide the audience, as Finch, steadying himself, made to leave the stage. "I give you time to think, gentlemen. Discuss the matter amongst yourselves at your leisure. Act as you see fit. But if you are caught violating the King's Law, I *shall* enact a fearsome punishment upon all of you for breaking our accord. What's more, I would take with a gratuitous helping of salt such extreme accusations from a man who refuses to even identify himself by his full name."

Finch then took the moment to step off the stage and light up a pipe outside, as his audience began to decide amongst themselves the fate of Hillsborough. An hour passed, during which time much shouting could be heard from inside the building. In time, a messenger appeared with a signeted envelope for Finch. Finch broke the seal and read the message within.

God save the king, it read in a shaky hand. Finch smiled grimly. It was clear not everyone would be convinced, but it seemed as though much of the populace would cooperate for now rather than risk further difficulties. He proceeded inside to some ragged cheers. Some town officials stood up from their chairs and approached him. Shaking hands with some of them, Finch heaved a sigh of considerable relief. He was glad *that* had not ended with violence.

"Now if you'll excuse me," he said, "I have to ensure the defense of the city." Finch made to stride from the hall when a shout of "We're with you, General!" echoed down the hallway. No fewer than fifteen citizens ran after him, forming up outside at attention.

Finch turned around as casually as he could, concealing his excitement. "I am glad to hear it," he replied, and he took a man by the shoulder, inspecting him and his compatriots. They were a motley crew, two Scotsmen and a Frenchman amongst them, but they brought their own weapons: daggers and broadswords as well as a few fowlers and pistols. "You know you will be enlisting to fight alongside Natives and Negroes, yes?" Finch said. "I trust you have no second thoughts about fighting alongside these ethnic groups, and that you are willing to take orders from a black man?"

There was some murmuring at this, some shuffling of feet.

"Ah . . . well then, I am sorry, General," one man said, wiping sweat from his brow. "I love my king and all, but I'll be hung before I entrust my life to a Negro." He stepped down from his position alongside the other men. Three others followed suit. Finch shook his head. "As you say, gentlemen. It is not as though I have any means of dissuading you. I wish only that you would give this Negro a chance. He is as experienced as he is crafty, and we are wanting for able-bodied heroes for him to command."

"Heroes we are, prejudiced we are not, but we don't need no blackamoor telling us what to do," one of the fellows replied.

Finch snickered at this remark. The gentleman who had said it glared at him, and Finch regarded him with a condescending grin. "You are aware, sir, that no one person roams freely in this army," he said. "That would lead to chaos in the ranks. Titus has proven himself time and time again as a valued soldier in this army. You have not. If you wish to fight alongside us, you will listen to Titus, and you will listen well."

"'Evening, gentlemen," came a soft, dusky voice that made the white militia prospects jump. Titus had marched past with a most businesslike gait to take over the men. With him were the Native allies and some of his black troops. "So these are the new recruits?"

"That's them, indeed." Finch replied. He smiled at the uneasiness some of the troops showed. "Drill them well, Mister Titus. I want an effective fighting force in the next two hours."

Titus grinned. "You'll have such a force in one hour." He turned to the individuals making their way back to the tavern. "And where do you think you're going, cowards? Do you wish to live out an eternity of oppression and torment, humiliated and cast out as Tories in the face of a Rebel victory? Or would you prefer to die, maybe even live, as heroes?"

"We want to live as part of the population that survives this conflict," one of the deserters retorted, glaring at Titus. "Operating alongside Negroes will only make us a target for the depravities of the enemy."

Titus nodded. "Indeed. And I cannot guarantee you a victory, much less that you will be able to survive. What I can guarantee you, however, is that if you fire your three rounds a minute at the enemy, and we win, I shall give you all full rights to pick over the dead. I understand you fight for yourselves and your families, and I respect that. I would do the same if I were in your shoes, but I have an entire race to prove worthy of respect in the meantime. To prove my people worthy, we must win battles, and to help us win, it behooves us to do business with your lot."

Finch was taken aback. He knew the captain was far from a romantic, but he had his ideals. Finch was surprised Titus was tarnishing his goals by working with these ne'er-do-wells. He turned to Titus and asked, "Are you—are you sure you wish to sully your hands with these pragmatists, out only for their own skins?"

"I think we understand each other well enough," Titus replied, smiling at the aforementioned men. "And if they do not commit to their goal in the skirmish lines, three rounds per minute, you have my permission to shoot them."

Finch was aghast. "Shoot them?"

"Politely. Meanwhile, if they hold their position in the firing line, we will reward them. Surely they will deserve to be rewarded like gentlemen for helping my noble cause, even if they are not gentlemen."

Finch saluted. "Splendid, sir. Go to!" He then proceeded to make his way in between various factions of his occupation force toward the north end of town. Peering out into the distance, he saw some black spots on the horizon. He pulled out his spyglass and trained it on the growing spots, only to take note of the Hessians and their ranger allies riding furiously for Hillsborough. As they made rapid gains toward the town, the garrison was able to open the gates to town just in time for the mounted infantry to file in en masse. As they did so, the jaegers and rangers dismounted and led their horses to stabling. Taking account of their numbers,

Finch noted numerous casualties. The units were badly shot up, and many horses were without riders.

He found Browne at the front of the column. "Sir, I beg you, report," Finch said. "What has happened to your men, as well as those of von Wurmb? Did you not take any prisoners of those men you routed?"

Browne spat upon the ground. "Oh, we took prisoners, alright," he replied bitterly. "Then they caught a glimpse of Rebel lines in the distance and made a break for them. Had to give them a taste of the hatchet before they could reach their allies."

Finch stopped dead. "Oh . . . oh no," he said. He kicked the dirt road beneath him.

"I warned him not to do it, sir," von Wurmb cried out from afar. "But he started it, and then all the other prisoners rose up and fought us, trying to pin us in place until their allies arrived!"

"Shut it, von *Worm!*" Browne snapped. He turned back to Finch. "We got the lot of them and made a fighting withdrawal under heavy fire to Hillsborough. We lost maybe thirty men total, but we killed a lot more. Thinned the enemy reinforcement line, too. We could have done some major damage if it wasn't for our overcautious commander over here." He gestured at von Wurmb.

"Hold hand, Browne!" Finch ordered. "We came into this war with orders to reduce casualties and bring the colonies to order. Though we are under a new commander-in-chief with new ideologies on war, it would still do us well to minimize losses. Soldiers though we may be, it is not only for our own good but for that of our comrades and country that we retain our lives. Better to live to fight another day than to die inflicting massive casualties. Our reinforcements have been slowed to a trickle and tend to come from across the ocean. Though better trained, our men are all the more precious."

Browne frowned. "I understand, sir. My apologies. I got carried away by my own personal vendettas." He scowled. "Some of those men were the remnants of the revolution's Georgian establishment. The fellows who defeated you at the Jewish cemetery. They were backed by Carolinians both North and South, and what seemed to be a Virginian regiment or two. It was a big force. At least six guns, too."

Finch raised an eyebrow. "That force is enormous! You're lucky to have come back alive. What possessed you to give chase to such a corps?"

Browne hesitated. "The initial force we saw amongst the reinforcements were *Georgians*. My neighbors."

It came to Finch at last. "You mean the people who walked you across coals and tried to scalp you because you are a Tory?"

"The same."

Finch clapped Browne and von Wurmb on the shoulders. "I comprehend and commend both your command decisions. Next time, work together. Now, help Ferguson's rifles and the lights establish a defensive perimeter around the town. The rest of the men will join you soon. See to it that we lock the town down. We cannot have civilians dying in the upcoming battle, whether by accident or on purpose. Dismissed."

The two colonels saluted before walking off to mind their men. Finch shook his head sadly. A lot of young lives had been lost on both sides to no real end.

And a storm was coming.

CHAPTER 8

Fortress Hillsborough

Hillsborough, North Carolina

7 April 1777, 8:00 AM

Boom! Boom! Boom! Boom!

Finch was jolted from his slumber inside his tent on Hillsborough Green by the thunderous noise of artillery, as the shrieking of round shot sounded overhead before impacting with sickening crunches below.

Looking out the window, he barely noticed the sun rising overhead, as screams abounded and men were sent flying from their positions, grotesque wounds inflicted on them. The injured were evacuated into more solid, brick and mortar buildings, crying in agony, whilst the remaining troops busied themselves with a perimeter defense.

For all the time and effort the lights and rifles spent fortifying the positions, Finch thought, *our defenses were ineffectual in the face of the Rebel cannon. After all, what have we to defend with besides a low picket fence and a few tables, chairs, mattresses, and additional planks of wood to support them?*

Finch looked at his men, scrambling about to prepare for the assured onrush of enemy soldiery. Many appeared shaken, quavering in fear. Finch considered giving a rallying cry but remembered that sometimes it was better to show more than tell. Gathering his own emotions, he attempted to put forth airs of confidence and went to work, gathering his officers.

It was not long before Browne, Titus, Grant, and the others were huddled around him, awaiting others. Grant looked shaken, and the energetic Browne, ever ready to push the attack whatever the odds, was not looking pleased, either, but Titus seemed calm and unshaken by the turn of events. They were all ready to take orders. Shots flew overhead as Finch cautiously observed the scene around him from behind the cover of a low brick wall that once offered support to a now dilapidated house.

"Gentlemen," he said, "I see our artillery is well positioned behind cover, but this protection does not sufficiently guard against their cannon, which is hitting us hard. Kindly withdraw our guns to bottlenecks in town. We will withdraw from all positions along the perimeter and wait for them to give chase. Then we will ambush them in a street fight, catching them with crossfire from the windows of buildings at all angles. We'll be sure to inflict massive casualties from a more defensible position."

Bugger, Finch thought. *I'm at it again. Ranting and rambling. I must be more to the point.* He cleared his throat. "Rifles, Titus's irregulars, take to the buildings. Lights, Indians, fight in support of the guns on the streets. Cover their withdrawal on recoil. Horse—" Finch paused as the artillery barrage fired low, nearly taking the heads off some men waist deep in the entrenchments. *These men are no engineers,* Finch thought. *Though I commend them for trying.*

He waited for the commotion to die down, surprising himself with his composure, before continuing. "The horse will attempt to make themselves scarce, acting independently and engaging the flanks and rear of the enemy as they expose themselves in their attempts to storm the buildings in town. Now take cover"—Finch paused to look about town for well-fortified buildings—"there, there, and there, for starters." He pointed at a few particularly strong stone mansions. *Those will be more than likely to repel shot of that caliber.* "File out amidst the town and seek shelter in the most stalwart of structures. Four men to a window."

The redcoats complied at once, seeking out bottlenecks along the cobblestoned streets with which to trap the onrush of Rebel forces and rolling the small four-pounders into position. They were soon followed by their Native allies and riflemen, who scanned the area for alternative tactical positions. Finding none, they took up positions in the windows. Meanwhile, the Loyalist rangers and jaegers mounted their horses and trotted off, presumably to view the battle from afar before committing their combined force. Finch hoped they had rested sufficiently after their exhausting skirmish.

At length, the makeshift militia, taking a good look at the battlefield ahead of them, sighed, shrugged their shoulders, and followed the rest of Captain Titus's men, who had already taken off toward the stone bastions. Finch looked after them as they went before turning around to review the progress made by the Rebel forces. He jumped, realizing that he did not even need to use his spyglass.

With their barrage complete, the Rebel artillerists and their guns fell silent, scoping the countryside for additional targets. Not far off, however, flew the standards of no fewer than nine full regiments of foot advancing at a rapid pace and backed not by dragoons but by lancers, garishly dressed, who galloped grimly along, intent on skewering Finch's mounted infantry with their spears.

Finch hoped they would see the British forces in full retreat and expect the Crown forces not to pose much of a threat. His forces were outnumbered and outgunned, and the engineer could not deny that this appeared to be the case from the outset. *But,* Finch thought, *does not terrain play a role?*

"Very well, gentlemen," Finch said, addressing his officers. "Time to spring a trap on them inside this very town. Hold your fire until they come near, then, as one, give them hell." With that, Finch withdrew into a relatively undamaged building alongside his sharpshooters, intent on observing the battle from above.

As the enemy came closer, Finch stole a glance at their forces through the window. They had trooped past the gate and into town. Their first rank, a force of blue-coated soldiers with red facings and white waistcoats, had their bayonets fixed forward, prepared to attack oncoming threats. The rest of the Rebel forces followed behind closely, ready to fill holes in the ranks where their allies had fallen. Some appeared prepared to march down back alleys and secure them as well. Finch smiled grimly.

He held his breath as the Rebel forces walked underneath his position. He hoped the lack of shooting from his position would cause officers elsewhere to order their men to hold their fire as well. Some of his men had taken up positions in the back alleys and would be able to stalk the Rebel forces as they made their rounds, and near the fountain in the middle of town were several gun emplacements, camouflaged and protected by what remained of the hay bale wagons, town fountain, and other debris to repel the occupation force. Finally, freely riding around the exterior of town were the rangers and jaegers, waiting for their time to act.

Continuing to spy on the enemy below, Finch saw some commotion playing out on the streets. Smith, the particularly outspoken Rebel plantation owner, was in intense conversation with the commander of the lead Rebel column. *Shite, the citizenry are ratting us out! Yet we cannot turn our weapons on workmen, can we?*

The light infantry crewing the artillery answered this question for him. With a resounding, nearly simultaneous series of

BABABOOMS, the now-revealed artillery, newly obtained by the British, fired great gouts of canister shot. Rounds of containers carrying hundreds of musket balls tore open upon being fired, indiscriminately shredding all in front of them in a cloud of viscera and gore.

Between the four guns, Finch felt he could safely assume that over one hundred men had fallen in the surprise barrage. Doing his best to keep his last meal swallowed down, he turned to Ferguson.

"Get your men on the rooftops and behind as much cover as you can, Patrick. We will make our stand from the buildings! Try to relieve their horses of their burdens." He then shouted out to Titus and his partisans, who were stationed across the street. "Form up along the road, gentlemen. Cut off their lines of retreat from behind cover. We shall send support shortly."

A crackle of musketry rewarded Finch's remarks as, not to be outdone by the artillery, Grant's light infantry and the collected Native allies made their muskets and fowlers heard from behind their barricades on either side of the town fountain.

Seeing themselves ambushed, the Rebels bravely attempted to hold their own. Finch could hear their officers shouting orders but was unable to decipher and counter them over the sounds of battle below. Fortunately, his subordinates appeared to be doing that job for him. Blasted by artillery, light infantry, and Natives to their front, rained with musketry from the buildings to their flanks, and sniped at from behind by auxiliaries, the Rebels were deeply imperiled. They braced against each other for support as they volleyed in different directions but failed to shoot their way to safety. Finch's men had followed his orders meticulously and had found good cover.

From the windowsill, Finch looked down at the carnage below. It was clear that he and his men had a distinct advantage over their entrapped foes. Only both sides' horse remained unaccounted for. Finch bit his lip, then nodded. These Rebels were valiant warriors. He could not kill them to the last man, and they were in no position to call for truce, with enemy fire raining down on them from all sides. Stripping a nearby mattress of its white sheet, he fluttered it from the window as a sign of truce.

Over time, the shooting stopped, and a dignified-looking individual of average build, wearing an epauletted blue and buff coat and crowned with a few wisps of white hair, bravely stepped to the fore. He was accompanied by a weedy subordinate, young and ruddy cheeked with a sharp nose.

The commander of the Rebel force smiled up at Finch. "Hallo up there, my good man!" he said, an apparently genuine grin crossing his features. "I hope you are well. It appears as though you have us, fairly enough. I am General Nathanael Greene, at your service. This is Captain John Laurens, one of my attachés."

Laurens gave a bow of his own. "Your reputation precedes you, General Finch. I commend you and your own on behalf of us abolitionists for your early emancipation of the Negro. Our own government is struggling to come to terms with the reality that whilst they are in bondage, we cannot consider ourselves freedom fighters, and—"

"Yet freedom fighters we are, in our own ways, out to set many free from your king's tyranny," Greene cut in hastily, his face falling. "The two of us, at the very least, personally hope to free blacks as well, of course. But let us dispense with the political discussion, for though we sympathize with one another's plights and recognize that good men abound on both sides, we will nonetheless kill over the few differences we have." He sighed. "This we have learned over the past year or so of warfare."

Finch nodded. "It is a tragedy indeed, sir." He thought a moment. *These men seem friendly, and to end a revolution, one must reach out to one's enemies.* "Come!" Finch interjected. "Let us take drinks in the local tavern. It must have been a hard fight, and a difficult defeat to stomach, I am sure. We will discuss terms of your surrender there." Finch craned his neck up toward the roof, where Ferguson and his men had drawn a bead on the Rebel officers. "Come now, Ferguson, you know that's dishonorable. Join us."

Ferguson lowered his rifle. "You know me all too well, General." The captain launched himself once more through the window of the tall building and soon stood before Finch in all his sweaty glory. "Let us drink to our victory."

The Pegasus, Hillsborough, North Carolina
7 April 1777, 5:32 PM

As Finch and Ferguson were finishing their third bottle of whisky with their two Rebel counterparts, Finch, at long last, began to realize that he was actually somewhat at ease. With his family nearby and safely quartered in one of the plantation houses and the enemy scattered, he could relax knowing he had just won a decisive battle, capturing at least two important officers in the Continental Army. Though unused to this kind of success, he accepted the role of conquering hero with what grace he could.

He offered his conciliations and even apologies to Greene and Laurens for their losses and promised them that he'd do his best to see proper justice served for both them and their men. Though he recalled his own prison sentence after his capture at Post Hill, Finch firmly reminded himself that these men were very much the opposite of McFadden and Burkett. His memories of the two made him shudder.

Indeed, Greene and Laurens were the perfect guests. They laughed along with Finch at Ferguson's intellectual jests and plays on words. Each person in question related tales of home. Finch learned a great deal about Scotland from Ferguson and decided he would have to visit Laurens's childhood home in Beaufort, South Carolina, all the while recalling many of the landmarks Greene spoke of when he described Rhode Island, having visited not long ago. The four men shared an excellent repast of pork and roast beef, as well, and were just about to part ways when Finch could swear he heard music in the distance.

Bagpipes!

Ferguson ran to the window. "It's the Seventy-First Foot!" he cried. "They're with Cornwallis! Reinforcements are here!"

If maybe a tad too late. Finch nodded. "Very well, Captain Ferguson. Please convey my deepest respects to General Cornwallis. I shall be with him shortly." He turned back to his prisoners. "And now, gentlemen, the terms. Your sentiments and good intentions have softened my heart . . . as if my heart weren't soft enough, damn you. But enough of this. Sirs, I see you are equipped with military-grade muskets. I do not know how you received them, but you will dispose of them . . . ahem . . . into our possession, that is. Your artillery will be similarly surrendered into our hands, whilst your troops will be divided into various labor camp details and, under guard, will help contribute to the construction of projects benefiting the surrounding communities. I feel this should be a fair course of action for genuinely well-intentioned men. This is, after all, our plan: to slow this revolution to a halt, killing it with good intentions and kindness. You two will be taken as prisoners to South Carolina, where you will stay in luxury quarters until you are ransomed or the war ends."

"Be wary, friend," Greene cautioned. "You may take us into custody and even attempt to befriend us with some success, but you will never truly snuff out our demands for independence." He smiled sadly. "You speak of rights for Papists and Jews, Negroes and Indians, but what about our own population? Until we have the rights to representation in Parliament, how can you call us truly citizens and not slaves, ourselves?"

Finch frowned. Politics was never his strong suit. Giving the matter some thought, he replied, "Well, do recall that, even after the various duties placed on you after the Seven Years' War, you still would have paid a significantly smaller amount of taxes per individual here than in Great Britain. That makes up for part of your lack of representation outside of your own colony. What's more, you were content with the arrangement for some time. Both sides should have definitely reasoned more, well, reasonably, certainly, but had you also shown that you truly cared about representation by freeing your slaves and treating other denominations with respect, we would not have ended up here."

Well, I'm not sure about that last part.

An awkward silence ensued.

Fortunately, a knock on the tavern door rescued either side from responding. Before one of the sentries could open the door, however, it opened from the outside and into the tavern stepped General Cornwallis with a pair of Highlanders of the Seventy-First and Colonel Grant in tow. The gentlemen officers stood up from the table, ready to pay their respects to Howe's protégé.

"Sit down," Cornwallis said smoothly, though Finch had heard that voice before and knew a tone of irritability was hidden within. The major general first recognized the enemy officers in front of him. "Mister Greene, Mister Laurens, I presume?"

"That's General Greene and Captain Laurens," began Laurens, but Cornwallis hushed him.

"Not only did you never serve in any army prior to this insurgency, but you have all but lost this war. You are no proper officers, gentlemen, but you are citizens of the empire masquerading as some. We shall be merciful. Seeing as you take responsibility for these misguided men you call soldiers, you will be imprisoned here, in Hillsborough's jail. Your men, however, will pay for their treatment of the citizenry and will be stowed aboard prison ships at Charleston Harbor. All your equipment will be summarily confiscated."

Finch was outraged. "General Cornwallis," he shouted, "I must protest! Show these men some dignity. They fought with honor and good intentions. There is no need to consign them to what may well be a death sentence. Just because the Rebels have, in the past, shown us similar indignity does not mean we must stoop to their level."

Cornwallis now turned on Finch. "And how do you describe what they did to your men, General Finch? You may have won the battle, but at what cost? Have you looked to your lights? Your mounted infantry? What, do you intend to plug your ranks with untrained Negroes? No, *no*! I will not allow it!" He cut off Finch as he was about to respond. "You would award the men who cut up your army so, and provide them with a potential escape?"

Finch took a few deep breaths. "It is to be expected, sir. Would you rather I had asked my foes to vacate the town politely, giving up the element of surprise?"

Cornwallis turned beet red. "This is *my* victory," he seethed. "You were merely to be the advance force of an operation I was to command overall. As your superior, I demand you turn over the fates of your prisoners to me. Any word of this made to Sir Henry will be your undoing. I outrank you, and you should feel lucky to not be punished for breaking with my commands. Instead, you should have obeyed my orders to the letter. This is how things are done in the British Army. I can only thank Colonel Grant for being so astute in his observations as to alert me."

Finch looked at Grant in hurt disappointment. *Some relationships never change*, he thought. He growled at Grant but slunk out the door with Ferguson in tow.

Stepping out into the town square, Finch could barely contain his remorse and rage, sullenly looking about as not just the Seventy-First but also the Forty-Second Highlanders patrolled the town, along with the Eighteenth and Third Foot from Ireland. It almost seemed as though England were barely present on the field this day, and yet Cornwallis, despite his traditionalist nature, managed to manipulate many of these provinces against Finch. He hung his head in shame. Somehow he'd fumbled it all up again.

"General Finch?"

Titus had walked up to the former engineer and extended his hand. "May I congratulate you on a battle well fought? You organized us well, and I hope my men performed well enough to receive your commendation."

Finch brightened a little. "Absolutely, Titus! A job well done. You've more than earned the commission you sought to form, and I hereby style you Colonel Titus."

Titus grinned. "Call me Colonel Tye."

"Colonel Tye it is. Have you further news for me?"

"Well, sir, the lads and I were beginning to organize patrols of the town to ensure all Rebel collaborators—collaborators, mind you, not mere sympathizers—were kept under close watch, and one of the men you sent us to reinforce our line, you know, the Frenchman, failed to appear for duty."

Finch frowned. "Deserters already?"

"Agents, sir. One of Browne's rangers caught him trying to sneak out of town with a letter." Titus handed a small dispatch to Finch.

"It's in French. I cannot read it," Finch replied.

"Neither can I, but Browne read it aloud to me. He's got a bit of a pedigree and education, as you know. Apparently, it says King Louis will declare war on us and is sending men to the

Caribbean, India, and here to fight for the land we both stole from the Natives."

Finch's eyes darted to the bottom of the letter.

Sure enough, the seal of King Louis XVI glared back at the former engineer, crisp and clean as the night sky.

The Mayor's Mansion, Hillsborough, North Carolina

8 APRIL 1777, 3:52 PM

As Finch stood before him, Cornwallis leaned back calmly in the office chair meant for the mayor of Hillsborough. This was a chair Finch felt *he* deserved after his share of the conflict the other day, but he was in no mood to contest the matter.

It was a dreary day, and rain sloughed off the caps of the Seventy-First Highlanders as they marched Greene's force off to imprisonment in Charleston. Cornwallis, after some soul-searching, had mercifully allowed the officers to travel with them, but they would stay as guests under guard in the townhouses of Charleston. "So the French are marching to war with us, eh?" he inquired.

"Yes," Finch acknowledged. "Well, at least they mean to. I wonder where they will land their forces, if they have not done so already."

"I would think they would take a leaf out of our book and help reinforce the beleaguered Rebel garrison in Wilmington. It's under siege by our forces under Prévost, and they could unite with the Rebels there and help them break out. It might be well for us, then, to reinforce our besieging army in turn before the Frogs spread their vitriol throughout the entire South."

There was a pause.

"Hm," Cornwallis said. "Your motley crew has served you well, Finch."

Respect, if in the form of a backhanded remark, at last!

"I shall reinforce Prévost at once," Cornwallis continued. "Between the force already arrayed against the Rebels in Wilmington and my incoming army, I am sure we will see to it that they receive a sound thrashing. You're on garrison duty here. Take your militia and partisans. Natives and blackamoors included, if you must. Dig in here, and win the population over with your great works of civic engineering. I will take some of your men and the artillery you found, if you don't mind."

Finch gave Cornwallis a forced smile. "General Cornwallis, you ask me to simultaneously guard the entryway to the Southern Colonies against any manner of Rebel counterattack and win the hearts and minds of Hillsborough with a paltry militia force and a band of partisans?"

Cornwallis cocked an eyebrow. "Have you heard of a support force of Rebels coming down from Virginia to assist the French and their allies in Wilmington?"

"Well, no."

"Good! Neither have I. Proceed with your fortifications and hold at all costs." He hesitated a moment, then sighed. "Keep Browne with you, if you must. He and his . . . irregulars may serve as our line of communication."

Finch frowned. *It is better than nothing.* He saluted. "As you say, General Cornwallis. My lads will win over the locals; worry not. I wish you well in your siege."

Cornwallis nodded. "You just be sure to maintain close control over the town. More Rebel traitors could be anywhere, and I will not stand for their sending word to their allies."

"I shall, sir," Finch replied, "though I have promised the people of Hillsborough that I will not impose martial law too harshly upon them. I have told them that the garrison I will keep will be approachable and willing to hear out their needs."

Finch's senior officer smiled. "I *am* impressed by the order you have kept in this town, and even the small militia you managed to raise in desperate times. I am sure General Clinton will hear of this, one way or another." He saluted Finch. "Carry on, sir."

Town of Hillsborough, North Carolina

10 APRIL 1777, 1:47 PM

With Cornwallis off on his crusade to lock down the final Rebel stronghold in the South, Giles Finch was left with a very small force to tend to a strategically important town and curry favor with the locals. Fortunately, he had found a way to keep them in line with his pleas for order in exchange for the promise that he would not enact martial law—a promise he had managed to keep despite the presence of senior officers and hoped to continue to keep. This was all very well, but other issues abounded.

Firstly, there was the matter of casualty clearing. The Rebels had suffered horribly in the past battle, and at least six hundred bodies were found wearing Rebel uniforms or identification in some way.

The British were not let off easily, either. True to form, the light infantry under Grant had been hit hard. The three-hundred-man battalion had faced down the enemy occupying Hillsborough and then the force attacking the town, taking some seventy-two casualties for their troubles. The Native allies who joined them also sacrificed dearly for the cause, losing at least twenty-three warriors of the approximately two hundred fifty who had taken the field. Though the mounted units were not far behind, it was these two groups that suffered the most on the Crown forces side, and Finch was unnerved by the small body of men he had with which to defend the town.

No matter how many men lay sprawled upon the city and its surrounding fields, however, it was the job of Finch and his men to entomb the bodies respectfully, and with them, Finch hoped, bury what was left of the hostilities with the townsfolk alongside them. And so, with shovel and spade, pick and axe, details of pioneers comprised of the remaining forces left in Hillsborough set forth to dig individual graves and mount crosses atop them. At least it was a relatively cool, yet sunny, dry day to enact such grisly labor. As the sounds of digging persisted after a good eight hours' work, Finch decided that he had had enough of the somber atmosphere.

"Gentlemen," he said, looking about the assembled pioneers, "we shall take a moment to remember these comrades who have fallen, for what is the point of paying respects to their graves if we cannot celebrate the persons?" He turned to the rotund, lovable Sergeant Daniels of the Loyalist Orange County Militia, newly formed with the British occupation. "Sergeant, see if you cannot strike up a band of musicians and gather some food to raise our spirits during this difficult work. Perhaps we can accompany our digging with a song from home!"

It was an unorthodox request, but sure enough, when Daniels returned followed by a quartet of musicians and a veritable cart of foodstuffs, the mood of the diggers visibly brightened as they stopped their work in favor of a sandwich or some other treat before continuing whilst the musicians set up. As the workers polished off their meals and set back to work, the quartet struck up an inspired rendition "Over the Hills and Far Away" whilst the pioneers labored. Things appeared to be looking up until Finch caught a glimpse of the face of the next corpse he was saluting before consigning it to the earth.

Amongst the fallen was Corporal James Simmons.

Finch's gaze lingered upon the body. It had again been struck by a musket ball in the side, and the poor fellow had bled out. Not the worst way to go, but by no means quick and painless, either. He knew he'd have to tell Constance, but the task would not be an easy one. *She is sure to bear the news with grace,* Finch thought. *But beneath that steady mask, she will be crushed. I should not even begin to think about how his father will react.* After secreting away James's cartridge pouch in the chance Constance would want a keepsake, Finch covered up the body in a funeral shroud once more, offered a prayer wishing Simmons a speedy deliverance to heaven for protecting the King's Law and citizenry therewith, then returned to his digging detail.

His mind wandered the rest of his shift as he quietly went about his duties, far more subdued than before. His men did not seem to notice, however, and continued to talk amongst themselves and sing along to the quartet's music, the better to encourage their own labors. The scene was surreal, and Finch felt terrible for helping to engender it. *Finding this body was surely a curse from God in exchange for bringing joy to a band of gravediggers.*

Finch shook his head and kicked the ground. *This is the age of enlightenment, damn it. I am a scientist with no desire for superstition in my life. I don't need to have religion guide my every step, and I don't need this guilt. I tried to entertain the troops in a somber moment. I will tell Constance of this tragedy, and we will all get on with our lives.*

The Mayor's Mansion, Hillsborough, North Carolina
10 April 1777, 7:04 PM

" . . . and so, to conclude: I . . . ahm . . . I fear young James has passed on, my dear daughter," Finch finished somberly, taking Constance's hands in her own and patting them gently. "I am so very sorry about this, my darling, I wish there were an easier way to tell you. He died a hero, and . . ."

As always dissatisfied with being absent from the life of her father, Constance Finch and the rest of her family had returned to the engineer's loving embrace with the end of the initial fighting at Hillsborough. Unfortunately, by the end of the Rebellion's counterattack, her beloved was found dead by their hand. There was no consoling her. Constance gave a high-pitched sob, pressing her hands to her mouth. "N-no," she remarked in between muffled breaths. "This cannot be happening! It's terrible!" Tears streamed down her face as she made to wipe them away. "Excuse me a moment," she said, before dashing for her bedroom in the mayor's mansion and closing the door with a loud slam. Wailing could be heard not long thereafter.

"*Gad*, Adelaide! What have I done?" Finch cried.

"You've done the right thing, Giles," his wife replied bracingly. "Give her time and space. After a while, she will come to you." She paused. "Possibly to me. Carry on with your planning of the town's defenses, dear. I'll keep an eye on her."

And so Finch went about his business. Calling together Colonel Tye and his Black Brigade as well as his indigenous allies and Browne's rangers, he tried to keep business and family life separate, much as he remained concerned for the well-being of his daughter.

"General?" the gruff voice of Thomas Browne rudely interrupted his ruminations. "We're ready for you."

"Wha—? Oh, yes!" Finch remembered he was in a conference, his mind having wandered once more. Trying to focus his thoughts, he addressed his superior officers as efficiently as he could.

"Black Brigade, your force now comprises some locals of Hillsborough, who know the general terrain around here. You will refortify what positions we have in town and prepare the city against another assault. I recognize there are only so many of you, so Browne's rangers will divide in two. We shall have some of their riders following Titus's building orders whilst the rest, alongside the Indians, will patrol the outskirts of town and keep a watch out for enemies. With the fortifications done, we shall work on improving the infrastructure of the town and repairing the damage from battle."

The officers nodded but stayed put, as though expecting something.

"Gentlemen, are you quite well?

Running Deer was the first to speak up. "My friend, you are aggrieved. Is there some way we may be of assistance?"

Damme.

"We lost a great many men in combat these past few days, my dear fellow," Finch responded. "Don't you believe I have a heart? Can I not be disappointed in the—"

"Come off," Titus demanded. "Something else wears at you, sir. I shall not lose this battle because my commander is not fighting at his best capacity. What has you down?"

Finch stammered a bit. "W-well, it is my daughter, Constance."

There was a collective groan.

"Come now," Finch defended himself. "She is lovely. Kind, beautiful, a fine nurse and craftswoman, and, though rather a traditionalist compared to her old dad, quite intelligent, I'd say."

"That's all well, but if she is causing you great sadness, she is posing a threat," She Who Laughs pointed out.

"How can we cheer you up?" Storm Crow calmly inquired.

Finch scoffed. "I'll be fine. I . . . thank you all for your concern, but I will be fine. I think. In truth, though I have been acquainted with many who now lie amongst the dead, I have never lost a lover to war."

"Ah, she lost a loved one, eh?" Browne sighed. He clucked his tongue in sympathy before continuing in a gruff voice. "You have given your orders, General. Give us a bit to carry them out and keep us apprised, but we shall take command of our men. You helped us clear the casualties after all and deserve a rest from your labors. Your greatest asset is your mind, after all, and not your brawn."

"But I need to set an example for my men!"

"Bugger that!" Titus retorted. "Do you think we cannot handle matters ourselves? Family first."

Finch smiled and saluted. "Yes, sir. Colonel Tye, sir."

The Mayor's Mansion, Hillsborough, North Carolina
10 April 1777, 9:19 PM

Finch strode into the mayor's mansion and saw Adelaide consoling their grief-stricken child. The other children waited nearby, as unsure as Finch was about what to do to help Adelaide in assuaging the ills of their sibling.

"Mother said to stand by and do our best to listen to Constance's woes, that lending an ear and the occasional considerate act might help her feel better," Caroline whispered to Finch as she and Archibald dutifully waited on their sister. Much as Adelaide fancied herself the great peacemaker in the family, it pained Finch to see his wife have a go at this alone, and though he felt he should look after the other children, here *they* were as well.

Finch turned the matter over in his head. After a moment, he strode up to Constance and said, "He was a good man, my dear, but many more of these good lads will come and go in your life at various times. Though some number of men on both sides will be claimed by this conflict, you are sure to find a good husband regardless. You are a woman of industry, heart, and a good mind. These are things that matter, though I may say you are beautiful as well."

Constance sniffed and looked up at her father, rubbing her eyes. Her tears still stained her dress, but she appeared to be cheered by this statement just a little. "I thank you for your kind words, Papa," she said, sniffing, "but you must understand that James was the man I was going to marry. He was so good to me. I do not believe for a second I could find a better man in this world."

Archibald awkwardly hugged his sister, attempting to help staunch her tears. Constance clung to him tightly.

"Aye, my darling girl," Adelaide remarked, smiling at her husband. "And yet let us not forget that one does not need a partner to confirm one's own existence—only to amplify the well-being and enjoyment of life when one is secure in one's own shoes. Why, though your father does seem to offer me some support and love, not to mention some finances, I am secure in my belief that I am a fine person without him."

The young girl chuckled softly. "I shall think on that, Mama. Thank you, Papa, Archi—"

"Cheer up, sister!" Caroline piped up. "We are in North Carolina now. A whole new colony of boys to watch and pick the choicest from. Perhaps you can teach me to catch an eye or two?"

This caused Constance to laugh. "It might help if you washed your face, Caroline."

Her younger sister grinned sheepishly. "You know me, sister mine. I could never commit to such a change lightly."

Constance smirked. "What if I told you that you might be able to charm information from your opposition, rather than have to hide and watch them?"

"But getting dirty is part of the fun!" Caroline whined good-naturedly. Noting the look on her father's face, she lowered her voice and continued, "Very well, you will teach me the arts of womanhood. And if you do not find another man, we'll live as sisters together till the end. Archibald will join us and be our devoted guardian, of course."

Constance giggled slightly, then swept her two siblings into an embrace.

Finch smiled at his family's ability to overcome loss and hoped their attitude would last. Deciding not to encourage them to nurse the wounded soldiers that day, he stopped by the plantation house turned field hospital and offered his own services to take his mind off his family's woes by helping assuage the woes of others.

Though he imagined his services could have been more useful elsewhere, judging by the fact that many of these men would not rise again and others would be entirely unfit for future combat, he personally visited with the soldiers and gifted them small favors, expressing his gratitude for their bravery. One man even asked to have the Bible read to him. Finch obliged, attempting to gloss over some of the more judgmental bits and emphasizing the parts that showed God to be forgiving.

"So you think God will forgive the Rebels and let them into heaven, sir?" one injured light infantryman croaked.

"If heaven exists, my lad," Finch clasped the man's shoulder. "There are many people with views that could be as correct or more so than ours. We have no way to prove which one is right until we die."

"*Right,*" a passing pastor broke into the conversation. He eyed Finch angrily. "That's quite enough of that, General. You win your war. I'll ensure the legions of Satan don't gobble up your deceased men's souls!"

Finch tipped his hat to the pastor and beat a hasty retreat. On his way out, he was nearly run over by a statuesque Shawnee warrior who growled at first, then gave a respectful bow when he noticed whom he had ploughed into. As Finch struggled onto his feet with the warrior's help, the tribesman said, "Most respected War Chief Blackhawk greets the good General Finch and wishes to report that his warband, of which I am a part, saw the enemy advance upon our town. They are many, and Blackhawk suggests we leave and fight another day."

Finch blanched. "Can you give me an impression of what we are up against?"

The Shawnee nodded. "I saw many hundreds, even perhaps a few thousand whitecoats marching under great flags emblazoned with flowers upon them. In support were both horses and siege cannon."

Siege cannon? Whitecoats? Flowered flags? Finch thought. *That would almost certainly be the French. There is no way my men could successfully defend against a force of that size and quality. We would be trapped like rats!*

"Thank you, soldier. I wish you a good day. Please send my compliments to War Chief Blackhawk and, if you could, assemble my commanders present in Hillsborough at this time. We shall meet at the mansion tomorrow at ten in the morning. I need time to plan our retreat."

The indigenous warrior nodded.

The Mayor's Mansion, Hillsborough, North Carolina
11 April 1777, 10:36 AM

"So you see, lads, we are up against a challenging foe," Finch said, before draining a glass of wine. "From what the Indians and rangers tell me, the enemy is advancing with a vanguard well deployed in a disciplined skirmish order and pickets aplenty. They will be hard to surprise, much less fight out in the open."

"Then how do you intend to engage this enemy, General Finch?" She Who Laughs inquired.

Finch frowned. He had been thinking on this topic awhile and had come to a conclusion that would make Pitcairn proud, but he was nervous that the concept would be lost on the others. "I fear that I have not defined a way to prevail over the Frogs. We must strategically displace. I do, however, have an idea as to how we can assist in our withdrawal."

"Oh?" Browne cocked an eyebrow.

"In the dead of the night, we will go into the forest and hew down trees, cutting them into the shape of eighteen- and thirty-two-pound guns and positioning them strategically. These weapons tend to have about the range of smaller siege guns, which could possibly be what they will be bringing with them, seeing as the terrain is difficult for larger ones. Because the enemy will be unable to have a good view of the guns until they come in close, which will take a great deal of courage, it will allow us time to evacuate men, women, and children aligned to us, as well as matériel."

Browne laughed. "A clever gambit!" he said, grinning. "Anything else?"

Another idea came to Finch. "Those plantation houses are symbolic of our peoples' excesses and cruelties. Once we evacuate the Negroes and offer them a chance to serve in our forces for wages equal to any redcoat, their houses of torment will be blown to kingdom come." He turned to Browne. "Whilst the Natives and militia cover the exodus of our people, your rangers will rig the plantation houses with explosives. When the French enter to inspect these elaborate houses as potential bases of operation, you will level them, with the enemy inside. From there you will fire one volley and mount up and get the blazes out of there. We shall reconvene in Charleston."

Browne gave an uncharacteristic bark of laughter. "By *God*, sir, if only the younger me would see me doing what I'll be doing now. Helping slaves? Destroying homes of fellow gentlemen? *Ha!*" He lowered his voice, more composed now. "I suppose I may not be seeing you again, sir." He held out his hand. "If not, it's been a pleasure."

Finch smiled and clapped Browne on the shoulder. "Shove that nonsense, Colonel. I have the utmost faith in your abilities. We'll see each other in South Carolina and respond with reinforcements of our own. Let us assemble the townsfolk. We must evacuate those wishing to go with us."

The Pegasus, Hillsborough, North Carolina

11 APRIL 1777, 6:52 PM

"You must understand, citizens of Hillsborough, your lives are in grave danger! An invading army has occupied the next few towns over and intends to march on your city in the near future. I understand some of you do not trust the armies of your king, and that is your prerogative so long as you don't commit any heinous acts against him or his men, but surely you realize that a French invasion will only spell doom for your town's well-being."

Finch punctuated his feelings with a frustrated stomp of his feet upon the floor. He did not like the idea of withdrawing and leaving the town to the barbarism of the French. The townsfolk looked on in shock. They were unimpressed to see the garrison commander in such a state.

Finch sighed. It had been several hours since the call for evacuation had been given, yet precious few townsfolk of Hillsborough had endeavored to pack their belongings and leave. Some had heeded the call for their own personal safety, but many more were proud of their livelihood here and were prepared to fight to protect it.

After a time, one man spoke out. "General, I understand your concern for our safety, but many of us, well, we won't be going anywhere. I, for one, am proud of the achievements this town has made and will be staying here with or without your forces. Nobody knows the town like us, and we'll be quite happy to fight the French for you, if we must, until you get your courage back." There was some snickering at that.

"Now then," another more elderly gentleman remarked, stroking at days-old stubble. "The general has had a rough time of governing over us, and he seems to have a good head on his shoulders. Perhaps we should listen to him, as he has our best interests at heart. What do you think our small band of soldiers and some militia could do against a division of French regulars? I say we *do* leave this town and return some other time." He nodded vigorously.

"G-g-general? Is it true the French like to raid wine cellars and ravage our livestock?" a young mother inquired. "My husband died in the fighting, and I'm ever so frightened. I do not believe I could start a new life alone outside of town, but I don't know what I can do here, either!" She began to sob.

Adelaide came over to the woman and embraced her. "All will be well, dear. The French will be civilized, or whether by the divine or by our own cold steel, they will be punished for their wrongdoings. Worry not. Things will return to as they should be."

"Nonsense!" a pugnacious-looking tough shouted. "The Revolution and her allies are our only chance for safety. Let us welcome the French. Down with King George!" he cried emphatically. Some muttering resulted.

Finch was tired of it. "Very well!" he snapped. "Come with me if you wish to live a life at all similar to your current experiences, under the standard of His Majesty. We gather outside on the green at six in the morning."

Orange County, North Carolina

12 April 1777, 6:22 AM

As Giles Finch led the exodus from Hillsborough, he could not help but feel a flood of mixed emotions. He was glad to have rescued a great many brave men, women, and children, yet he knew in his heart that if only he were more diplomatic, he could have saved more. Nonetheless, he thought, sighing as he heard the resounding *KRAKABOOM* of an explosion as a plantation house went up in flames, followed by another, at least he would give the enemy pause and inflict a few casualties upon his retreat. He could only wonder what would become of Browne and his riders as he did so.

Not to mention the town of Hillsborough, delivered into the hands of the French.

CHAPTER 9

The French Invasion

Governor Campbell's Mansion, Charleston, South Carolina

28 May 1777, 5:24 PM

It was unfortunate that such a retreat had been necessary, but Finch felt he had nobody to curse but himself for landing his soldiers in such a plight. He should have protested Cornwallis's orders more directly. To his relief, however, the soldiers under his command and even most of the citizens making up the exodus from Hillsborough had taken the situation well. They knew what they were getting into by fighting this war and by leaving their homes. Nevertheless, judging by the faces of many soldiers who took part in the expedition, there was still some shock at what this reality entailed.

Upon Finch's return to Charleston, Governor Campbell and Sir Henry showed they understood the difficulties he faced, but their comforting manner did little to alleviate his mood. As they stood about awkwardly in Governor Campbell's once beautifully furnished mansion, now blackened and smelling of smoke, under renovation after a recent Rebel attempt at arson, Clinton clapped Finch on the shoulder.

"You did well, my boy," Clinton said for the third time in a vain effort to cheer him up, thumping the engineer turned lights officer on the back. "This is war. Sacrifices must be made."

"Y-yes," Campbell stammered, face pallid at the thought of any more sacrifices to come. "And think of all the citizens you saved!"

Finch sighed and looked out to the countryside. The French took little time to dally. Now that they occupied Hillsborough, they had surged across the South Carolina mainland, taking Camden from the small force under Prévost, or so surviving stragglers reported. Finch's efforts to send Native troops out on a series of missions to reconnoiter the surrounding territories had confirmed his fears: the Crown forces in South Carolina, Georgia, and Florida were cut off. An attack on Charleston was imminent.

The garrison of three hundred militia and the small remnants of Finch's force numbered a total of approximately eight hundred men. Finch was unsure what he could do to halt the French advance. With Ferguson and von Wurmb reassigned to Cornwallis in North Carolina and the rangers missing, only a quarter of his command stood ready to combat the forces of the enemy.

Fortunately, the bulwarks of Charleston stood firm, having been undermined almost a year ago by Clinton and his men not through force but by starvation. That meant the British now stood in control of a fully serviceable palmetto and stone fort around the town. Even so, unless they could silence the siege guns the French would bring to bear against Charleston, they would be sitting ducks.

Finch recalled his easier days as an engineer. Perhaps he was not ready to command a brigade, or perhaps poor fortune dogged his every step, but he was prepared to tender his resignation and return to what he loved best in military work: building. How he missed the hammering of steel on steel, the therapeutic sounds of digging; even the odd explosion was welcome from time to time, and he found it a lot more pleasing to construct buildings than to destroy families. This he related to Clinton and Campbell, who frowned at the suggestion of his resignation.

"Absolutely not, General Finch. I will not have a man of talent and wisdom throwing away his career over war-weariness. We must see this conflict through. So Cornwallis scattered your force? We shall form a second one. You did not so much abandon Browne as save a great many civilians. What's more, is there any *evidence* Browne is indeed gone?"

"Rather an optimistic viewpoint to take when I sent him off on an assuredly suicidal mission," Finch replied darkly.

"There is that, yes," Campbell admitted. "Do we have estimations as to the enemy's strength?"

"Three thousand elite troops, sure to be backed by Rebel militia and their Continental brethren," Finch remembered from reports. "We are outnumbered at least four to one, not to mention outtrained, as well."

"Outnumbered, you say? Surely our defensive cannon could wreak a little mischief upon these blackguards, and your Natives and partisans could train our militia into a more mobile force." Campbell was smiling as he spoke, but it was clear he felt the weight of the odds against him as well.

"The scouts reported the French as having possession of siege guns, Governor. I do not believe this will be an easy fight."

"Nor I. But it is a good thing we have many guns of our own to spare."

That gave Finch an idea. He turned to Sir Henry.

"Sir, if we have access to so many guns, do you think I might borrow a few?"

The commander-in-chief furrowed his brow. "What have you in mind, Finch?"

"The guns, sir. A map, if you please."

A map of the surrounding territories was sent for and unfurled.

"We could establish flanking positions amidst the trees facing perpendicularly to the town in that forest across the road," Finch explained. "We can erect trenches, barricades, camouflage, and other cover for our skirmishers, partisans, Natives, and smaller cannon. The fort will still be protected by your militia, as well as the largest guns we have to offer. Then, when the French attack, our force shall be perfectly positioned to blast them from the rear. It will buy us time."

"That . . . ," Governor Campbell started, pausing to let it all sink in. "That might just work, General Finch. Let us see to—"

"And *then*," Finch continued, growing excited, "if they continue their charge toward the city walls, they will be forced to either form along the road in a column or bog down in the swamps. We can continue to hurl rounds at them till they break."

"By God, sir, a fine plan!" Clinton boomed.

And so the entire township of Charleston, including the governor and his dignitaries, rolled up their sleeves and began to make preparations for the town's defense. Even some of the revolutionaries of the town, harboring no love for the French, assisted in rolling fort gun emplacements into positions overlooking the swamplands, soon to be drenched in blood, as well as moving several twelve-pounders into the forest and camouflaging them with leaves and other greenery.

After that, they fortified the town walls, boarded up houses, and armed themselves, drilling for the conflict to come. As the sound of industry rang through the land, Finch once more felt at peace in his profession. Alas, he could not take time to revel in his work. The Frogs would be upon Charleston at any time.

Outskirts of Town, Charleston, South Carolina

3 June 1777, 7:12 PM

As the job neared completion, Finch heard the sound of marching feet from the north. Turning sharply, he saw a column of greencoats approach. Several men appeared injured, and their once-resplendent coats appeared a little worse for wear, but their fifes and drums nevertheless trilled and beat the tune to the "The British Grenadiers" with an upbeat lilt. As they came ever closer, Finch noticed the royal seal of the colony of Georgia imprinted upon their standard, next to the King's Colors.

Though both appeared tattered, Finch could barely contain his joy. It was the battle-hardened men of the First Georgia! Straining his eyes out to the horizon as the evening turned to dusk, he could just make out a second force of Georgians behind them.

"Finch—a delight to see you. How are you this day?" asked Reverend Peabody, puffing on his pipe and smiling, as though there were no conflict to fear at all and the two men were walking along Kensington Square. Finch envied him his tranquility but wondered whether it made others around Peabody as uneasy as it made him.

"We have come to reinforce Charleston," Peabody continued. "A French army has pushed us—that is, my men and those of Silverstein—from Camden. Let us unite as one force to halt the Catholics' heathen advance!"

"I do not believe we should vilify Catholics so much as the enemy forces specifically, but it is nevertheless a pleasure to see you, too, Reverend," Finch replied. It was not long until the second unit, in a similar state, fell in with the first. At the head was Silverstein, who bobbed his head awkwardly in Finch's direction.

"General Finch, it is a delight to hear of your successes, both in combat and in evading certain death! I trust you are well? Have you any words for our readership back in Georgia?"

Finch shook the reporter-colonel's hand. "I have been better. Won and lost a brigade, you see. But now is the time to fight with what we have. I shall tender my resignation to Horse Guards after we survive this battle."

"Are you sure there is a need, my dear boy?" Peabody asked. "Many a great general has lost battles. The Crown commands the impossible sometimes. You are a man of some talent and great intelligence. Freethinking, too. I know you have heard this frequently, but your light brigade needs a commander such as you."

"An officer who sacrifices whole regiments just so that others might escape?"

"The men signed on to fight, sir, not to waltz through a war unscathed," Silverstein piped up. "You put us to good use and to a valiant cause, might I add. Those men, so endangered, were all detached with competent commanders. I am sure they will do you proud."

Finch pondered Silverstein's words. True, he did not know the fate of those men he lost to Cornwallis during his march on Wilmington. They could be alive and well. Just because they were detached does not mean they had been killed. Far from it. It was often the role of the light infantry, be they rangers or bobs, to be detached as a battalion or even company and fight as an independent command—to raid and to live off the land.

"We shall see," Finch admitted. "For now, we have prepared a warm welcome for our French foes and will call it a night." He turned to Reverend Peabody. "We shall have a good, long smoke after this battle is done, but to win the day is of foremost importance. Bolster my forces in the forest, sirs. Help us prepare a camouflaged position. Though Campbell may be terrified by the dearth of soldiery at his command, he must understand that we need a large sallying force, as well."

"How many do they have, Papa?" came the sweet voice of Caroline from behind the officers' backs. The congregation began to murmur as the young lady advanced to join them. They were used to her presence by now, but it still scandalized some of them.

"Several thousand, sweetling, though we do not know how many will march on Charleston," Finch replied, back turned to her. "I am going to have to ask you to return to the city, where you will be safe from their onslaught. Stay there until one side triumphs, do you comprehend?"

"I comprehend, Papa, that you will need—"

"A scout, yes, but it will not be you. I will need someone resourceful, who won't draw attention to himself."

"Herself, Papa. You need your men for fighting, whilst I can easily slip amongst the French. They would never expect a girl to inform on them and would be too confident to care if they did."

Finch groaned, palming his face. She was right, of course. It was hard to admit this fact in the face of outside company, and even harder to consider risking a family member, especially one willing to volunteer her life at such a young age.

"Very well then, child, we shall put you to good use. I will visit with the French and pretend to see if we cannot come to some accord, stalling for time on behalf of our citizens of Charleston, allowing them to prepare, whilst you count their numbers and determine their disposition."

Caroline saluted as well as any grenadier. "Yessir."

Finch sighed heavily, feeling his pulse in his temples. He loved Caroline but worried that she was shaping up to be a troublesome young adult in the eyes of society, if for no other reason than because she was a very bright if reckless girl and would become an even brighter and even more reckless woman.

On the Road to Charleston, South Carolina

9 JUNE 1777, 3:11 PM

The French, burdened by heavy artillery, took their time in their approach to Charleston. It was over a week before they slowly, casually made their way down the road from Camden. Still, it was a mighty force that retained much of its previous strength, even after their occupation and garrisoning of towns along the way.

Clinton had come down with a cold, so it had fallen to Finch alone to step forth and parley with the enemy. Taking a handkerchief and wrapping it around a stick he found in the forest, the engineer stepped forth with his daughter in tow. A pair of gruff-looking, white-coated grenadiers stopped them at the perimeter of the French position. Though they seemed to comprehend the rag of truce, they scoffed at the symbolism before turning to let Finch and his daughter pass. They had not gone far before they came across the French general, getting his shoes shined.

The general was a rotund, baby-faced, and lavishly dressed man who, judging by his uniform, served King Louis as an admiral as well. To his right, scowling at Finch, was the Rebel Brigadier General Lachlan McIntosh, the Georgian commander who had parleyed on behalf of Major General Lincoln when their forces had been defeated whilst besieging Savannah.

Finch put on an air of confidence to throw his enemy off balance. "Welcome, guests. McIntosh! What a surprise to see you again! One repulse wasn't enough? I see you've brought company this time."

The expression on McIntosh's face shifted from annoyance to mortification. He gestured Finch toward the French general's seat without a word.

"Charles Hector, le Comte d'Estaing," the French commander introduced himself lazily, sipping a glass of wine as Finch came closer. "Please might you dispense with your young lady? She is not welcome here."

"You heard the man, Caroline," Finch said to his daughter, who frowned. "Run along home." Caroline nodded, her curls bobbing, and made toward the edge of the encampment.

"You will surrender your town to us at once, or we will take it by force. Tarry, or choose the latter, and it will be a waste of life," Hector continued as Caroline disappeared around the corner of a tent.

Finch smiled. "Of course, General, it will be a waste of *your* men's lives. Your casual advance has permitted me to summon reinforcements. They are now en route. Even if we fail to achieve victory this day, we are well entrenched. At what cost do you suspect you will purchase your win? I assure you it will be more than you would desire."

The comte blanched momentarily before setting his jaw. "Battle it is, then."

Finch smiled, trying to exude confidence and ignore Lachlan McIntosh's glare as he faced the comte. "I see General McIntosh, but otherwise no Rebel forces in your advance party." He turned from Hector to McIntosh. "Has General Washington hired you now to play advisor to his allies? Do they no longer trust you to command men?"

McIntosh's look turned from mortification to barely suppressed rage.

"Or," Finch continued, "have you turned coat? Do they pay you in Continentals or francs, Monsieur?"

"*Enough!*" Hector cried, turning red. "Return to your encampment at once, Anglais, or you will face your doom."

Finch bowed politely and withdrew in the direction of town. Not long thereafter, Caroline followed on short, stubby legs. As she caught up with her father, she pressed a dispatch into his hands.

"I counted approximately three thousand soldiers, Father, along with eight siege guns. All French except for General McIntosh. He's turned coat, you know. The Rebels think he's still one of them, but the French are out for themselves. Did you read the letter yet?"

"Patience, child," Finch laughed. "Let us wait until we return to camp."

And yet, upon returning to camp, it was Caroline, as a gift to her from her father for her diligence, who read the letter aloud, in halting French, with the assistance of a translator, to the assembled staff of Sir Henry, Peabody, Silverstein, Campbell, the Native allies, and, of course, Finch.

Admiral D'Estaing, it read.

> *Congratulations on your headway along the American South. Soon it will be in our possession as our glorious nation has long dreamed.*
>
> *You have done well. The British are on the run, the Rebellion is exhausted. It is only necessary to capture Charleston, where a large army and their commander-in-chief, Sir Henry Clinton, sits, to deal the British war effort a terrible blow.*
>
> *Meanwhile, the Americans have proven incompetent, as well as noncompliant, and stingy with their offers of compensation for our efforts. You will destroy them next, all with the exception of General McIntosh, who has proven useful in our efforts. Then, alongside the Spanish relief force sent over by Don Bernardo de Gálvez, we will divide up the colonies between us and the Spanish.*
>
> *We have the enemy by the throat this time. You need only remain calm and not become too ambitious. Follow my orders and I shall expect to see you in Paris showered in glory.*

Long live King Louis, I am your devoted ally,
Jean-Baptiste Donatien de Vimeur, comte de Rochambeau

Forest Outskirts of Charleston, South Carolina

9 June 1777, 7:20 PM

Night began to fall on Charleston as Finch carefully replaced the tree branches he had parted, the better to view the approaching enemy. In doing so, he again camouflaged himself and his loyal band of Natives, partisans, and provincials. *Shite! Here they come!*

He collapsed his spyglass. "We are in for a fight, gentlemen," he whispered to his fellows hidden amongst the trees. "The French are en route."

One of the provincials looked to Finch. "Shall I inform the governor?"

"No need. They might see you anyway. We just need to be careful and quiet. Load round shot for the field guns when we fire the opening volley. Conserve canister for when they have deployed a wide line of their men."

Finch surveyed the soldiers hidden alongside him before stopping short at the Cherokee warriors. Some he had never seen before and seemed awfully light-skinned for Natives. One was also rather young and chanced to wave at the general, a smile crossing her features.

Finch groaned. He recognized Caroline and Adelaide.

"Prime and load," Finch whispered to Peabody, attempting to ignore the presence of two of his most beloved on the field of battle, much less in the attire of Natives. Surely they could have assisted Constance in her first-aid work behind friendly lines. Alas, were they to attempt to return home at this juncture, they would attract the attention of the French. They were now safest here.

Finch heard them before he saw them with the naked eye: several snaking columns of whitecoats tromping across the countryside in perfect chorus. Seeing his own pistols unloaded, he promptly made to rectify this.

"Hold your fire, lads. Wait until they come in to about sixty-five yards," Finch said quietly, waiting a moment to ensure the message had made it to the end of the line.

The whitecoats began wheeled into position until they stood facing Charleston from across the swamp. The artillery on Charleston's side stood silent as they organized, instructed to hold their fire against infantry at this distance. When the French artillery began to unlimber from their horse mounts, however, the fortifications were suddenly enshrouded in great gouts of smoke accompanied by thunderous explosions. Artillery rounds—three-pound, six-pound, nine-pound, twelve-pound, twenty-four-pound, and even the great thirty-twos from the front gate—slammed into the high ground above the swamp where the French were positioned.

As they were the main targets of Charleston's great guns, several enemy siege pieces were dislodged from their mounts or rendered completely inoperable as they arrived on the scene. One battery's powder supply was struck, resulting in a great explosion that rocked the guns nearby. Horses, some still attached to the gun carriages, whinnied in terror and shrieked in pain as they were struck down, many more skittering away from their handlers as men ran amok. Some attempted to see to their wounded whilst others withdrew the remaining guns behind the French lines.

Meanwhile, the remaining shots struck some of the infantry regiments, crushing bone and burning flesh, as screams and curses followed. Even as they did, the well-trained soldiers of the French Royal Army carefully extended their forces into a well-spaced skirmish line, as though oblivious to the bodies of their compatriots beneath their feet. Finch admired their resilience and calm in the face of the barrage.

For all their order and discipline, however, the French were distracted by the enemy to their front and prepared for their inevitable charge against the town. This gave Finch an idea. Noticing the French had only just begun setting up their ravaged siege artillery in their new position, he put a finger to his lips, gesturing to the provincials not manning his own artillery to follow him. With the other hand, he halted the Natives, gesturing to them, and presumably his wife and child, to stay with the artillery.

"Very well, lads," Finch said. "Now is our chance—let us disable their guns!" The message was delivered down the ranks, and the provincials proceeded to scurry along the tree line, taking care to stay out of the French whitecoats' line of sight.

As the tree line thinned, they came into full view of the artillerists, busy setting up their guns. Finch smiled. "Fix bayonets, lads. Let's go!"

With a loud "Huzzay!" Finch and his men burst from the brush, wincing and dodging as the branches tore at their clothes and skin. Still, they carried on, locked in step as they made to plunge their bayonets down the throats of the artillerists. The French gunners jumped, fear clearly written across their features. Noticing their terror, Finch pushed the assault, realizing the enemy were scrambling to unlimber their guns. "Give them a volley, lads!" he commanded.

Krak!

Krak!

Kaarakkk!

Several artillerists fell, nursing terrible wounds as the musket balls splattered muscle and splintered bone. As blood flowed freely, Finch prepared to sound the advance once more, but the Georgians surged ahead with a bloodthirsty battle cry of their own volition.

"Onward!" yelled Silverstein, flourishing his blade as he did his utmost to maintain order amongst the men.

With Finch not far behind them, the Georgians waded through the mass of moaning bodies toward the remaining French gunners, who, protected by a small band of fusiliers, met them with sabers and bayonets of their own. As the Loyalist troops came ever closer, however, even the fusiliers began to waver. This moment of weakness was what Finch had been waiting for.

"Drive the froggies back across the pond!" Finch cried.

This was the final straw. The majority of the French artillerymen, beset by a band of howling, hostile colonists out for blood whilst their own defensive cover was otherwise occupied, took to their heels. Those who stood and fought for their King Louis were quickly subdued.

"Stupendous job, friends!" Finch shouted. "Now, spike the siege guns. We cannot let them crack open our walled city!"

After a cursory search of the batteries' supplies, a few hammers were found amongst the inventory of the French gunners, but to Finch's surprise, he could not find any spikes with which to render the guns useless.

Suddenly, he heard loud cries coming from the front lines where the French infantry had begun entrenching. Not long thereafter came the sound of marching and cries of "Vive le roi! Vive le roi!"

French reinforcements.

Stealing a look, Finch saw a large force of burly men wearing bearskin caps forging their way toward him, chanting in bone-chilling unison.

"Vive le roi! Vive le roi!"

It came to him.

"Gentlemen, hammer your bayonets down the touchhole of each siege gun. *Now!* I don't care who does it, but we need these guns out of action. The field guns, too."

The officers complied at once.

"Spike the guns, spike the guns! We're falling back!" they cried, running for the wooded position. Hundreds of French soldiers advanced on their guns like a swarm of angry hornets. Whilst most of the provincials attempted to hold them off with musketry from behind the cover of the guns, a few raced to unfix their bayonets and smashed them into the touchholes of the cannons with the hammers, rendering the siege guns useless before taking flight.

Charleston was now relatively safe. Finch's men were a different story.

The French army, stymied in its attempt to bombard Charleston, turned its sights on the provincials instead. A collection of grenadiers formed up, muskets at the ready, their officers doubtless taking them through firing orders. Finch did not wait to find out.

Huffing and puffing after his provincials, he ducked and weaved, a hail of musketry following him as he ran to the safety of the trees. Whipping a look over his shoulder, he saw at least twelve of his men lying on the field and the French following close behind. As he made haste back toward the encampment, he noticed the position of the artillery he had brought with him and realized it posed a problem: the three-, six-, and twelve-pounders he had taken from Charleston had no angle from which to hit the enemy battalion companies without shredding some of his own men. *Blast!* Finch thought. *And the Natives have no orders to defend us, and—JESUS!*

At that moment, the Natives struck with a loud war cry. The Cherokee, Creek, and Shawnee warriors leapt from a number of hiding places and fired a volley at the pursuing French grenadiers before charging into the fray. Having displaced from their strategically placed grove, the Natives meticulously struck from all sides with a great fury. At first caught off guard by their attack,

Finch then delighted at their arrival onto the field of battle but almost immediately felt abject terror.

Where are Adelaide and Caroline? Did they lend themselves to the attack? Looking about wildly, he dodged under the recklessly swung blade of a French officer before viciously stabbing him in the groin and kicking him off his blade. Working his way around the battlefield, he at last noticed Caroline and Adelaide sitting in a tree, a smoking trade musket in Caroline's hand whilst Adelaide loaded another firelock feverishly. Beneath them, some of Titus's partisans fought with grim determination.

Meanwhile, the provincials comported themselves heroically in battle. Heads rolled, torsos were disemboweled, and both sides fought viciously in a terrifying melee. The Loyalist troops, initially shaken by the sight of their well-trained and disciplined enemies, now saw the odds evened with the timely intercession of their allies, the Natives. With another "Huzzay!" they brandished their bayonet-fixed muskets and met the enemy's steel. Suddenly, Finch found himself in the middle of a deadly maelstrom.

The stench of blood, shit, vomit, and sweat, the sounds of clashing steel, the yells of rage and agony, the groans of the dying, along with the touch of moist linen, pissed upon in terror and bloodied with wounds, made the brigadier yearn for an engineering role more than he ever had before. Desperate to survive, he kept moving, striking from behind as he needed to. Finch kept up the fight for his life, discharging a pistol shot into a Frenchman's skull. The poor soul died instantly. Then he shot another man with his second pistol, lodging a ball into his ribcage. After this, rather than finding individual opponents one at a time, Finch kept himself attentive for any foe with his back turned.

Taking a hatchet, Finch bashed in the skull of a third gentleman, cleaving through the hat and into the gray matter of the Frenchman, where it stuck. Unwilling to expose himself to an attack from behind, Finch left the hatchet and drew his sword. He stabbed a fourth Frenchman in the back before finally meeting the hanger blade of a fifth with a resounding *clang!* The officer exchanged blows with Finch awhile before Finch parried a wild overhead slash, stabbing the attacker in the gut. This officer dispatched, Finch began to see that his side might stand a chance after all.

Though the French grenadiers were armed with bayonet-fixed muskets, useful in line combat, the melee had degenerated into a cluster of small skirmishes. Such weapons were unable to move with the speed of a hatchet, sword, or dagger. This gave Finch and some of his partisan and Native allies an advantage. Unfortunately, he saw French reinforcements charging onto the scene. This fight was far from over.

As he dodged another bayonet strike, his arm was grazed by the attack of yet another Frog, and he began to bleed. Finch's counterattack, however, cut deep into the bone of his foe's neck, felling him at once. Just to be sure, he struck once more across the man's belly, splattering his white coat with red.

As time passed and the butchering continued, Finch stopped to take stock of the enemy. Many had crudely bandaged themselves with their uniforms and were limping back to their base as fast as their mangled limbs could carry them. Moans of agony filled the air, awash with the smell of the dead and dying from both forces. As they fell back, Finch heard the thundering of hooves. Grasping for his spyglass, he put it to his eyes and thought he could make out in the distance some angels in green and red.

Finch's jubilation lasted all of five seconds before he was knocked over the head with a musket butt. As his vision grew hazy, he saw a whitecoat, murmuring under his breath as he clambered to his feet and drew a blade, intent on running Finch through.

Krak!

The man clutched his torso and fell, a pool of blood oozing from his chest and muddying his already sullied white uniform.

Finch's last sight was that of Caroline dropping her musket behind her and running toward him, a concerned look on her face. Suddenly, Adelaide's voice rang out.

"Caroline! Come back—"

KA-RACK!

Another shot resounded in the evening sky as Caroline doubled over.

Then everything went black.

Governor Campbell's Mansion, Charleston, South Carolina
11 JUNE 1777, 7:39 PM

"Oh thank goodness, the man's come to his senses," came the relieved voice of Doctor Harold Brewster, one of Finch's field surgeons. Finch blearily opened his eyes and saw the doctor's and Sir Henry Clinton's faces swim into view.

"FINCH! DO YOU HEAR ME?! YOU DID A FINE JOB!" Clinton roared.

Finch's eyes widened, then he smiled weakly.

"We're goddamn heroes, Finch, and it's thanks to you," came the husky voice of Thomas Browne from behind him. "I won't be surprised if even Ludwig here gets some female attention thanks to that splendid cavalry charge he led." He grinned a wide, terrifying grin.

"*Ja*, we made a fine company," came Colonel von Wurmb's high-pitched, academic voice. Finch looked around Clinton's head to find von Wurmb sitting in the corner of the room, his nose in a book.

"Well, erm—" was Finch's eloquent reply, as Sir Henry Clinton let out a loud guffaw and drank deeply from a wineglass he was holding. Finch's head pounded as he shifted uncomfortably on the table to look around the room. He appeared to be in a makeshift field hospital in one of the fancier houses in Charleston. Titus and some of Finch's indigenous allies had looked up from a conversation not far off, having heard Finch stir.

"Very well, gentlemen," Doctor Brewster said, his green eyes nervously squinting as all other eyes fell on him, "the general needs his rest. I shall have to ask you to leave."

"Bother the bedrest!" Clinton cried, tossing the wineglass behind him. "The men have yet to have a party in honor of the general and their glorious victory!"

The pint-sized doctor sputtered, flailing his small hands, and tried to speak, but Clinton cut him off. "Finch, you can talk. Can you walk?"

"I—I think so? W-Where are Adelaide and C—"

"Then there is no need for further examinations. Perhaps some pipe smoke to stabilize his nerves, but beyond that, the man's fine. Release him at once, Doctor Brewster!"

The doctor gave a good-natured smile, but with no shortage of concern.

"General Finch, you are released from my care."

"But—"

"AND ABOUT TIME, TOO!" Clinton roared, clapping Finch on the back as the doctor cringed. "More wine, please!" Sir Henry barked at a servant who'd entered the room to sweep up the shattered glass.

As Browne, von Wurmb, She Who Laughs, Titus, Clinton, and Finch exited the governor's mansion, they were met with a rousing cheer. The people of Charleston had stepped out in force to meet with the defending heroes and celebrate their achievements.

"Bravo, heroes!" Clinton joined in the applause and then took another glass of wine off a serving tray and drained it. "You have saved Charleston and offered us a staging ground from which to retake our possessions here in the South. I cannot begin to fathom the frustration the French must have felt with a full quarter of their southern expedition dead or captured!"

The audience gave three cheers and toasted the king. Reverend Peabody offered a sermon of thanksgiving, and everyone cheered again before the guests began to talk amongst themselves.

Finch felt woozy as well-wishers passed by to offer them their goodwill and thanks. "One quarter?" he asked. "And where are Adelaide and Caroline?"

Clinton nodded jovially before his countenance changed to a more solemn expression. "They're fine. Well. One is. That is to say—"

"*Where is my family?*" Finch hissed with all the rage he could muster.

"Caroline didn't make it, Finch," Browne said regretfully. "I'm sorry. Shot near the end of the conflict. French chasseurs. I picked off the gent who did the dirty deed, though," he went on thoughtfully after a moment of silence.

"We'll return you to Adelaide and Constance and your boy soon, but for now you must listen," Clinton said, but Finch was going into shock.

Dead? God, no. She was young and so full of life! So sweet and such an idealist! Why?

"Finch? Are you listening?" Clinton barked, jolting him back to his surroundings. The engineer stared at him, stupefied. "Do you remember the plans? The French ones?"

Finch nodded slowly, and Clinton grinned. "Good. It is only necessary to expose their evils to the Rebels and press them into an alliance. It should not be a problem to declare a truce, as we have the Rebels on the run. However, both sides have fought hard, and we may not be able to convince them to join us. You have ever been fair to them in our dealings, and though I strongly feel it will take a man made of sterner stuff than you to crack the egg that is the Rebellion once and for all, the rabble respect you. If you can use kindness and reason with the scum, we may yet see victory, with their help, over our foes. I know you are tired. And you just suffered a terrible blow, but so have the Rebels. Their morale is flagging as much as ours is, but we are winning the battles. We can do this, but we need your help . . ."

But Finch was slipping into the past, meditating on Caroline's birth and early days. The Seven Years' War against the French had concluded, and he was at last able to relax with his family for a time in Boston. Adelaide had had some complications delivering the twins, but after prayer and assistance by the midwife, she had given birth to two beautiful infants. Though sickly at first, both Archibald and Caroline, in addition to Constance, born earlier with no complications, had grown into such wonderful and children.

How could fate deprive him of his beloved younger daughter, secretly his favorite child, prior to his own death? Her many talents were wasted, by no fault of her own. She lived a life of disappointment, being a woman with interests in the men's arts, and then she died. *It's not fair!*

He was again brought back by Clinton shaking him another glass of wine in hand. Upon getting Finch's attention once more, it was then that he remarked, genuine sorrow in his eyes. "I tell you, Finch, I am sorry. We must both find another pastime besides warfare. It wears upon us before o'erlong. Good, brave men *and* women die; the malevolent and cowardly do not. It's terrible, the fate of your daughter and so many others. Finish the job, sir, and do so with haste. I tire of this conflict. Far more enticing to start conflicts than to endlessly carry them on, wot wot?" He patted Finch on the shoulder.

"I have Charles Grey under orders to capture Philadelphia with a force of lights," Clinton continued, "as well as Iroquois warriors under that marvel of an Indian, Joseph Brandt. If we can scatter the Rebels from their capital, this shall help a long way toward achieving our goal. I want to be sure a tragedy of this sort will not happen again. Meanwhile, you will meet General Washington and his aide, Benjamin Lincoln, in Williamsburg, Virginia. Convince them of Franco-Spanish duplicity and offer an alliance. If this fails, you must at least dissuade them from fighting us any longer. Prevail upon their weariness and do not tarry. Return and I shall grant you all the time you desire with your family."

That bastard. He doesn't give a damn for Caroline. Betrayed by my own friend. Nonetheless, Finch nodded, and the two shook hands. As he did so, Finch's hands trembled with rage. *Talk to Washington? After his allies killed my daughter? After all the cruelties he visited upon Lord Dunmore and his Ethiopians? My Archibald, Constance, and Adelaide, not to mention Titus and the blacks, would never forgive me. If we must side with the Rebels, could we not send a man more willing to compromise his morals than I?*

Sir Henry gave Finch a thin-lipped smile. "I know what you're thinking, Mister Finch, and no, we cannot send another. Washington respects warriors and self-made men. You are both and more. He knows you and will listen to you, perhaps all the more because you hate him, yet you visit him regardless. This will be a jolly good conference for all of us, except maybe you, but we all must make sacrifices sometimes." His eyes became stern. "End the war between colony and country with us remaining in control, but try your utmost to appear charitable. The Rebels are but a minor threat on their own, but the fewer wars we fight at a time, the better. With the French and Spanish on the scene, they shall become a damnable nuisance."

Finch grunted his agreement, his thoughts swimming.

"Thank you both, sirs," Governor Campbell remarked grimly, "for hammering the final nail in the coffin of our foe's assault.

Between the losses they suffered this day and the reinforcements we have received, I do believe we shall be in prime condition to recover our lost territories. We shall push them back!"

"That's the spirit!" shouted Clinton. "Though should we not enjoy the party and our guests before attending to such sordid matters?"

"No," replied Campbell. "My colony is still threatened by the Frogs. What's more, according to young Caroline Finch's report, the Spanish intend to engage in a sneak attack from the west." He fixed Clinton with a stony glare. "I assure you this is no time to celebrate."

"Very well, very well," Clinton conceded quickly before drawing himself up, proud as ever. "Let us repair to the study. If it is a stratagem you want, it is a stratagem you will get. Finch? You are to rally two other officials of the Crown and present your reasoning to convince the Rebels to stand down. Batman, call in General Murray. I shall provide him with his orders next. Can't tell Finch of the details lest he be captured by Washington."

Once they were assembled in the study, Clinton took out a pen, paper, and ink, and began scribbling a letter detailing his orders. Meanwhile, Finch racked his brains for a General Murray. He could think of no such commander, yet that name sounded ominously familiar. "General Murray, sir?" Finch inquired.

"Why, John Murray, Lord Dunmore," Sir Henry replied. "I released him from house arrest. Now get ye gone. Your ship awaits, chartered and supplied."

"Fine, sir," Finch growled as he stumbled away back to his room to pack, cursing the world. *I am not going to be upstaged by that balmy old sod*, he thought. *I don't care if he has a title. I shall not be making nice with that bastard Washington whilst Lord Dunmore reaps the glory of a victory over whatever force he engages . . . if he wins, which he may well not!*

The Marquis de Lafayette's Headquarters, Williamsburg, Virginia

16 June 1777, 8:50 AM

The table spread at the dean's house of the College of William and Mary was grand, Finch had to admit. Seven courses, including pigeon, venison, turkey, artichokes, and French beans, made up the main brunt of the repast, whilst chocolates and tea were brought in to encourage conversation over dessert. Finch could not help but admit the Rebels appeared to bend over backward to please him. Entertainment, comprised of firework displays, unmanned balloons powered by hot air, and feats of marksmanship, proved most impressive and a delight to watch as well. Despite this, Finch could not help but feel slighted.

There he sat in an uncomfortable but ornately carved chair, in a stately room with shelves positively spilling over with books that were stained with old age. Atop them were a collection of firearms—muskets and pistols. Gazing across a mahogany table groaning under the weight of food and draped in the finest of lace was Finch's contact.

For all the indignity he has caused me, all the cruelties he visited upon my men, Washington slights me further by sending a proxy in his place? He glared across the table at not Washington, nor even his second-in-command, Benjamin Lincoln, but a third fellow. A ruddy-faced youngblood with a receding hairline and an aristocratic but idealistic fervor in his eyes.

A French fellow, thought Finch. *So much for this expedition. This Gilbert du Motier is sure to attempt to keep the Rebellion in the war regardless. I might as well try to enjoy myself.*

Humming along to the tune of the string quartet currently providing the entertainment, Finch looked about the room. None of the individuals he had invited on the trip to Williamsburg had deigned to come along for fear of missing out on greater honor and glory in fighting the French and Spanish. It appeared the boyish marquis had suffered the same difficulties, appearing both bored and lonely, with a lack of diplomatic attachés assisting him. Indeed, the room was sparsely populated. A few upstanding members of Virginian high society and the two diplomats were all that comprised this meeting, and the Marquis de Lafayette was quick to pick this up as well.

"This is some party," the young Frenchman said with a surprisingly good command of English. "I suppose we shall have to take some of the food home with us. What is it, Mister Finch, that you wished to discuss with us of the Continental Army and our great cause?"

"I fear it would not have much impact upon your excitable and unshakable passion for your cause, young Marquis," Finch said, shaking his head sadly.

The marquis burst out laughing, and suddenly, Finch saw it, too: the absurdity of two of the most fervent warriors on each side, stuck together in the same room as diplomats. "Such curious times," Lafayette remarked, chortling. "I wonder why our sides chose us."

"Most likely to prove that they tried the peaceful approach, only to be rebuffed," Finch replied, a broad grin on his face.

"Played for fools it is. I suppose I should have suspected it when General Lee recommended me for the job. He hates my guts."

"And I suppose," Finch said, laughing softly to himself, "I suppose Clinton wanted me out of the way for my"—he adopted Clinton's loud, boisterous tone—"unpredictable behavior."

"*Ha!*" Motier replied. "So I've heard!" The two shared a chuckle. Finch then leaned over the table and spoke more conspiratorially.

"I understand you preceded the French alliance into this conflict, my dear Marquis," he observed. "Do tell me, what caused you to become so excited about the possibility of separating us from our colonies?"

"Ah, Finch!" the marquis replied, setting down his wineglass. Both parties were drinking liberally. "Ah, Finch!" he said again. "Do remember that I am but a little boy, a romantic, spoiling for victories over a traditional foe for the good of my nation." He coughed. "This alone should give you and your fellows cause for concern. But toss into the witch's brew a desire to end tyranny in another nation? Even as England has advanced the rights of many in time, not all rights were addressed or fulfilled by your Magna Carta. It is clear we can push for the greater liberties of many and end these unjust tyrannies your king pursues."

Finch felt himself tiring of debate on this topic, especially with those who presumed to believe the Rebellion brought liberty and justice for all. He nonetheless once more took a puff on a pipe offered to him before wading into battle. "So you speak of tyrannies. I take it you mean the taxation without representation that started the conflict in the colonies?"

Lafayette nodded. "Your Magna Carta, a brilliant piece of literature for its time, ensured rights to many. Why did you aid in depriving the colonies of those rights?"

Finch smiled. This was a point he had turned over in his head many times before. "It was a balance. The colonials agreed to having no representative rights in England in exchange for being only indirectly ruled by the Crown and paying fewer taxes. They still benefited heavily. All the infrastructure and spending and defense from the Crown in exchange for minimal taxes and no say."

"Indeed, but they had no say over their rights as years went on. And did you not tax them thereafter?"

This was a strong point. Finch appreciated this kind of discussion but had a defense of his own. He leaned forward. "The taxation was based on new circumstances—namely, the colonists began a war with your empire, and indeed much of the world, without our consent. We joined on their side only to protect them from the results of their own folly. It bankrupted us, so naturally, we felt it fair to request a token stipend in exchange for our services. They resisted violently, even as we tried many different ways to peaceably extract the money before fighting back. They persisted, refusing all our overtures, some on behalf of the lack of representation, yes, others simply because they did not wish to pay taxes."

He straightened up. "I understand revolution is poetic and dramatic, but to watch your allies die by inches because they would not pay a small, provisional, and justified tax seems rather asinine to me. Even more so is rebelling for the right to keep slaves, discriminate against Papists, and allow for the invasion of Indian lands protected by the Crown. Doesn't seem very in keeping with 'All men are created equal,' especially when restricting the opposition's freedom of press."

He smiled, his confidence growing for the first time in a while. He had crushed the young man's argument and, through him, Washington's, too.

Gilbert du Motier gritted his teeth, then smiled politely. "A truth. And yet, is defending the disenfranchised of your colonies truly the aim of the British Empire? Who is to say whether they will uphold these promises of emancipation? Will not the Crown do anything or say anything to keep control over her colonies and exploit them?"

Finch's resolve briefly began to crumble. He bit his lip. *I do have a reputation for taking everything at face value.* Then he stopped, eyeing the young marquis. "I know Sir Henry personally. He is a man of honor and kindness and has moved with the times to put up with Lord Dunmore's shocking activism thus far, whether or not it was the initial aim of the Crown." He eyed Lafayette. "Surely he will be fair to the black man—at least more fair than Washington, whose policy with black people was to own them, and only to emancipate them for combat purposes, even then as an equalizing measure, since we emancipated them first." He took a sip of wine, smiling haughtily. "And if you mean to speak of Crown policy toward Natives and Papists, we had sympathetic diplomats in positions of authority for years before this bloody insurgency."

"Nonetheless," Motier replied, pounding the table with his fist and beginning to pace about, "it seems that for all *your* cries, the white Protestants of the Crown will want to look out for each other first, whether or not it is the right thing to do."

"This is true, and a damned tragedy," Finch replied. "Just because the black slave will gain his freedom and the Indian will retain his lands does not mean most people will see them in the same light we see each other as white men. I fear, alas, it shall be some time before true equality will reign across the colonies, regardless of the flag under which it flies. However, I firmly believe that it may well happen under the Crown first."

Motier started, raising an eyebrow as he took a drink of wine. "And why is that? Surely the American colonists have fought for the right ideals, and even if their practice is misplaced, they will come to realize their mistakes."

Finch nodded. "Indeed, the colonists possess that drive in the correct direction. But modern Britannia was formed after years upon years of our own civil wars, and each time we had to rebuild ourselves anew. Though we have grown ever closer to achieving these goals, it took us a great deal of time and restructuring. I wonder whether the Americans will grow based on our past or in their defiance will have to start somewhat afresh, no matter what their initial intentions were."

Motier snorted. "I disagree. Did not your empire grant suffrage through the Magna Carta shortly after rising up against King John? True, there was some backwardness amidst your Stuart kings, absolute monarchs that they styled themselves, but I firmly believe the colonies have no reason to betray their ideals, nor fall prey to such idiocy."

"Ah," Finch replied. He blushed. He hadn't studied up as much as he should have on his monarchs. "Perhaps I was impulsive. I . . . shall think on this. That being said," he added weakly, "you must admit that, even if they did manage to triumph, a transition of power over time, rather than an instantaneous one, would benefit the Rebellion, for they have no experience in self-rule."

Lafayette scoffed. "Let us be realistic, Mister Finch. There is no chance on God's Earth or beyond that General Washington would agree to that. I know *him* personally."

"Yes, you are right, of course," Finch said. Then it came to him. "Your Grace," he went on, bowing his head. "What of the comparative financial predicaments? In America, are there not plantations and agricultural labor required to run them? Do planters and people of means not own slaves on many levels both as aid and as status symbols?"

He cleared his throat carefully. "Not to be too cynical, but would it not be a terrible difficulty to extricate these laborers from their masters if one American were to command another in the name of liberty to do so, for some would consider the right to own others a liberty? Namely, a great number of those in government?"

Motier pondered this a time, hand on chin. "And why would this be less difficult in Britain? Freeing the slaves, I mean?"

Finch pounced. "Because the black man is *already* free in England proper, and this is a monumental start, as they are the sole region in our empire, for better or for worse, with governing power. The abolitionist movement in our home country which affected this development is now spreading to the far reaches of that empire, if not the world. This has, in part, sprung from the ideology of our ruling class, which has little use for slaves. And with our merciful king's approval, there is little to stop us from freeing slaves across a vast number of other territories. That is more than can be said for what the colonials can or will do."

He stopped to sip some wine before he continued. "And it is not limited to slavery. We are also making great progress legalizing freedom of worship, much to the chagrin of many Rebels. We already have legalized Catholicism in many of the colonies under our command, whereas surely you have heard of the myriad reports of Rebels etching 'Death to the Pope' upon their own artillery? Many equate the Catholic Church with oppression equivalent to our own and entertain considerably more anti-Catholic sentiment than we do, of this I can assure you. Their alliance of convenience with France, possibly even you, is just that."

Lafayette stared.

Got him.

Finch toasted the marquis with his glass. "You're a good man, Your Grace. Perhaps just a tad thoughtless."

"Perhaps."

Another thought struck Finch. He extended his hand. "Consider the words of an old man, Gilbert. War? It is hell. I would heartily suggest you never involve yourself in conflict unnecessarily. For me, I shall fight this one out, then, having cemented my family's position, retire a made man. I suggest you do the same. And if this war does not make you a legend, look to a different industry. Perhaps engineering."

The Marquis de Lafayette paused at this suggestion, thinking over his response carefully. At length, he sighed. "It is merely that . . . when Mister Franklin came across the Atlantic and spoke to us, he was so charming, so charismatic. He promised such great things for the new country and its people. I just wanted to help them. And anyone who could have charmed Franklin, that General Washington . . . he is not much of a warrior, but he is so handsome and strong and devoted. He had persevered so many times. I felt I could follow the man to hell and back."

He hesitated. "I understand that must sound like rubbish to one who has met neither man, but believe you me, if they became rulers of this great land, they will make this country flower."

"Perhaps they would," Finch replied, smiling, for he remembered Washington from the Seven Years' War—a brash and impulsive young Virginian. "It certainly has been difficult stamping out any belief in their capabilities. They have spread propaganda like none other."

"So you would have the French abandon their allies?" the marquis inquired, raising an eyebrow. "Back out from the war?"

"Not as such," Finch replied. "I already happen to know that there is more to your mother country than meets the eye. I imagine, based on your impassioned defense of the colonies, that you have not heard of France's plans with Spain?"

Lafayette's eyes narrowed. "They mean to win America for the colonists and divide up the rest of Britannia's possessions if they triumph abroad, no?"

Finch shook his head. "They want the colonies for themselves, too, Gilbert. These men you are fighting for, you will betray them to the French and Spanish Crowns."

Finch took the moment to unfurl the dispatch he captured from the Comte d'Estaing. The Marquis read it with disbelief etched across his face. Having finished the document, he set it down, looking shaken.

"This is . . . this is Rochambeau's script," he said, his voice quavery.

"Indeed," Finch replied. "Gilbert, I come before you today under orders to ask for a ceasefire. As you can see, we have a common enemy, and must face them, first, before determining the future of the colonies, whose interests we both hold dear."

Gilbert stared. "Truly there is no honor in politics. It is a dark day when your mother country manipulates you and turns against you. You shall have your ceasefire, General Finch, and if the Rebellion has no permanent alliance with France or Spain, I do believe our cause is ultimately doomed. I shall see the document reaches General Washington and urge him to rethink his stance on revolution. I think you should leave now. Though Williamsburg is largely aligned with the king, it is occupied, as you have seen, by soldiers of *my* former king. Stay safe." He paused. "And thank you. For the lesson in the diplomatic sciences. Nationality is a fleeting concept. Integrity is eternal."

Governor Campbell's Mansion, Charleston, South Carolina
17 JUNE 1777, 7:22 AM

Finch woke up with a throbbing headache. Whilst in transit from Williamsburg he had dreamed of disasters to come, of Lord Dunmore leading a campaign against the European coalition arrayed against the Crown. He understood the governor to be a strong propaganda symbol and thus worthy of some respect, but the man was even more unpredictable than Finch himself, with half the engineer's tactical acumen.

Meanwhile, he thought, *Sir Henry delegated me command of a diplomatic expedition. Unacceptable!* Taking deep, heaving breaths, he reached for his pipe and took a long puff. *It is decided. I must seek out Lord Dunmore and aid in his expedition.*

But first, it was time for a drink.

Lord Dunmore was discovered at one of the inns in town, the Barge House. He was carousing with some of his soldiers, amongst whom were black freedmen whom the governor had emancipated with his own money upon landing in South Carolina to swell the ranks of his army. It was clear that the Ethiopian Regiment was reconstituted and ready for action. This time, however, it was part of the provincial establishment. Not only were the men officially trained and equipped, but each soldier had a uniform: hunting shirts, trousers, regulation cartridge boxes, and haversacks. A vibrant red sash with the words "Liberty to Slaves" emblazoned across it in gold completed the look.

Apart from the fact that the forces were not racially integrated, Finch thought, Titus was likely proud to see this force of freedmen regulars trooping through Charleston with the rest of the British, Loyalist, Native, and German forces, a fellow named Prince at the head. Whatever the reason, Lord Dunmore was keen on making the statement that he intended to abolish slavery wherever it could be found.

The presence of the hawk-nosed former governor of short stature, garishly kilted and bonneted, yet already drunk at eight in the morning, seemed to frighten off most of the regular crowd, as Lord Dunmore greeted Finch with a raised tankard. "Hail to ye, Finch!" he slurred. "I surely hope your command skills have improved since last we met! Of course, it doesn't matter. You're to be diplomatizing with Washington, I hear, whilst I shall be appropriating your corps. Should be fun!"

Finch was immediately annoyed. "Yes, about that. Lord Dunmore, you must understand that I know my men and their capacities. It is important that I come with you."

Lord Dunmore whistled. "Why, sounds like someone is trying to wrest control from high command. After your last error, you'd think you should leave matters to Clinton. He's a fine gentleman, you know, and, after all, a *fair tactician*." He smirked. "So am I, you know. We lent ourselves to some of the fighting and rescued your men at Charleston. What were you thinking, taking on the whole French army with partisans, provincials, and Indians?"

Finch's eyes narrowed. "I spiked the enemy guns, thus preserving the town, and contributed to the fighting pretty heavily myself, you know. It was a matter of teamwork." He forced a smile, though he suspected it came off as something of a grimace. "In that vein, again, please, let me come with you. I can handle myself and take full responsibility if Sir Henry is wroth with us."

Rawdon, a husky colonel with a bulbous nose and bushy eyebrows who was under Dunmore's command, grinned grotesquely as he pinched the buttocks of a passing barmaid. He turned to look Finch squarely in the eye. "Maybe that is so, but the less danger I place myself in, the better. How can you think of exposing yourself in battle against the French and the Spanish when you have a bevy of pretty South Carolina girls baying for your body?"

"Hardly sporting, Rawdon. You know perfectly well how women are the weaker vessels," came the high-pitched, aristocratic voice of a man behind Finch. Fresh off his horse came a lean yet well-muscled man in green, young and effeminate, with straight black hair and a dragoon helmet under his arm.

"Hear, hear, Tarleton. Let us drink to it!" cried Rawdon, sliding the colonel a drink across the bar as the two toasted, laughing as Finch pulled away from them.

"Lemme tell you something about my brigade," Lord Dunmore interjected, pulling Finch aside and gesturing to his officers as they conversed merrily with each other. "They've contributed only to victories, never to defeats, and have done good work at all times. I trained them myself," he boasted loudly. "So if you're thinking of going on any madcap adventures, like last time, know this: you won't be doing it with my lads. We are going to be winning battles, not sacrificing ourselves for some fool activist's cause."

Finch was about to roll his eyes at the hypocrisy of Dunmore's words when the quiet, intense remark of a shadowy figure from the other side of the bar made him jump. "I would not mind sacrificing myself for an activist's cause."

As Finch screwed up his eyes to take a closer look, he noticed an older, heavyset fellow with a fashionable mustache drinking some mead with a slender, blond-haired woman of comparable age. Finch instantly recognized them and felt an enormous pang of remorse and embarrassment for interacting with Dunmore's boorish officers in front of them. He bowed humbly. "Greetings, your Graces! Baron Riedesel, Baroness. Brigadier General Giles Finch, at your service."

The baron smiled. "You were the lucky engineer who married my wife's favorite handmaiden. You should have heard her laughter for days thereafter. Frederika here was most excited to have brought such joy to her best friend." He chuckled. "I have heard of your endeavors and think highly of your actions. Word of your activity has earned the commendation of many throughout the German states." The hulking gentleman turned to face Dunmore, tapping his cane on the floor twice. "Again, I see no issue in activism or in ending this war early, whichever comes first. The more bodies we win to our side, the less likely we need fight much longer and the fewer bodies we sacrifice."

"Major General Riedesel here is one of our cause's more refined warriors, a jewel in our Crown," Lord Dunmore remarked, playfully taking the baron by the shoulder. The German stared at him quizzically. "He sailed in with some gentlemen from Brunswick and Hesse-Hanau to bolster our forces."

"Forces that I can inspire and help lead against the enemy!" Finch said with a smile. "With my command of German, I can serve as a go-between for our troops and those of the enemy if Riedesel falls." The Brunswicker chuckled. So did Tarleton.

"Ha. Surely the other Brunswickers know English?" Tarleton inquired of Riedesel, whirling around from his conversation with Rawdon. The German shook his head. Tarleton was aghast. "We have a vast empire, allied with your nation, and your own officers cannot speak English?" He smirked. "Very well, I say Finch can come. We shall surely need him. Moreso than we need Negro troops, anyway."

"Thank you, Green Dragon," Finch replied and bowed to Tarleton, so nicknamed amongst the men. "But you will find black troops will be essential to our cause." He turned to Lord Dunmore. "Governor Murray? Let us keep up the fight."

"You are sure high command will allow your presence?" Lord Dunmore asked.

"Come now, *Lord* Dunmore, since when have you heeded high command?"

The governor smiled mischievously.

Realizing that there was no time like the present, especially in war, when one might never see a friend again, Finch called for pen, paper, and ink from the bartender and quickly penned a letter to Clinton explaining his intent.

To the intrepid General Clinton,

You will find me gone from this place before the day is out, off to do my duty during the beginning of this slow grind toward the end of the war. It has been an honor serving with you and our fellow officers, and despite our setbacks, many of which were my fault, it has been a learning experience I shall not forget.

Should I die on the field, know that I looked upon you as a tremendously stalwart, forthright, honest, and talented man. That is why I hope you will not begrudge me, or at least hope you will forgive me, for one last change in our

*plans. I did not have the time to discuss it with you whilst
in Charleston, as time is of the essence.*

*Though Lord Dunmore and I will, in time, march on
Augusta and continue to roll up the French flank as you
request, we feel it best that we push back and sever the supply
lines of the Spanish before they become a true threat to our
colonies. As such, we shall sail to New Orleans, forcing the
Spanish to double back to defend their side of the Mississippi
River. Should we capture their position in one final assault,
I believe that may end their contribution to the war effort.*

*A thousand pardons for not confirming this stratagem
with Your Honor, for, again, I felt it best to move quickly.*

*Your perhaps not so much obedient but ever admiring
servant most sincerely,*
FINCH

The die had been cast. Finch had subjected himself, by his own design, to a maneuver that would once again jeopardize or bolster his career.

As he stood up from his stool to return to his quarters and prepare for his mission, however, the doors to the tavern opened to reveal none other than Sir Henry himself.

"Thought I'd find you lads here," he said, smiling at Lord Dunmore and his command. "Lord Dunmore, I wish to tell you that we have decided to postpone your march on Augusta. The French in this region are on the run. Their numbers and morale are devastated, and we believe Simcoe's Queen's Rangers will do a splendid job of harrying the remnants of the enemy force. The local militia will help them."

Lord Dunmore smiled in Finch's direction. "Very good, Sir Henry. This is most heartening news. What will you have me do with my force, then?"

"Your brigade, as well as that of Riedesel's and Finch's, will sail with Admiral Byron to New Orleans and contribute to an attack that will capture the town. We need to deprive the enemy of their supplies and resources. That will place the Spanish troops between a hammer and anvil, wot wot."

"I see," Lord Dunmore remarked, nodding. "And who will lead this delightful little expedition? I take it you'd want a man in possession of the king's commission? British born and such?" He puffed out his chest.

Clinton pointed in Finch's direction. "Him."

Both Dunmore and Finch started. Riedesel silently munched on a sausage.

"Finch is unpredictable and has not always been successful on the field, but he has had his moments and is an engineer. Trained to be a good judge of the land, wot wot. Beyond this, he is resourceful. I know he will worm his way to command somehow regardless." He winked at Finch, who couldn't help but smile sheepishly.

"Indeed," Clinton continued, pointing at Finch. "Take time to bury your daughter, then bury your feelings, take Lord Dunmore's brigade, your own brigade—including the Natives and Negroes—and also Riedesel's corps, and set sail for New Orleans.

Finch, realizing his jaw still hung open, finally managed to close it. "Sir Henry, are you quite certain of this arrangement? Surely General Riedesel is better equipped for this engagement."

Clinton frowned. "I do not recall asking for your advice. You are my friend, not my equal. You are also *supposed* to be still in dealings with the Rebels in Williamsburg. Would you prefer that?"

Finch shut up immediately.

CHAPTER 10

The Final Campaign

HMS Reliant, off the Coast of New Orleans,
Louisiana Territories

4 JULY 1777, 12:45 PM

As he gazed off the starboard bow at the city of New Orleans, Finch found himself recalling Caroline's memorial service.

It had been a beautiful but simple ceremony. He had ensured it would be the way he imagined his adventurous daughter would enjoy it. Though a few flower bouquets festooned her casket, as per tradition, Finch had also called upon some favors to take an honor guard with him as he gave his daughter a heroine's burial. Drawn from the feldjaegers, they fired a six-rifle salute after a brief service.

Clinton and Dunmore had accompanied the family, standing with Constance and Adelaide as Giles and Archibald helped to cover the body with dirt. When that was done, Dunmore looked on and nodded whilst Clinton offered his sincerest regrets to each of the bereaved.

"My condolences, General Finch," Clinton said, a somber look clouding his features. "She was a heroine on and off the battlefield. I thought her a grand example of womanhood, and her services were invaluable. Here, sir! I am having this commissioned in her honor."

243

He passed along an illustration as a sad smile crossed his face. Finch took it curiously, and was surprised to behold the likeness of Caroline emblazoned onto a small disk, attached to a ribbon. "The Finch Medallion of Excellence in Espionage," Clinton proclaimed proudly. "I shall see to it that some of our best spies are awarded with one, however covertly, at the war's end."

Finch nodded. "Thank you, Sir Henry. It is much appreciated. She would have been thrilled." He turned to Adelaide, who was marveling at Caroline's likeness. She caught his look, smiled, and nodded. The two were then surprised as an enormous hand laid itself on Finch's shoulder. He turned around to find the Baron and Baroness Riedesel, who made to lay white carnations at Caroline's grave.

"You are not alone, Brigadier Finch, Frau Finch," Baroness Riedesel said, taking General Finch's hands in her own. "A child to you is a child to us as well. We must be there for one another and see each other through this war."

Finch nodded and turned away, tears in his eyes. The baron tutted him, however, and held him and Adelaide close. "We must stand by one another and wear our emotions on our breast." He smiled. "From what I hear, your Caroline would have liked that."

Adelaide nodded. "I agree. She would like those she loved to stand together against all the troubles life has to offer."

Finch smiled sadly. "Much as I appreciate your encouragements, Baron and Baroness, I do believe Caroline would also want me to finish the war without grief hanging over me." He turned to Clinton and Dunmore, lounging about smoking cigars. "I understand we have a war to win, and–"

"Sir?" a voice piped up, startling Finch from his reveries as he leaned on the ship's rail.

He jumped, then regained his grasp on reality as he marveled at the beauty of the town before him, soon to be flooded with blood. Seagulls laughed as the waves lapped against the sides of the small fleet of ships, battered by storms that had slowed the convoy. The walled city stood not far off, the standard bearing the Cross of Saint James flying proudly in the distance. Cannon dotted the fortifications, but Finch knew that the duty ahead of him had to be done.

"Sir?" the seaman inquired again. He gestured toward Dunmore, who was in conversation with a well-dressed naval officer. "Lord Dunmore requests your company." Finch sighed and followed the officer across the ship. As Finch tromped along the deck, he could overhear the conversation the two were having.

"Jack," Lord Dunmore was saying, "you will support our landing and bombard the ever-living shite out of those defenders, sir."

"Yes, sir," Admiral "Foul Weather" Jack Byron replied, rolling his eyes. "This is not my first crack at a fortified town."

Dunmore smiled. "Good. Whilst you take action, your marines, in addition to our blue, green, and frock coats, as well as those savages without any coats, will then row ashore and charge the fort with gunpowder kegs, make breaches, and—"

"*Yes*, Lord Dunmore."

"Ah, good!"

Finch checked his timepiece. In about an hour, the bombardments would begin. He looked about. She Who Laughs was particularly excited about the concept of a landing action, rallying her warriors, who looked seasick and woebegone, with some motivational speaking in her native tongue, making several dramatic slices with her hands.

As the vessels neared shore, Finch turned to Reverend Peabody of the First Georgia. "Now would be a good time to send out an appeal to God for us all, Reverend."

Peabody, his lips trembling and knees knocking, nodded vigorously and fell to his knees in prayer.

"Loudly, sir, if you please." Finch pressed a flask full of rum to Peabody. The reverend took a long pull and reached for his pipe, puffing rapidly.

"God of power and mercy." *Puff, puff.* "Maker and lover of peace. To know you is to live"—*puff, puff*—"and to serve you is to reign. Through the will and guidance of the Father, Son, and Holy Spirit"—*puff, kaffkaff*—"be our protection in battle against all evil. Help us to overcome war and violence and to establish your law of love and justice." *Kaffkaff, puff.* "Grant this through Christ, our Lord."

"Amen," the company chorused.

Reverend Peabody remained on his knees and persisted in his prayers, clinging tightly to a cross around his neck.

"Reverend Peabody, I would not think you so bothered by the thought of battle against the Dons, sir!"

Peabody turned a wary eye on Finch. "It be not so much the Papists I worry about, but the fishes that swim below. Many are man-eating, and I fear drowning as I fear the devil. Indeed, sir, there be no comfort in that form of death, a meal for fishes—without last rites or a prayer? No, sir, not for me!"

Finch understood, though he felt death on the battlefield sounded dismal as well. He didn't want to excite Reverend Peabody further, however.

He decided to take a nap, informing a batman that he should like to be awakened five minutes before the bombardment. The batman saluted smartly and went on his way. Finch returned to his cot and soon fell asleep to the rocking of the waves.

Minutes later, he was awakened by the loud crackle of cannon fire from ship guns. He rushed amidst the sailors crewing the vessel, dashing up the stairs to the foredeck to find a small sloop darting from the Spanish port, attempting to run the British blockade.

Defiantly flying the Rebellion's naval ensign, a great snake on a red and white striped field, she threaded the white-capped waves. Suddenly, the Rebel vessel turned sharply to port, struck by a high wave. This proudly displayed her name for all to see. It was the *Liberty*, John Hancock's personal vessel.

Clearly, Hancock, whose Sons of Liberty had defied Governor Thomas Gage so long ago, sought refuge in a town within Spanish possessions. Now, sensing trouble, the very man who brought about all this carnage, which endured to the present day, was scuttling off to avoid capture in some other far-off realm. Finch's blood boiled.

A Royal Navy frigate, the HMS *Anvil*, began to turn about in an effort to block the *Liberty*'s path, but the sloop was too quick. Maneuvering between many of the thirty-two-pound shots hurled her way, with any one direct hit meaning certain destruction, Hancock's vessel cleared the blockade in a hail of smoke and fire, ball and shot.

However, as the *Liberty*'s sailors cheered, putting their backs into setting a course for open sea, they neglected to note the frigate coming about in slow but steady pursuit. Unable to hit the vessel with a broadside from this angle, the fore cannons on the *Anvil* blasted away, damaging the forecastle on the sloop and ripping into her decks and sails. Undaunted, the *Liberty* continued to tack toward an escape route, making her way toward billowing clouds in the distance. The *Anvil* whipped itself about at the fastest speed she could muster. Having done so, she fired off one last desperate salvo from her thirty-two-gun arsenal with a barrage from her port side.

Though on the other end of the fleet, watching this action through a spyglass, Finch could not help but cringe away as the resounding explosion echoed in his eardrums and the vessel swayed in the water. The shot from this blast spewed hot iron all over the decks and into the side of the *Liberty*, knocking down one mast, which felled the second. This left the vessel dead in the gulf, small fires licking the decks.

With her captain taking note of this, the *Anvil*, far beyond the range of New Orleans's guns, gave chase and prepared to offer assistance to survivors, rapidly deploying lifeboats as the sloop began to sink. From afar, Finch again put his spyglass to an eye and made out, amongst the Rebel sailors, a mustard-coated figure striking a heroic pose aboard one of the tenders. Finch allowed himself a moment of pity before gesturing over a marine.

"I should like to be rowed over to the HMS *Anvil*, if you please," he said, crossing his arms. "It is a matter of some importance."

HMS Anvil, off the Coast of New Orleans, Louisiana Territories

4 JULY 1777, 5:23 PM

Giles Finch stood aboard the deck of the HMS *Anvil*, once more across from the famed smuggler who had caused all this ruckus. Hancock sneered as Finch loomed ever closer.

"Ah . . . the general approaches. Good day, General . . ."

"Finch. Giles Finch. We met before some two years ago." The engineer grinned predatorially, surprising himself. "I wondered whether I would see you again, John Hancock. You have some nerve, taking cover in Spanish New Orleans whilst your men die by inches."

Hancock's eyes shot up before setting his jaw. "Oh, you. Well." He shrugged. "It's what leaders do. And better to be revered as a leader and make some quick money than to forever be seen as a second-rate smuggler." He dipped into a pocket for a snuffbox. He took a pinch from within, then inquired, "Perhaps you might release me in exchange for a cut of the profits?"

Finch couldn't believe his ears. All the respect he had for the man who had told off Thomas Gage and fought for alleged liberation of his people, however flawed, disappeared in an instant.

It was all an act. Pure tax evasion.

The engineer turned on Hancock with a newfound rage. "You start a war costing thousands of lives over ego and profit, endanger my countrymen the world over, *kill my daughter*, and now you expect to bribe your way to safety?" He turned to the marines restraining the Rebel leader. "Gentlemen? Show Mister Hancock to the brig and imprison him forthwith." As he spoke, he searched Hancock and extracted a bag of coins from inside his coat.

Hancock shrugged. "I shall be seeing you again, General Finch. Money always prevails."

That did it. Gripping the bag of coins firmly in hand, Finch swung the monies with great force into the nose of the offending Rebel, resulting in a satisfying *crunch* as the weighted container hit home. Hancock let out a bellow of pain.

"I daresay you're right." Finch smirked at Hancock before gesturing to the marines to escort the dazed and humiliated smuggler belowdecks.

Finch then turned to Admiral Byron, who had just come aboard from a tender of his own. Looking around, the admiral inquired, "Where did the prisoners go? I was hoping to meet them."

"There is no time, Admiral. We must prepare the ship guns for a two-hour bombardment on New Orleans."

Byron's face fell, and Finch remembered that Byron was technically the highest-ranking officer in the expedition. "Very well, General Finch," Byron growled, clearly not used to being ordered about. "The guns shall be ready." He stalked off.

"Upon that note, would it not be best to attack by night, General Finch?" Lord Dunmore said, having appeared at last behind the sailor and soldier. "They would not suspect such an approach, and the enemy could not see us coming as easily. We would have those walls down in seconds!"

Finch considered his options. At length, he remarked, "Whilst it would certainly increase the likelihood of a more decisive victory to attack by night, it would also increase the possibility of an unmitigated disaster when we would already be in a position to carry the day. Much as I appreciate your candor, Lord Dunmore, to win the final battle of the war through treachery would be chaotic and bloody. A nighttime bombardment would also be inaccurate. It might harm the town, you see. The iron cover of round shot offered by Admiral Byron will be all the protection I need for my pioneers and lights."

"Fine then. Though I would be most cross if my brigade were to lose a battle," Dunmore said.

"Worry not, Your Grace. This territory will be ours." Despite this remark, Finch could not help but worry his troops might be slaughtered to a man for his display of honor.

A bit too late for that, he thought, shaking the concerns from his mind, as the time for the landings to commence was upon them. As transports began lowering flat-bottomed boats into the churning waters below, soldiers clambered over the sides of the ships and down to the long boats, beginning to row toward the enemy fortifications. Joining his pioneers and lights in the first few boats, Finch could clearly hear the gunner's mates bellowing their orders to roll out the starboard cannon. Frigates and ships of the line lowered their anchors whilst the gunners hungrily eyed the port city.

Fort Galvez New Orleans, Louisiana Territories

5 July 1777, 7:39 AM

BOOM! BOOM! BARABARABOOOM!
The thirty-two-pound guns of the Royal Navy sang, battering away at the walls of Fort Galvez as a number of small boats

containing Finch and his force watched, the round shot of their allies sailing overhead. Many iron balls sailed too far, crossing over the walls of the city and hammering the town itself. *That will not bode well for our cause amongst the citizenry*, Finch thought.

Fortunately, the navy noticed this, too, and after a few test shots that fell short of the fort that surrounded the city, a salvo rocked the walls proper. Finch watched in fascination, calculating in his mind the right trajectory, powder, and force needed to strike the walls at a good angle and cheering on the sailors with every hit against the wall.

"Nearly there, fellows! God be with you!" came the distracting cry of a sailor in front of Finch. Whirling around, he remembered that he was being rowed toward shore.

Boom! Boom! Ba-BOOM!

The fort batteries echoed, returning fire. The shot rained down, splashing into the depths and barely missing the boats, stirring up the waves and rocking them dangerously. As they held on for dear life, more than one man retched over the side of the ship, their vomit slowly mingling with the hue of the ocean as fish darted about, terrified by the havoc of the whole affair.

Then the vessels reached the beach with a resounding thump, jostling the black soldiers about. Finch's men clambered out of the craft, taking with them large kegs of explosives. Hurrying behind the cover of a boulder with some of his pioneers as small-arms fire nipped at their heels, Finch surveyed the area with his spyglass. Thanks to the naval bombardment, many enemy guns were unseated, and the walls had certainly sustained damage, but Spanish soldiers nonetheless lined the parapets. Finch sighed. *Let us end this.*

As he watched the soldiers land in scores, Finch gestured the rest of the newly arriving Ethiopian Regiment and Black Brigade, led by Colonels Prince and Titus, over to the boulders and cover. As they dashed out of their boats, bravely weathering fire from the ramparts, they were soon followed by a boat full of Natives, then elements of the German establishment under the rotund Riedesel. The rangers and other Loyalists were slated amongst the last to arrive, only now piling into their boats. Somewhat upset at the landing order, Finch kicked himself for not predicting that the sailors would deliberately engineer the landings so that the non-British and nonwhite, and thus "expendable," Crown forces landed first. *I should have stopped them.*

Deciding he'd have to have a chat with Admiral Byron later, Finch gathered his courage and drew his blade. "Front march, lads!" he cried. "March! March! We shall only be able to take this fort with speed and efficiency. Come! Forward the charges! *For your homelands and loved ones!*"

As the men advanced into a withering fire of round shot and musketry from the fort defenders, a rank of Brunswicker light infantrymen ahead of Finch fell, the soldier in front of him exploding into a mass of gore and viscera that covered the engineer. Stunned and shaking, Finch did his best to recover his senses and brushed the blood off his face and coat, unsteadily forcing himself forward.

The pioneers, couched amongst the black troops, equipped only with charges and axes with which to undermine the main gate, put aside their fears and continued their advance, their spaced-out skirmish line formation giving them hope as they ran full tilt at the enemy positions. As they came close, however, the dreaded sound of canister—the cacophonous noise of scores of musket balls hurtling out of a small container, rending and tearing into soft human flesh—assaulted Finch's ears. Like wheat cut by a scythe, at least thirty soldiers fell, and the remainder wavered as the Spanish cheered on the success of their artillerists.

The cheering was too much. Breaking out from the middle of the Ethiopian ranks, the pioneers began to run for cover. Having exposed themselves, they quickly became a target for Spanish sharpshooters as they backtracked toward the ships. Finch, sensing disaster, retraced his steps.

"Rally, pioneers!" he called, waving his hat. "We may end this war today. Do not thrust the day into the hands of the enemy! Come back!"

"Not a chance, sir!" cried one soldier, quaking, his burden slipping from his hands. "We love our country, we really do, and that is why we are going home to it!"

Finch had no real answer to that.

Then came footsteps along the shore as Titus planted himself between the two soldiers.

"Sir"—the partisan officer frowned as he addressed the pioneer—"your patriotism is commendable, but my men have no sympathy for your flummery right now. Cower if you must, and die in disgrace 'pon these shores, but hand over your charges, that we might win the day."

"That is well by me!" The pioneer shifted his burden into Colonel Tye's arms.

Finch was impressed. "How did you get that response?"

Titus grinned before passing a keg off to an Ethiopian soldier. "I learned from the best."

Now that the charges were once more in the hands of an inspired force, the operation forged ahead. The Ethiopians cautiously carried them, whilst the Brunswickers, grimly led forward by General Riedesel, provided additional cover for their attack. As iron and lead balls kicked up columns of sand all over the beach around Finch, the world suddenly went red, and a stinging sensation permeated his body. Finch checked himself for wounds and found a scarlet ribbon of blood issuing from his shoulder. A rifle bullet had struck him. He roared in pain as he crumpled to the ground.

Fortune had caught up with him at last. *I've failed,* Finch thought. *My family will fall into destitution and be forgotten. I shall be forgotten. It was all for naught.*

Just as his eyes were closing from the exertion and exasperation of his failed attack, as the world was turning to black, he caught sight of the elderly Running Deer striding up to him. The wizened old man held out a hand.

"You must fight on," he urged as bullets and balls whipped up around them, ricocheting off the rocks of the beach. "For my people, and for yours." He gestured back toward Charleston. "Remember the loved ones you left at home."

With great exertion, Finch craned his head toward New Orleans. His eyes opened wide as, at that moment, the gates exploded open with a resounding *KABOOM!*

Masonry and men flew far and wide as a great portion of the city's walls, caught in the shock wave of the explosion, tumbled down with the gates, leaving a huge breach through which the Crown forces could pour.

There was hope.

Slowly, his wound stinging like a thousand nettles, Finch rose to his feet, allowing his shoulder to be bound by the warrior, who took him by the hand and led him to cover up against the ruined walls of the city. Finch's soldiers, regarding his injuries and woebegone look, held back a time, unsure of their next move. Finch weakly waved them on.

"Men," he cried through the pain, "our victory is at hand. If ever you have loved me, or sought to do me, as well as yourselves, honor, you will carry the day!"

Upon hearing Finch's words, the men of the Crown forces rushed the fallen gates of Fort Galvez. As fierce as the tiger, as swift as the roe, they pushed the enemy back toward the governor's mansion.

Noting the arrival of the black, Native, and German troops at the walls of Fort Galvez, Lord Dunmore advanced a force of his own. The light infantry of his British Legion and line infantry of the Volunteers of Ireland regiment, each comprised of crack New York Loyalists, made their way onto the field along with the battle-hardened New Jerseyans of the decidedly more aptly named Fourth Battalion, New Jersey Volunteers. They soon caught up with and eventually overtook Finch's force. Inspired by their bravery, Finch and his men followed them with a cry of "Huzzay!"

As they threaded the many streets of New Orleans, Finch noticed with discomfort the quietude of the breached city. The town seemed almost abandoned, when only a little while ago the ramparts had been crawling with soldiers.

Suddenly, there was a flash of movement from behind a fence and a cry from the ranks: "Down, lads!"

Finch sprawled upon the earth as the world around him exploded.

KRAK! KRAK! KA-RAK!

A force of Spanish militia fell upon the Crown soldiers from behind the cover of crates and barrels, fences, windows, and doors. After discharging their weapons, they made to withdraw. Finch sensed a trap.

"After them!" Dunmore shouted, discharging a pistol in the direction of the fleeing guerrillas. "British Legion to the front! Death or glory, lads?"

"Glory!" shouted the green-coated lights as they pushed the advance, giving chase to the guerrillas.

"*Flaming idiots*," Browne muttered, holding back his rangers and their Native allies with a gesture. "It's a trap!" he cried between cupped hands.

Too late.

Mere seconds later, the Loyalist lights were engulfed in smoke as a second rank, this one of white-coated Spanish troops, suddenly made their presence known, jumping up from behind a low wall of crates and firing a volley of scattered shots. The pursuit bogged down into heavy melee fighting.

"Shall we help them?" inquired Sandsnake as his Natives looked on, champing at the bit.

"You may attack," Finch said. "The rest of us will hold the force in reserve and lock down this town. Take She Who Laughs and the other Cherokee with you. The Shawnee as well."

"It is done!" Sandsnake shouted, and his Creek warriors took off with the Cherokee and Shawnee, ululating, hot on their heels.

"Right, lads!" Finch addressed the remnants of the force, nervously picking at his shoulder dressings as another burst of agony made him hiss in pain. "It is the will of Sir Henry that we force the surrender of this town's governor. Set off along the side streets and surround the manor house. New Jerseyans, Volunteers of Ireland, strike to the north and south. Ethiopians, Black Brigade, east and west. Browne's rangers and Riedesel's command will act as a mobile force and provide cover for all of us. Use what stealth you can. If we can get Lord Dunmore to draw the enemy's fire, we will do well."

There were a few murmurs of approval before Abraham van Buskirk, lieutenant colonel of the Fourth New Jersey Volunteers, spoke up. "Chop chop, lads! Today, if you please. The Spaniard waits for no man, and the more we delay, the more heads will roll. Now! Onward! Staunchly! Bravely!"

As the forces of the king broke off along their various routes of attack, Finch found himself lost in thought. *This could be it*, he said to himself, *the last battle I'll ever need to fight. I will have achieved what I could to bring honor to the family.*

And about time, too, he considered in an afterthought as his shoulder blossomed into another maelstrom of pain. He shook his head free of the clouds forming in his brain and started after the New Jersey Volunteers.

In the distance, the fight continued strong. Finch could hear the cries of the wounded, the musketry, the clanging of steel on steel, but the route the New Jerseyans took remained eerily silent.

"Keep a sharp eye, gentlemen," Finch hissed through the relative quiet. "The enemy could be anywhere, and—"

"Yes, sir, we understand," came the hushed voice of van Buskirk. "Please, if you could keep your voice down and take cover— we must be as stealthy as possible."

Finch nodded and kept his head down as they crept amongst the tombs of a cemetery. Suddenly, van Buskirk raised a palm and pointed in the direction of the far gate, which led ever closer to the manor house.

There in the distance was a band of cazadores—Spanish light infantry. They were well equipped and nervously awaiting an assault. Their crisp white uniforms betrayed them as freshly deployed, but they were doubtless well trained.

Smart, Finch thought. *They will bottleneck us using the tombstones.*

He considered his options before realizing he and the men with him had none to speak of. No clever maneuvers. Time was of the essence.

"Give them hell, New Jersey!" Finch roared, attempting to sound like Sir Henry Clinton and, for once, nearly succeeding. "Don't leave one alive!"

Van Buskirk briefly turned and glowered at Finch before also urging his men on with great shouts as the New Jerseyans quickly made their move on the cazadores.

The Spanish light infantry's response was swift and harsh, scattered musket shot slamming into the New Jersey line as a consistent line of fire was sprayed in their direction. Finch counted seven greencoats go down as the force advanced. This did not stop van Buskirk.

"Onward, volunteers!" he roared through the turmoil. "We will not be spared, so if we must fall, why not die fighting? Take the fence and gate!"

"Huzzay!" the New Jerseyans responded, and they surged ahead with nothing to lose. The cazadores fired one last round of shots, this one a bit more scattered, then moved to withdraw through the gateway and over the fence behind them.

Bergen County was prepared for them: seeing their quarry dashing away, the volunteers ran up to the cemetery fence and fired a rolling volley at their retiring backs.

KRAKKRAKAKRAKAKRAKAKRAKAKRAKA!

A thick smoke engulfed the fence and obfuscated all. Finch instinctively took cover to avoid any stray return fire from the vacating cazadores.

"General, they've retreated! They're heading for the governor's mansion!"

Finch looked up to see one of the New Jerseyans looking down at him with amusement. Blushing, Finch peered over the picket fence to count twelve cazadores littering the ground like unshapely white leaves, stained red, after a stiff autumn breeze. In the distance, he could see the backs of several more running for the open back gate of the mansion.

Before they could reach safety, however, a crackle of muskets resounded throughout the trees, and a detachment of Browne's rangers pounced on the retreating cazadores. This was too much for the Spaniards, who laid down their arms. The colonel of the ranger squad saluted Finch before displacing once more with his men and their prisoners. Finch smiled and turned his attention back to the manor house.

Guarding the gates, their scarlet coats glistening in the noonday sun, was a formidable force of redcoats. For a wild minute, Finch thought the marines had beaten them to the governor's mansion. Sadly, this was not the case. Instead, before them stood the Regiment of Hibernia. Racking his brains, Finch recalled their history and shook his head sadly. This was to be a challenging fight. The enemy was a force of Irishmen loyal to the Spanish Crown having fled British rule. A fierce veteran regiment, they were prepared to die hard and were deployed in a square formation, five hundred strong, around the governor's mansion, protected by cannon and barricades.

And it seems they currently have their forces trained on Lord Dunmore's fellows, too, Finch thought, noting their guns blazing away at what he perceived to be Lord Dunmore's position in the city below. He sighed and said, "Very well, lads, let us save our beloved governor once more. Charge those guns."

There was a pause as the men looked at him. *Disbelief, perhaps? Waiting for confirmation? Maybe an explanation or a morale-raising speech?* "They won't be able to bring their full force to bear," Finch said, dryly, by way of explanation. "Roll them up and we might win the day."

"Skirmishers, deploy!" van Buskirk roared. The greencoats spaced themselves accordingly, remaining out of sight behind the cover of the fence. "We will charge on one pipe from the whistle and form ranks from a skirmish line into a battle line on two pipes. Again I say! On the whistle, sirs! One, two—"

Tweeeeeeeeeeeeeeeeeeeeeeeeeeeeeeeet! The sound of a piercing whistle from van Buskirk's lips permeated the air. For a brief moment, it seemed as though the fighting stopped. Finch took the initiative.

"Onward, New Jersey!" he barked. "Riedesel and van Buskirk, to the front! Britons never will be slaves!"

In an explosion of motion, the New Jerseyans vaulted the fence and made a mad dash toward the Irish Spaniards. Made aware of their presence by the action against the cazadores, the Hibernians were ready for them. Finch, however, expected this.

"Tree!" Finch cried as the Hibernians leveled their muskets at the New Jerseyans. He dashed for cover behind a formidable bald cypress. The New Jerseyans, comprehending the old Seven Years' War command, dashed for cover behind the nearest tree. Many were able to find safety just in time as a loud volley shredded the foliage around Finch.

"Quick! Whilst they reload!" Finch roared.

Tweeeeeeeeeeeet! van Buskirk piped shrilly.

The soldiers leapt from the thickets and trees whilst the canister opened fire in a deadly cone, forty musket balls at a time flying from each cannon and striking down several men.

How many? Finch thought. *It doesn't matter. This is not a time to count, not a time to count,* Finch told himself as he maneuvered amongst the dead bodies. *It is a time to* fight.

TWEET TWEEEEEEEEEEEEEEEEEEEEEET! van Buskirk replied defiantly in the face of this bombardment, ordering his men into a dressed battle line. Not sparing the time to shout "Huzzay!"—still shaken by the bombardment or perhaps just too caught up in the rush of battle——Finch's men nonetheless dutifully hurried into a battle line.

"Crown forces!" Finch roared as he ran. "Fix your bayonets and bloody well give them a hiding!"

"Sir!" van Buskirk brandished his hanger blade. "Let's go get the bastards!"

Newly inspired, the hard-hit New Jerseyans swept in again, shrugging off one last scattered, desperate Spanish volley before thrusting home across the barricade with the bayonet and taking the battle to the enemy. Once more, steel rang on steel, and eviscerated and pummeled soldiers sang out in anguish, cursing their fellow man as they fell.

Empowered by the energy of his men, Finch followed in their footsteps, taking care not to tread on the corpses as he launched himself over the barricades and engaged the Irish-Spanish soldiery in melee combat. Bellowing like a madman, he threw himself at a soldier with reckless abandon, moving as quickly as he could to work his way around the makeshift spear facing him, the result of a bayonet-fixed musket.

The final fight! The final fight!

Thrust!

Parry!

Slash!

An Irishman went down, clutching an eviscerated belly.

Red on red, leave him for dead.

Flèche!

Parry!

Balestra!

Lunge!

With this lunge, Finch managed to run his blade through another enemy with a great squelching sound. Blood permeated the Spaniard's coat and splattered onto his own.

As he kicked the man off his sword, Finch paused to take a look at his surroundings. The Irish had fallen back to the manor house, and the New Jerseyans had taken the barricades and guns. Some had taken axes to the front doors of the house and were close to breaking them down.

Then he saw it.

A second battalion of Spanish Hibernians, swinging around from the other quadrants protecting the manor. *Shite! We've been flanked!* Finch looked around for allies. *Fellow Loyalists, Germans, Dunmore's men—anyone!*

The red-coated enemy Hibernian soldiery marched ever closer, their bayonets gleaming in the sun.

"New Jersey! Form up! Face the enemy!"

With a resounding crash, the doors to the manor house broke open and the New Jerseyans poured into the structure. Finch froze in a panic. He was suddenly almost entirely alone and utterly outnumbered and outgunned. Dropping his blade, he reached for his pistols, about to go out in a blaze of glory.

The enemy captain smiled. "It's alright, lads. Stand down. It's only an officer." He gestured for Finch to lower his pistols and fished in his haversack. "End of the line, General," he said, grinning. He held up a long, slender cigar. "Final smoke?"

Finch spat upon the ground. "Save your tobacco, traitor."

"And you, your life, oppressor. Your King George has heaped nothing but trouble upon my people."

Finch sighed. "King George has heaped nothing but trouble on many people, I'll not deny it. I fight for Parliament and our collective empire, not the king, and hope to make it a better place in the process. Why do you fight for a foreign people who would make it a worse one?"

The Irish officer frowned. "Any enemy of King George is a friend of mine." He gestured to two of his enlisted men. "Take him, lads. Let no Paddies back the Crown!"

As the two soldiers advanced, triumphant grins upon their faces, Finch raised his pistols once more. Seeing this, several other Irishmen raised their muskets in turn. Finch took aim, closed his eyes, and fired.

KRAKRAK!

KRAKRAKKRAKRAKKRAKRAKKRAKRAKKRAKRAK-
KRAKKRAKKRAKRAKKRAKRAKKRAKRAKKRAKRAK-
KRAKRAKKRAKRAKKRAKRAKKRAKRAKKRAKRAK-
KRAKRAKRAKRAKKRAKRAK!

KRAK!

KRAK!

Finch stared at his pistols in disbelief as the smoke cleared.

"Trouble, General?" a familiar voice inquired dryly.

Oh, that makes more sense.

He smiled in comprehension as several black and Native American soldiers appeared out of the smoke, a mass of fallen

Hibernians in their wake. Titus and She Who Laughs were amongst them.

"Thank you for the assistance," Finch remarked, taking off his hat to wipe sweat from his brow. "A damn fine rescue."

"A . . . damn fine charge," She Who Laughs replied, as Titus laughed.

Around them the remaining Irishmen fought bravely but were outnumbered. It was not long before the Emerald Islanders realized the futility of their mission and clubbed their arms in surrender.

Finch processed the scene. The shots echoing around town below them had slowly begun to fade, and Lord Dunmore's men had begun to troop toward the manor house, badly bruised but victorious. The commander of the Hibernian Spanish troops, clearly humiliated by his detachment being routed by a band of "savages," caught Finch's eye, drew his sword, flipped it hilt-wise toward the engineer, and offered it in surrender.

Finch pointed toward She Who Laughs and Titus. "The victory is theirs."

The Irishman glowered at him but complied, and the manor house suddenly exploded in great cheers. Through the window in the midafternoon light, Finch could see the New Jerseyans celebrating the capture of what must have been the governor. A small band of them clambered up to the rooftop and up a flagpole to tear down the flag of the Cross of Burgundy, replacing it with the flag of the Crown. As Finch looked on helplessly, the Loyalists then mischievously paraded the Spanish governor down to meet him. The Spaniard submitted himself to this without a fight and looked Finch warily in the eye.

"Governor Antonio Luisa de Córdoba at your service, señor," was the governor's courtly introduction. He unsheathed his sword. Finch smiled and gestured him over toward Lord Dunmore's men. He then saw Riedesel running down the last of the

Spanish partisans. Along with Browne, he had run admirable defensive cover for the attack.

"With me, Riedesel," Finch called. "The honor is yours as well. Rally on Lord Dunmore."

Lord Dunmore, however, was in a bad state. Having been riddled with shot, the Virginian governor had no time for Córdoba's pleasantries. Eschewing all courtesy, he nodded curtly to the Spaniard as he was carried toward the mansion, bleeding from several wounds.

"Our victory is at hand, Lord Dunmore," Finch said as he passed. The governor weakly ordered his pallbearers to halt a moment.

"Job well done, Finchy," he replied with a soft smile. "This is your prize, not mine."

He then gestured the New Jerseyans forward with the flag of Burgundy. Finch looked it over closely, feeling its delicate stitching and turning over the folded banner in his hands before gently taking Lord Dunmore's clammy hand and placing it on the flag, as well that of Riedesel's.

"This is *our* banner, not mine." Finch proceeded to walk toward the mansion, joined by Riedesel and the stretcher bearing Dunmore. Germans, Loyalists, Natives, and now some British sailors and marines, curious to know the outcome of the battle, milled about the mansion, crowning a town still smoking from the bombardment.

Finch addressed them all. "Gentlemen, we have achieved a great victory this day."

A silence followed.

"It came at high cost, but the day is at last ours. I daresay this is the beginning of the end, and many lives shall be spared because of our heroics. It is because of our valor today that Britannia still rules with her noble German allies on land or sea." He gestured to Riedesel and Foul Weather Jack, who had at last made it onto the scene. "That our colonists, black and white, stand true against the invader and insurgent." He signaled to the Loyalists. "And that the lands to the west remain in the stewardship of their rightful owners, the Natives." He pointed to She Who Laughs. "May this alliance forever endure in our mighty league of Crown, Colony, Ally, and Indian!"

"Let us hear three cheers for General Finch!" Titus roared, brandishing the Hibernian colonel's hanger blade.

Several huzzays followed.

Beaches of New Orleans, New Orleans, Louisiana Territories
5 July 1777, 6:50 PM

Two columns of soldiers, one significantly shorter than the other, snaked onto the beaches of New Orleans under the scarlet setting sun. As waves crashed upon the rocks, surrender documents were signed by sputtering torchlight.

"The tenets of the surrender document are as follows," Finch said to Córdoba as he scribbled hastily with his left hand on a bit of parchment using a quill provided for him. His right shoulder still ached but had been seen to and was in fresh dressings.

"Rather lenient, really. Your people of New Orleans will be permitted to keep their firelocks so long as they subject themselves to citizenship under the Crown. You fought a good battle, and your men"—he gestured to the Spanish side of the gauntlet, some six hundred of the original alleged thousand who had appeared for duty—"conducted themselves bravely. If the numbers were more even, well, who knows what may have happened? My only regret is that we wounded citizenry in the process. They should not have been harmed."

The governor smiled sadly. "Collateral damage from the horrors of war. I would have done the same, then felt the same." He toasted Finch with a glass of wine. "You have won the day. My men are at your mercy, and yet you have treated those who have surrendered well." He nodded to himself. "Thank you for this, General Finch. That is all you can do."

Finch returned the toast. "You, Governor, will be replaced, of course, but allowed to live in housing as befits your honor. I wish I could do better for you."

The governor looked crestfallen, but Finch paid him no mind. He looked at the remnants of his own task force: 3,000 men had been brought to bear against the 1,000 men and countless citizenry in the fort. According to reports, Finch's victory had come at a high price. Though he had captured the fort and taken the lives of many soldiers and some townsfolk, Byron had lost a frigate and a few landing craft to counterfire from fort batteries. Meanwhile, on land, Finch's pioneers had suffered especially, losing 54 men from 100 in their battalion alone, with light infantry casualties numbering 71. Despite his worries and cavalier maneuvering with the New Jersey Volunteers and their allies, only a total of 102 greencoats had been lost amongst all provincial line regiments, with 22 frock-coated partisans rounding out the Crown casualties that day. Now, however, began the unenviable task of bringing the rebellious citizenry to heel.

As a final blow, though Finch's shoulder injury had been seen to and dressed in time, Lord Dunmore's case was another matter. Though some of his many wounds appeared treatable, a few days' worth of examination and treatment under less than stellar conditions saw the leg wound quickly grow infected. The final conclusion of the surgeon, Finch was informed, was that it was "a leg, and a wonder it was not more."

Epilogue

Fort Finch, New Orleans, Louisiana Territories

17 July 1777, 9:11 AM

As the sun shone brightly over the crashing beaches of Louisiana, Finch stretched luxuriously in his four-poster bed, still uncertain of his next step.

Having taken the seat of Spanish power across the Mississippi, he and his allies had rendered the Spanish unlikely to continue the fight in any real capacity, but the engineer still worried about uprisings from the local population and had anxiously awaited instruction from high command for the past two weeks.

Out of the loop, Finch felt increasingly on edge and prepared to carry the war against the Rebels and their former allies to its bitter conclusion. Despite the injury done to his shoulder, he knew it was high time to push forward.

Looking around, he noted that a letter had been slid under the door to his room. Groaning from exertion as he reached down, he proceeded to slip his thumb under the seal and read the inscription within.

FINCH!

I should like to commend you and thank you for a job splendidly done. New Orleans, upon capture, will make a fine staging ground for our forces attacking Spain's holdings to the west.

That is, it would if they were still in the war.

We have just received word from their home offices that they intend to stand down from the fight.

This, in fact, concludes the conflict.

We've won.

Sir Charles Grey has captured Philadelphia and successfully called upon Rebel forces under Mister Washington to surrender themselves, per the demands of Lord George Germain, offering amnesty in exchange for their loyalty and obedience. I do not know what you did during the time of your audience with General Lafayette, sir, but it worked. At this time, however, we received rumors from our spy networks of a French expedition headed in the direction of New England. This inspired Sir Charles to recruit from amongst these misbegotten Rebels, citing, as you once did, common language, religion, and culture.

Though Mister Washington refused to command these men, preferring instead to retire to the Virginian countryside, Mister Nathanael Greene, newly released from prison after a highly profitable exchange, came to the fore, next in command after Mister Charles Lee and Mister Horatio Gates, one killed and one incapacitated by past battles. Greene was outfitted to lead a division of soldiers of the erstwhile Rebellion to battle in what the coming and hopefully final storm that was our war against France.

Thankfully, this storm never came, and France, bereft of allies, Her economy in ruins, has withdrawn from the war as well, taking Her soldiers with Her. A peace conference has been scheduled, which Sir Guy Carleton and I will attend. We expect to win back a sizable fortune for the woes we suffered at the hands of our traditional enemies.

Though I am sure many wars lie ahead before our days are numbered, you shall be partaking in no more of them, sir, as I feel it is high time I discharge you, albeit honorably, for your sterling, though dangerously independently minded, work. I would have you live out the rest of your days in joyous retirement with your wife and children, a hero of the realm, but no more a danger to this army.

Most sincerely, with many thanks for your service,
Clinton

Retire?

Finch opened the door to the balcony of the governor's mansion, pipe and letter in hand. After a war hard fought, the ability to take a respite and smoke should be most welcome indeed. The prospect of time with the family delighted him. True, he loved Britannia and all it had done for him, but he had paid his dues to the Crown. The time had come to move on.

Crossing to his desk, he then picked up a letter from his wife that had arrived a few days earlier. He pored over it once more with great excitement.

My dear Giles,

You cannot imagine the revelry and joy that has pervaded Charleston, thanks to your great victory over the Spanish. Whilst the remnants of the French forces are beginning to withdraw from the South, constantly harried by the forces of Colonel Simcoe and his combined force of rangers and militia, the citizenry rejoice, as banners fly high in the skies, music fills the air, and there is much dancing on the streets. Britannia has prevailed once more, and, as Caroline would say, "The Rebels can suck eggs."

Well done, husband!

Archibald, Constance, and I have secured transport to New Orleans, where we hope to see you and spend time with you as you go about your duties as a garrison commander.

There, I hope to spend what hours I can with you and trust you will find time in your hours off duty to favor me with the local delicacies and walks on the beach alongside our children.

With Caroline gone, I and the rest of the family have especially missed you, and you'd best make up your time to us for your absence, as we shall have only further difficulty overcoming Caroline's untimely passing without your peculiar wisdom and love to share amongst us all.

What's more, we must assist Constance in finding, if she so chooses, a man who suits her tastes, which, she has learned, is more important than prestige, wealth, and connections.

Archibald looks forward to hearing your stories and depicting them by interpretation, as well as to painting the seascapes. It sounds so beautiful over there.

With love, as well as the sincerest congratulations in your victorious campaigns. We look forward to seeing you soon.

Your wife,
Adelaide

Finch closed the letter with a satisfied grin. This was all well and good indeed.

The Thirteen Colonies and Beyond

1778 ONWARD

And so, after three years of vicious fighting and mourning the lost, the Finch household slowly began to show signs of a return to a status quo.

Finch never forgot Caroline, who, beyond being an empowered and delightfully forward-thinking figure in his household, had also saved him in the heat of combat during the Siege of Savannah, along with her mother. He made it a point to return to her grave site every year with his family to keep their lost child up to date with their recent events.

He also became a more attentive father to the children he had been forced to abandon at various times. Indeed, for all the loss and remorse her death brought her family, Caroline Finch not only fought valiantly and performed well under duress as a spy but brought the Finch household closer together.

With the conflict's resolution, Finch could remain in New Orleans as a hero of the realm. Whilst he and his family grieved their loss, he knew that their love for each other would conquer all. He and Adelaide, with the assistance of Constance and Archibald, founded a home for wounded veterans. The two elder Finches made many friends amongst the veterans and spent much of their later years trading tales with former comrades and bonding with one another.

Constance remained traumatized by Caroline's death. Seeing her dead sister with every injury she treated, she eventually ceased working as a nurse and instead sought out a husband. In time she found one in Hans Muller, a Brunswicker jaeger she met at a victory festival not long after the war. Gentle and eccentric, he had a zest for life that kept the two of them entertained for years. She convinced him to stay in New Orleans, and they helped her parents establish the home for soldiers in need. The activistic approach of young socialite Constance Muller allowed her many opportunities to fascinate high society with tales of her past for some time to come.

Archibald, after dabbling in many crafts and having served out the war alongside his sister as a nurse, at length decided to put his clever fingers to use as a painter. Backed by Uncle Jacob's funding, he set off on the task of traveling the colonies and interviewing veterans of the war before eventually setting up shop in New Orleans and orchestrating many imaginative and, to Finch's reasoning, somewhat stirring renditions of the major conflicts of the war. His unorthodox style of painting symbols and themes from many different battles onto one canvas raised the eyebrows of the locals; this, along with his peculiar, direct personality, won him the love of no woman. He seemed content, however, living alongside the rest of his family in one sizable mansion.

With the war's end, His Majesty George III, fearing additional repercussions, promised limited punitive action. Though the Rebel leadership was imprisoned, with the exception of those who pledged to fight for the Crown against the French, he did recognize the will of the people and, for fear of a second rebellion, offered the colonies representation in Parliament in exchange for demanding a greater volume of taxation closer to that which England bore. In the end, both sides had not only won something for their cause but learned something in the process, including the importance of communication.

Commander-in-Chief Sir Henry Clinton, however, had ideas of his own. With Lord Dunmore's emancipation of the African American slaves belonging to the revolutionaries of Virginia and his own proclamation that followed, which expanded emancipation throughout the colonies, Clinton, now empowered by his new position of secretary of state to the colonies, busied himself with methods of manumitting slaves owned by former Loyalists as well as those owned by the Rebels whom he had already freed.

Calling upon the fact that Parliament now deemed the colonists represented by themselves and thus free men of Britain, he exhorted the Americans to, like their British islander brethren, free their charges similarly within the next generation. By means of taxing slaveowners for their additional "property," Clinton incentivized cheaper labor from the British Isles to replace that of slaves. Though these factors gave the African population some healthy competition for jobs, it would free them of their bonds and, also helpful to Clinton's position of employment, would further populate the North American Territories, all factors attractive to His Majesty, which garnered Sir Henry even more influence and favor.

While excessive colonization would naturally lead to conflict with the Natives, Clinton was careful to respect the treaty lines of the Royal Proclamation of 1763 and was sure to strike a balance between the needs of his constituents and those of the First Nations, whose lands to the west of the Appalachian Mountains were declared to belong to the Natives unless business arrangements were made with them to the contrary.

For now, there was good land for all.

Finch hoped that commerce and trade, not active conflict, with the Native nations would become the norm, as Clinton dispatched a British expeditionary force to build forts and patrol the moving frontiers in what was to be a joint effort with local warbands. All of these factors would provoke, without a doubt, some resistance from particularly bitter slaveowners and frontiersmen, but the colonies, disheartened and defeated from the war and grateful for their newfound representation, largely counted their blessings.

The better to further assist his past allies and the black populace at large, Finch took action alongside Clinton in helping to raise funds for Colonels Titus and Prince in their establishment of the Institution for the Advancement of the Negro, an organization founded to garner the funds to buy, educate, and free slave populaces in the shrinking territories where slavery still endured. Though still a fledgling organization and frequently wanting for money in its ambitious activism, its noble deeds were nonetheless the toast of King George's domain and through Titus's excellent leadership won over many a wealthy donor.

It was, to Brigadier General Giles Finch, hero of the Attempted and Failed American Insurrection, a satisfying conclusion to a life well lived.

Acknowledgments

With special thanks to:

Madhav Ajjampur
Gilah Benson-Tilsen
Sanda Cohen
Christopher Culler
Carl Duff
Scott Edelstein
Alexander Farrell
Patti Frazee
Ralph Fuhrmann
Jason Grossman
Carrie Harshbarger
Veronica Hatala
George Hill
Amber Johnson
Deb Johnson
Sean Lowman
Elizabeth Motich Gross

Jennifer Munnings
William North
David Oppegaard
Anne Osberg
Sarah Ravely
Madeleine Vasaly
Jacob Waldman
Antoine Watts
Naida Wharton
Ralph Wharton
Beth Wright
Serena Zabin
The Royal Provincial Fourth
   Battalion, New Jersey
   Volunteers Reenacting
   Group

And many thanks to countless others for their contributions to the Finchverse.

About the Author

A native of New Jersey and resident of Minnesota, Daniel H Lessin has a history degree from Carleton College and is a seasoned Revolutionary War reenactor. When he is not writing books and chasing doodles, Daniel enjoys the company of animals (especially dogs), designing board games, wargaming with figurines, computer gaming, and partaking in rituals with his Reformed Druids of North America grove.

To learn more about Daniel's other books and his board games, visit blacklabradorcreations.squarespace.com.

www.ingramcontent.com/pod-product-compliance
Lightning Source LLC
Chambersburg PA
CBHW072056190726
48294CB00005B/1556